WHILE MY BABY SLEEPS

BOOKS BY NATALI SIMMONDS

My Daughter's Revenge

NATALI SIMMONDS
WHILE MY BABY SLEEPS

bookouture

Published by Bookouture in 2025

An imprint of Storyfire Ltd.
Carmelite House
50 Victoria Embankment
London EC4Y 0DZ

www.bookouture.com

The authorised representative in the EEA is Hachette Ireland
8 Castlecourt Centre
Dublin 15 D15 XTP3
Ireland
(email: info@hbgi.ie)

Copyright © Natali Simmonds, 2025

Natali Simmonds has asserted her right to be identified as the author of this work.

All rights reserved. No part of this publication may be reproduced, stored in any retrieval system, or transmitted, in any form or by any means, electronic, mechanical, photocopying, recording or otherwise, without the prior written permission of the publishers.

ISBN: 978-1-83618-473-7
eBook ISBN: 978-1-83618-472-0

This book is a work of fiction. Names, characters, businesses, organizations, places and events other than those clearly in the public domain, are either the product of the author's imagination or are used fictitiously. Any resemblance to actual persons, living or dead, events or locales is entirely coincidental.

To all the mothers who swallowed down their tears

PROLOGUE

I'm covered in blood. My eyes are stinging, too sticky to open, my mouth coated thick with the taste of iron. I don't know how long I've been standing here. There's something in my hand but I can't see what it is; cold and hard, heavy like a brick, the edges sharp and jagged against the soft pad of my thumb. I drop whatever I'm holding and hear it fall to the ground with a loud crack, shattering at my bare feet.

I use my knuckles to dig into my eyes, the heels of my hands to rub at them until I'm able to blink, the watery blur of the deserted street slowly coming into focus in hues of dark blues and blacks. I'm not far from my house. The amber glow of a distant streetlight is too far away to show me whether the blood coating my skin belongs to me or somebody else.

A shiver runs up my spine and I look over my shoulder. Nothing. Yet I know I'm not alone. All is still, the night holding its breath, and every window black; behind them people sleep, unaware of what just happened on their street. Bushes rustle, their branches speckled with brown leaves and tattered ribbons of old plastic bags. I turn all the way around, the soles of my feet scraping along the damp paving slabs. Glowing eyes blink back at me amongst the dank foliage. A fox, no bigger than a tomcat, is watching me. It's just us: the predator and the street vermin.

There's a hum in the distance somewhere behind me, a drumbeat slow and steady like an impending death march. Music? My heart trying to escape my ribcage?

The sound continues, a relentless thud of techno beating in time with the pounding in my head and my chest. Whose blood am I covered in? I don't think it's mine.

Rage simmers hot beneath my slick skin, like bubbles breaking to the surface – a familiar buzz I cannot escape. My jaw aches as I grind my molars together, my sticky fists opening and closing. I clench them as hard as I can, my broken nails digging into my flesh, ensuring that I'm really here. That I'm inside my body and not imagining this.

I try to remember why I'm here, but I can't. All I know is that I want to do something bad. Really bad.

Maybe I already have.

ONE

I gasp, sitting up in bed so fast the duvet is flung to the floor. The glare from the bedroom light, no more than a single golden bulb swinging above my head, forces me to shield my eyes. We really need to buy a lampshade.

'Riley?'

'It's me, babe.' Tony is standing in the doorway, filling it whole like he tends to do, his hand still on the light switch. He's fully dressed yet his hair is wet, which doesn't make sense until I hear the rain at the window. His shoulders are dark from the water, his damp polo shirt straining against his torso. His clothes used to be too tight on him because of his beer belly; now they're tight because he goes to the gym. I don't think he can move his arms easily in that top anymore, but he appears to like the discomfort, proud of the way the fabric pulls against his chest.

'Didn't mean to wake you,' he says, turning the light back off. 'Thought you'd be up by now.'

I pull the duvet back over me and glance at my phone on the bedside table: 6.07am. Tony is home, having finished work for the night. He's right, I'm normally up by now.

'Is Riley OK?' I mutter.

Our son is turning one at the end of December. How many weeks away is that? I try to remember today's date. I know what day of the week it is most of the time, but never the date. Is it November yet? Yes, the shops are already decorated for Christmas.

'He's sound asleep,' Tony says.

I'm not surprised. Riley got me out of bed four times last night to the point where I was racing to him before I'd even opened my eyes. I wiggle my feet beneath the duvet, testing where I stubbed my toe last night running to his room. It's throbbing – I didn't imagine it.

'Go back to sleep,' Tony says.

I suppress a sigh. 'There's no point. I'm awake now.'

'In that case, maybe you can rustle us up some breakfast before I go to bed?'

He turns on the bedside lamp and pulls off his work boots one after the other, letting them fall to the ground with a thump. I wince at the thought of him waking the baby up and take a deep breath, holding back the sentence forming in my mouth like too much bubblegum. *I could be sleeping still. I could be sleeping if you hadn't woken me up. I really need to sleep.*

I stay silent though because it's all I talk about lately. Sleep. Lack of sleep. Needing more sleep.

It wasn't just the baby that kept me awake last night. One of the neighbours, I think it was the man three doors down, was playing loud music until two in the morning. Between that and Riley's constant crying, I feel like bursting into tears myself. How many hours of solid sleep have I actually had?

I do the maths. Three hours, maybe four. My waking hours are filled with me doing mental arithmetic, calculating how little I've slept and marvelling at how my body continues to keep going even though my mind is always partially buried beneath something heavy and unyielding.

'What've you got in for breakfast?' Tony asks again.

I haul myself out of bed, slipping my feet into the flip-flops I've been using as slippers because everything I need is still inside the many boxes piled up in every room. We moved house a few weeks ago but no matter how many boxes I unpack, I don't seem to be getting anywhere.

'There's bacon,' I say.

'Lovely,' Tony replies as he strips his clothes off to have a shower. I'm already heading for the stairs when he calls out to me, 'Don't suppose you've had a chance to get any more unpacking done, have you?'

I close my eyes and hold on to the banister. Why is his voice so loud? I can hear the sounds of Riley stirring, a small whine that makes me hover outside his room. A box room, they call it. Ironic, really, considering it's too small to have any boxes in it. This house isn't as big as our last one. It's a standard two up, two down, in one of the many crappy streets of London that the tourists don't know about. But we weren't exactly spoiled for choice when Tony got a new job. It made no sense for him to commute from the suburbs and, as he said, it's not like the baby and I had anything tying us to our old neighbourhood. My brother, Dan, lives miles away and my parents are out of the country, so now we pay a higher rent for a lower quality of life and I'm more alone than ever. But at least Tony can get to work easily.

I wait on the landing until Riley settles, then head downstairs.

Our son wasn't planned. Riley came along before Tony and I even knew what we were to one another. Before we'd had a chance to dig deep with our love and think about what a future together would look like. We've never had much in common, but one thing we did know was that we wanted this baby desperately and we would do whatever it took to make things work. And we have. What we have is good. It's fine. It will get better... so all the motherhood blogs say. Once Riley sleeps through the night everything will be easier, and Tony and I can get back to enjoying one another again.

I fry the bacon, the smell of raw meat making me think of blood. I've been thinking about blood a lot lately, forever batting away all the dark and twisted scenarios that play out in my mind. All the worsts that can happen to those I love. A slide show of paranoia and pessimism. I can't escape these visions, day and night, even during my few snatched hours of sleep. My nightmares are often more real than my days: sharper, clearer, more acute. They make more sense to me than reality sometimes.

'You just need to relax,' Tony said to me last week when I woke up having a panic attack. 'Don't worry so much.'

Silly me. I never thought to simply... not worry.

Am I the only one fighting these fears or are all the capable-looking mums out there pushing their babies around also imagining every horror that could ever befall their precious bundles? All of us keeping the same secret. I looked up how I was feeling, and Google said it was normal, that new mothers often have intrusive thoughts. Apparently, I'm meant to ignore them – which is what I'm trying to do – and they will go away. But even if all mums *are* struggling with terrible thoughts, it's not like we can tell anyone how crazy we feel. Not even one another. No mother is going to take that risk because we're judged enough as it is.

I think I've been sleepwalking. Last week I must have got up in the night to tend to Riley and woke up on the sofa cradling a soiled nappy like a baby. Tony doesn't know about my night-time wanderings. He normally leaves for work late afternoon, depending on what night shift he has, and returns at dawn as his son and I are starting our day. Sometimes we have breakfast together as a family because Tony likes to wind down a bit before he gets some sleep. It's important he gets his sleep, he says. He drives lorries and works with heavy machinery. You can't drive lorries and work with heavy machinery if you're tired. At least if I'm tired, I won't kill anyone.

As the bacon sizzles in the pan, I heap a tablespoon of hard, greying coffee granules into the only mug I can find amongst the towering stack of boxes that I've been promising myself I will unpack this week. The old stained mug says GIRL BOSS and has a chip on the rim, but I don't care. I don't even like coffee that much, but right now I'm living off caffeine, sugar and the hope that this thick fog of exhaustion will lift.

I knew that feeling tired was part of motherhood, I was expecting it, but this is fatigue on a different level. There isn't a word for what I'm feeling now, but complaining about it gets me nowhere.

'You have to ignore Riley when he fusses at night,' my mum says. 'You're too soft on the boy. Let him cry it out.'

I've tried, but it's easier to get up four times a night than lie there hearing him in distress.

'At least you don't have to go to work,' Tony says. 'You have all day to rest.'

He has no idea, and I don't have the energy to keep explaining what I do all day.

'You should cherish the baby years,' another mother told me last week in the street as she wrangled her toddler. 'Time goes so fast. And it only gets harder.'

Harder? I can't imagine life being harder than this. Yet every other mother I see out and about with their baby seems fine. Happy, even. So maybe it *is* just me. Maybe my expectations are too high, and everyone has accepted their lot. I simply need to get the hell on with it because it's all worth it in the end. Shut up, put up and cherish every moment.

I can't find the spatula or any tongs to turn the bacon in the pan, so I use my fingers, making them red and sore. I suck on my greasy fingertips while I survey the towering pile of boxes next to the door. I'll unpack them today. Or maybe this evening once Riley is asleep and Tony's left for work, otherwise the baby will want my attention and his cries will keep Tony awake. He works weekends too at the moment. All the time he spends away from us is because he's making money for us. Because he loves his family. Tony and I are both trying so hard, in our own way. It's not his fault I'm so tired and irritable all the time.

I'm yawning, stretching my arms so high my fingers touch the ceiling, when something moves out of the corner of my eye. I peer out of the window. The street is dark and still, every house identical, squashed up to one another like they're huddled against the winter wind. It takes me a while to work out what it is that I'm staring at. Crouched on my kitchen window ledge is a round ball of black fur, trembling against the cold.

The cat looks healthy but skinny. No collar. Maybe he's a stray. They say no one ever sets out to own a cat, that cats choose you. I wonder why he's chosen me. He must have smelled the bacon.

I open the window a little and the cat tries to squeeze his black head through the gap.

'Not inside,' I whisper, placing the scraps of bacon rind I trimmed on to the window ledge. 'This should put some fat on your bones.'

The wind shoots up my pyjama top and I shut the window before the whole house gets cold. I've always loved cats. I suggested getting one when I found out I was expecting and moved into Tony's flat, but he said cat faeces are dangerous for pregnant women, and what if I tripped over it and fell? So we didn't get one. Riley will be a toddler soon, so it wouldn't be fair to get a cat then either. Maybe when he's older.

'Shadow,' I say, tapping on the glass. 'That's what I'd call you if you were mine.'

The cat's eyes flash gold then he's gone.

I pile the bacon sandwiches on to one plate, the cheap bread bouncing back up as I cut them into neat triangles. Triangles are fancier than rectangles. My stomach rumbles in anticipation, remembering that I had no dinner last night because I couldn't work out the oven in our new house. I ended up boiling some pasta but then Riley started crying and I forgot to eat it.

This is nice, having breakfast together before dawn, before the baby wakes up, just me and my man getting a few minutes of peace as one shift finishes and another begins.

I had a thing for Tony way before he ever had a thing for me. I've loved him since the first day I met him at my brother's wedding. Dan is a year and a half younger than me, and Tony is a couple of years older. I'd have corny daydreams about Tony asking me out and us going on brunch dates that would last all day, with sunny walks in the park and dinner out before catching a movie. We never did do any of that. But it's fine. Once Riley's a bit older we can have those fancy brunch dates as a family.

'Get me a towel please, babe!' Tony shouts down the stairs.

I wish he'd stop shouting. Nostalgia flips to annoyance in an instant like the flick of a switch, sharp rage climbing up through my stomach, clawing at my throat, fizzing beneath my skin. I never used to be like this.

When I was younger, I was the chilled child, the mediator, the one who would calm my parents down when they were arguing or tell my little brother to take it easy. I didn't let things bother me. No one annoyed me, not really. Now everyone does.

The anger began as soon as I discovered I was pregnant. I never got morning sickness – instead, I got twenty-four-hour rage. I put my negative emotions down to fear, anxiety, money problems, the fact that Tony and I hadn't been a couple for very long. We went from friends to lovers to expectant parents within a few months, before we'd had any practice at being an 'us'. I read about rage online back then too and got the same answers I get now.

'Thanks to fluctuating hormones, it's common to experience major mood swings in pregnancy,' the website said. The solution was simple: eat healthy, get lots of sleep, talk to people about it. They said it would go once the baby was born, but it didn't. It got worse.

I put down my coffee, which is too hot to drink, and rummage through the pile of clothes on the sofa. I'm not entirely sure if this is the washing I took off the clothes line yesterday or if it's dirty laundry. I smell the towel. It's fine.

'How did you get on unpacking the boxes last night?' Tony shouts down the stairs again.

Why does he keep asking me the same question? I hold my breath and count to ten. It's not him making me angry, it's the stress of the house move. It's not getting enough sleep. It's normal to hate everyone when you're tired. Everything will get easier soon.

'Lu!' Tony hollers. 'I'm freezing my balls off here, babe.'

This time Riley doesn't whine but screams. A sound that shoots through my core like barbed wire. I stomp upstairs, throw the towel at Tony, who's standing dripping water on the hall floor, and gently open the door to my son's room.

It's stuffy in here and smells of warm pee and talcum powder. When he sees me, he hoists himself up on the bars of his cot and holds out his arms, his crying reaching a crescendo. I lift him up, and his sweaty, pudgy hands grasp for me, pull at my hair, his face buried in the crook of my neck as his legs kick like a frog's. I sing and I coo, and he calms in my arms enough to let me change his nappy and clean his face. His Babygro is damp, so I change that too, brushing his soft, feathery hair with an even softer brush and breathing in the scent of him. Even though my eyes are heavy and gritty with invisible sand, my love for him is so big nothing else matters. That's what I tell myself when I'm so exhausted I'm swaying on the spot and my legs threaten to give way. *Cherish him*, I tell myself. *You wanted this. You wanted this so much.*

'Should we go and say good morning to Daddy?' I sing-song, my chest swelling at the sight of Riley clapping his hands – a new trick he learned only yesterday.

Tony, dressed in nothing but boxer shorts and an old, faded t-shirt, is coming out of the kitchen as I reach the bottom of the stairs. His son is already launching himself out of my arms, waiting for his father to catch him.

'My boy!' Tony cries out, swinging the baby around and making him laugh.

Tony has always found it so easy to be a dad, never once questioning whether he was a natural or doing anything wrong. Maybe it's because Riley was just an abstract notion for so long until suddenly he was real, a proper baby, clean and bundled up, ready for cuddles when Daddy was available. Tony didn't have to be responsible while Riley was growing inside of me; he didn't have to worry about failing his boy before he even existed. He didn't suffer any pain bringing him into the world, not while carrying him or pushing him out or breastfeeding him. And now? Now he gets to make him laugh and squeal and hand him back to me when he needs to work or sleep or take a thirty-minute shit.

I smile as I leave them playing, returning to the coffee and the bacon sandwiches I made. But back in the kitchen I see my coffee has grown cold and Tony has eaten all of the sandwiches. All of them. He didn't even put the plate in the sink.

My stomach rumbles and I have a glass of water instead.

I turn back to the scene in the hallway, but it no longer makes me smile. Tony needs to stop swinging him like that. Something bad is going to happen. I can see it, literally, like it's unfolding in slow motion before my eyes. Riley's head smashing against the wall. Tony dropping him and breaking his little legs. I can see him, my baby, still and crooked like a discarded doll on the floor. This is what happens when I don't get enough sleep; my nightmares rise to the surface and join me in the real world. I shake my head and rub my eyes, but nothing clears my visions. I don't choose to see any of this. I'm not asking for it. I only want to think happy thoughts.

I snatch Riley out of Tony's strong arms, making the baby cry again.

My man smiles, like I'm doing him a favour.

'Time for Daddy to get some shut-eye,' he says, kissing his son's sweet head and forgetting mine.

'Yeah, you get some rest,' I mutter at his retreating back. 'Don't worry about me.'

TWO

Riley has been crying for so long it's faded to a dull whine, like a persistent mosquito or tinnitus. He's not unwell, he's not hungry, I changed him. He's just over-tired. He wouldn't go down for his usual two o'clock nap and was keeping Tony awake so I've taken him for a walk. His cries don't sound so loud amongst the traffic.

'Please,' I say quietly, more to myself than him because he can't hear me over the wailing.

I pass him a breadstick, the last one, and he throws it to the pavement, where three pigeons fight over it. He won't stop straining against the straps of his pushchair, his back arched, his whole face bright red. Maybe it's his teeth hurting, piercing his delicate little gums like roots pushing through soil. A wave of guilt and shame washes over me as I try to replace my irritation with sympathy. God, I'm so selfish sometimes.

I'll buy him some rusks to bite on and some Calpol. That should calm him.

There's a supermarket on this street, I'm sure of it. I went with Tony last week when we did our first big shop. Everyone warned me about moving to this area, said it got rough at times. I tell myself that one London high street is much like the other and, anyway, crime doesn't happen during the week, at midday, in the winter. Bad things don't happen to tired mums pushing babies around in the rain, because we don't have anything anyone wants.

My wet hair is sticking to my face, eyes blurring and stinging. It's raining the kind of rain that's not really rain, more like mist. A fine drizzle that gets into your socks and under your hood, your face becoming a tight, frozen mask. I have no idea in which of the dozens of packing boxes my warm gloves are, so I'm not wearing any. After grasping the handles of Riley's buggy for twenty minutes, the skin on my hands has gone pink and raw, and I can't feel them anymore. Or maybe I'm holding on too tight, as if the more I squeeze the quicker he'll stop crying.

'Look! A bus!' I exclaim, pointing at a red double-decker as it rumbles past. It sprays my legs with water, but my grey jogging bottoms are already dark from the rain, so it makes no difference. I grip the handle of the pushchair tighter until my bloodless knuckles resemble popcorn.

I can see the light of the supermarket up ahead, but I can't go in, not yet, not while my son is in this state. I slow down outside a church to adjust Riley's rain cover and check he hasn't escaped the straps of his pushchair. He looks me dead in the eye, and for a moment he stops crying long enough for us both to hear the sound of 'Old MacDonald' being sung from inside the church hall.

'Friday afternoon playgroup,' the handwritten sign beside us reads. Someone has covered the yellow card in cling film to make it waterproof. It hasn't really worked. 'Free! Come and make new friends!'

I blink the rain out of my eyes and squint into the gloom of the interior. It's warm inside and there are toys. Maybe Riley will finally quieten down if he's distracted.

WHILE MY BABY SLEEPS

. . .

The woman beside me has been talking solidly since I got here thirty minutes ago. She told me her name is Daisy, and the child with the round cheeks and sticky mouth playing on the floor is her daughter, Tilly.

'What did you say your name was again?' she asks me. Did I tell her when I came in and sat down? Probably not. This woman hasn't shut up since I first gave her a hesitant smile.

'Lu,' I say. 'It's Louise but everyone calls me Lu.'

'Ah, that's right. And little Riley.'

Oh. So I did tell her.

She smiles at my son asleep in his pushchair. I've been shaking it side to side for the last ten minutes and now I'm too scared to stop in case he wakes up.

The second we stepped foot into the musty-smelling room he stopped screaming. I set him free, and he crawled over to the toys. Then within ten minutes he was asleep, so I put him back in his pushchair. I should probably take advantage of the quiet and do some food shopping, but I'm comfortable now and I'm dry. I don't want to move.

'How old is he?' Daisy asks.

'Nearly eleven months.'

'Lovely.'

'Is it?'

She laughs like I just told her a joke. Daisy has one of those laughs that sounds fake.

'As I was saying, I had such a rotten morning.' She sighs and rolls her eyes, gearing herself up to tell me something fascinating. I know it won't be interesting because she's already told me her life story and none of that was memorable.

I grab a biscuit, the first thing I've eaten today, and nod encouragingly. It's rich tea. The plain kind. I start to chew, and it immediately turns into a hard ball of mush in my mouth, but I have nothing to wash it down with. I was handed a flimsy plastic cup of watered-down orange juice when I got here, but Riley knocked it out of my hand, and it went all over the lino. The woman who runs the mums' group made a big fuss about not knowing where they keep the mop, so now I'm worried about looking greedy if I grab another cup of weak juice.

'I was changing my bed, but I couldn't find the pillowcases anywhere,' Daisy continues. 'And I hate not having matching ones, you know?'

Not really. I found our duvet the day we moved house, but I still can't find the duvet covers. Why did I pack the bedding in a different box?

Daisy is still talking.

'So I spent a good ten minutes looking for another matching pair of pillowcases. In that time Tilly managed to tangle herself up in all the dirty sheets on the floor and hit her head on my bedside table. Thank God there was no blood because I've already done five wash loads this week. And everyone knows blood is a nightmare to get out of clothes.'

Blood and stains and laundry. What a fascinating thing to bond over.

'Never ends, does it?' she says. 'So I had no choice but to use my white pillowcases.'

I keep nodding, the masticated biscuit now a solid lump on my tongue. I can't spit it out and I can't swallow it, so I just leave it there like a gobstopper.

'So there I was, shaking out the clean duvet cover, when I noticed something inside. And guess what it was? The blinking pillowcases. The ones that match! Except they'd dried all crumpled up and smelled of damp. So back into the wash they went, and I had to use another duvet cover. Thank God I had playgroup to come to, or that would have been my whole day wasted.'

Daisy thanks God for a lot of things. I wonder what He

thinks of that. I'm sure He has more important things to worry about than Daisy's duvet drama. She starts prattling on about something clever her daughter did involving Play-Doh or plasticine or something and I switch off.

Daisy is one of those mums who talks for the sake of talking, but I can't hate her for it. I know what it's like, that desperation to connect. To have someone listen and respond, even when you have nothing of any interest to say.

I find myself doing the same thing to Tony as soon as he gets in from work. I have no exciting news to share – all my days are the same – but I still talk and talk, trying to elicit a response.

'You're not listening,' I say to him.

'That's because you're always talking,' he replies. 'It's a bit intense. I'm knackered, babe.'

I try and explain, but he's already zoned out. 'I'm on my own all the time. You're the first person I've spoken to all day,' I say.

'You're not on your own. You have Riley.'

That's what he always says, as if talking to a baby isn't the same as talking to yourself. I spoke to the stray cat this morning too. Shadow. But he didn't talk back either.

'I'm boring you, aren't I?' Daisy says.

My eyes are aching and gritty again, as if sand is lodged beneath the lids. I blink. Hard. Once, twice. I keep doing that. People must think I have a twitch.

'No, you're not boring me. Not at all. I'm just tired,' I say.

'Bad night?'

'Every night is bad.'

Daisy makes an exaggerated sympathetic face.

'Tilly was a terrible sleeper too when she was a baby.'

Oh. Daisy has my attention now. I lean forward, still sucking on my biscuit ball. I need to hear this. I'm hungry for it. I soak up stories of mums who survived sleepless nights and lived to tell the tale like an addict hunting down a quick fix. I need to know how long I have to wait until it's bearable. Until I can go to bed, sleep through and wake up in the morning refreshed.

'How bad?' I ask. 'You know... how much of a bad sleeper was your daughter?'

'Oh, Lu. It was tough. The little love didn't sleep through until she was five months old. Then she'd sleep from seven until six but still wake up at midnight. But it was fine because Mark did the night feed, so I got to bed at nine.'

I do the maths. Always doing the sleep maths. Is this woman seriously telling me she's had over eight hours' sleep a night since her kid was half the age of mine? I don't say anything. I can't. I'm scared that if I start to talk, my throat will close up and I'll cry. Or scream. Or punch her. Or maybe the lump in my throat is just the nasty biscuit. I swallow it down whole and smile.

'Your husband sounds helpful,' I say.

Daisy nods so fast her messy bun gets even messier. I bet her hair smells of coconut.

'Oh, he is! Mark works from home, so I get to nap in the day too.'

Nap? Why does she need a fucking nap? She's getting eight hours of solid sleep a night.

'Mark is ever so handy around the house too. He's going to build a treehouse for Tilly to play in when she's older. Well, I say treehouse, but we don't have a tree in our garden. More of a clubhouse. A shed. One of those tiny ones that I can paint pink and decorate with flowers. I saw it on Pinterest once. He's great at DIY, my Mark.'

Now we've exhausted our own life stories, we've moved on to the dads. Great. I wish she'd bloody stop talking, but she can't. Neither of us can. Because if we stop this painful small talk, then what are we going to do? Just sit and stare at our kids like we do all day at home anyway? Mine isn't even doing anything interesting.

I keep rocking Riley while eyeing Daisy's cup of juice. My mouth tastes like wet cardboard.

'What about your husband? Is he good at DIY? What does he do for a living?' she asks me.

I'm watching Daisy's daughter play with a plastic plate and a spoon. She's kind of cute. Tilly looks about two years old and is practically bald, which Daisy has tried to disguise with a huge bow that matches her daughter's outfit. The child is very dressed up for a crappy playgroup in a musty church hall in November, but I know what it's like. People want to buy your child nice gifts, so they get them a frilly dress. Posh baby outfits are cute, but people forget we never take the kids anywhere posh.

Daisy's waiting for me to reply.

'I don't have a husband,' I say.

'Oh. I'm sorry. That must be hard.'

Great. Now I've made her uncomfortable. I could leave the words there, hanging in the air, and enjoy the way Daisy's face and chest are growing all motley and red. But I'm being unfair.

'Tony, that's Riley's dad, he and I live together,' I say. 'But we're not married. Not yet. Maybe we'll tie the knot one day. He just got a new job, actually. He works in haulage. You know, trucks and stuff.'

Daisy nods, like she's an expert on transportation and logistics.

She hasn't asked what I do. No one ever does. I'm here with a baby so that's who I am. What I am. Lu The Mum. End of story.

I can see she wants me to ask what her Mark does, but I can't be bothered. It will probably be something boring yet important that she'll have to explain to me anyway.

My bum has gone numb, and I shift around on my chair. Daisy is sitting on one of those wooden classroom chairs you get for little kids. It's yellow. She doesn't look uncomfortable though. I chose a plastic adult chair, the white garden type, because I'd never be able to get one arse cheek on one of those tiny ones, let alone be able to balance. Why can't they find enough big chairs for all the parents here? It's not much to ask, a chair that's not made for a five-year-old.

Daisy is wearing leggings with a top that doesn't cover her stomach or behind. She's what clothes shops call 'petite' but she's actually just skinny. Thin neck, tiny wrists, dainty ankles. I worry about women like Daisy, so quick to talk to strangers, to form new friendships, to give all of themselves away in one fell swoop.

My mind instantly shows me a film reel of all that could go wrong. How easily Daisy could be tricked by a man pretending to ask for directions, dragged into the bushes, blood on the leaves.

She'd make a pretty dead person.

Girls like Daisy are the easiest to murder. I bet she wouldn't make a sound. She's too polite for that, the kind that wouldn't like to draw attention to herself, even in her final hours. She'd probably whine a bit, like a scared puppy. An apologetic escape of breath as her neck was being snapped in half; every dainty limb splintered and cracked – a pile of mummy twigs, delicate and white like when the bark's been peeled off. A pretty, fragile marionette whose strings have been cut, lying out in the rain like a pile of kindling.

'This is the first time I've seen you here,' Daisy says, draining her plastic cup of juice.

'We moved here three weeks ago.'

'Oh yes, the new job!' Her eyes widen and she gives me a big smile. 'I live in the new development, the one with the hedges. Have you seen the hedges? They're shaped like different animals. Do you live near there?'

Jesus. I wouldn't have come into the church hall had I

known how much hard work this would be. She's got a nice face, though, when I'm not imagining it covered in blood.

'No. I'm just off the high street. Next to the big estate, the one with the high-rise flats.'

She doesn't say it. She doesn't need to; I can see it in her face. I don't live in the nice part of town.

'Do you like it there?' she asks.

'No one likes it there, Daisy.'

She gives me a smile, the kind with closed lips pressed in, and mumbles something about getting more juice for Tilly. I let her go. There was nothing left to talk about anyway.

THREE

I can't get the front door open because Tony has left his keys in the lock on the inside. I know he has because he does it all the time. I ring the bell and hold my breath as the thud of footsteps gets louder and louder.

'I wasn't sure if you'd be up,' I say as he opens the door with a heavy sigh.

'Good job I was, with the racket you're making.' He's talking about Riley, who hasn't stopped screaming since I took a corkscrew off him at the supermarket that he somehow managed to snatch off the shelf.

With a grunt I manoeuvre the pushchair and all the bags that are hanging off it through the front door.

'Your key was in the lock,' I say.

'Don't start, Lu. I haven't slept a huge amount.'

It's quarter to four in the afternoon so Tony has had plenty of rest. He went to bed this morning after the bacon sandwiches, but I could hear him watching something on his phone until around nine. He pretends he's sleeping but I know he just likes to unwind alone. How luxurious. He's still slept over seven hours though. Seven solid hours. I can't remember what that feels like.

His face is still crumpled with lines from the pillow, and the t-shirt he's been sleeping in is halfway up his middle. Our days overlap a few hours at each end – at the crack of dawn when he's getting in and mid-afternoon when he's getting up.

Riley has seen his dad, which means he's ramped up the volume of his screaming and is straining against the straps of his pushchair, arms stretched out to be lifted up. Tony unstraps him and Riley stops crying straight away. It feels like a betrayal. Without the weight of the baby, the buggy tips backwards, sending the shopping crashing to the floor.

'Shit, the eggs,' I mutter, scooping down to get the bags, one arm still stuck in my coat, which I'm trying to peel off.

'You got eggs in there?' Tony asks, pointing at the bags I'm trying to loop over my wrists.

'I just said I did.'

'Oh dear, someone's in a bad mood,' Tony says in a high-pitched voice to Riley. It takes all my strength not to take the eggs out and hurl them one by one at his head. I half drag the bags into the kitchen and plonk them on to the worktop. Two of them have already split.

My kitchen was a lot bigger at our old place, and it wasn't bright green or full of half-unpacked boxes either. I thought Tony would have taken a few days off work to help with the move and settling in, but he said he couldn't take the piss, not with a new job.

He follows me around the kitchen while blowing raspberries on Riley's neck.

'Do us an omelette, babe. I think Riley's hungry too.'

'Why don't you make a start while I put the shopping away?' I say, but Tony has already left the kitchen.

I start to unpack the groceries then stop at the sound of the baby fussing. I peer around the door of the living room. Tony has put Riley in his walker and gone upstairs without telling me. The baby is fine, he's safe. Tony clearly doesn't think it's an issue leaving him alone. Must be nice to do your own thing without feeling like you have to explain yourself, justify yourself, to everyone.

Our son has been showing signs of wanting to walk lately. His favourite thing is coasting along the furniture, grabbing on to the sofa and coffee table as he tiptoes from one dangerous edge to the other. I know he's safer in the walker than stumbling about unattended, but I read that those things are bad for a baby's physical development. Their backs or legs or something. But Tony saw some fancy Fisher-Price one cheap on eBay and bought it anyway. Riley has manoeuvred himself to the foot of the stairs and is screaming for his dad.

'I'll have cheese in mine,' Tony shouts down from the bedroom. I can hardly hear him over the wailing.

I didn't buy any cheese because the price has gone up since last week and I thought I'd find it cheaper somewhere else. I didn't. No wonder cheese is the most shoplifted food item.

I whisk the two eggs that cracked, then three, then four, then all six because all I've eaten today is that dry biscuit. I'm so hungry and tired I feel shaky. I put some toast on and take a plastic plate out of the half-full dishwasher, brushing off the crumbs because Riley won't mind.

It never used to be like this. When I was pregnant and Tony and I both worked nine to five, we split the bills and we both cooked and cleaned. But now that I'm home in the day and he's the one making all the money, we've fallen into these old-fashioned roles. It wasn't conscious, we never discussed it, it just happened. And I don't have the energy to get into a petty argument about it. I was going to feed Riley and myself anyway, so I don't mind making a little more. It's fine.

The baby has stopped crying now. I panic for a split-second and check on him, careful he doesn't see me in case we make eye contact and I set him off again. He's fine. He's gone back into the living room and is glued to the TV screen, where someone is being shown around a house in Spain they want to buy. I can't imagine being able to buy a house, let alone a second one in the sun. My parents live in Spain now, although they sold everything they had to make it work, and their tiny, high-rise apartment looks out over a car park and a fish and chip shop.

I glance out of the window at the dank drizzle, cars lining the kerb like dominos, litter swirling around in circles in the winter wind. I wonder if Shadow the cat is still out there, braving the elements. Does he belong to anyone?

'What time do you start work tonight?' I call out to Tony.

He appears in the kitchen doorway wearing a football top and some tracksuit bottoms I didn't even know he had.

'Nine.'

I glance at the kitchen clock. It's four thirty. All that free time. What must that be like?

'Perfect.' I slide the omelette on to his plate, butter the toast and chop up some more of both into tiny little pieces for Riley's plate. I put them both on the kitchen table, where Tony is already seated. 'So we can drive to dinner with Dan tonight?'

Tony looks up, a piece of omelette hanging from his mouth like a floppy dog tongue.

'You what?'

'My brother.'

'Yeah, I know who Dan is. I didn't know he was in London.'

I set up the highchair and go and get Riley. As I bend over, a wave of exhaustion hits me and I stumble, my ears humming like I'm underwater. Voices, even my own, melt into the distance, faint and muffled. This always happens around this time in the afternoon. I'll be OK once I've eaten.

'Dan's on a romantic weekend with Kayla,' I tell him. 'It was their wedding anniversary last week.'

Engines are revving outside, and someone has started to

play techno music. I bet it's that idiot who had the party last night. Don't these people sleep or work?

I bring Riley into the kitchen and attempt to slide him into the highchair. He goes ramrod-straight, making it impossible for me to put his legs in. He starts to cry then stops as soon as he sees his plate of food. I wish he hadn't had that nap earlier; it's totally messed with his routine. Is this a late lunch for him or an early dinner? I can't remember.

'Where are they staying?' Tony asks as I fry the last of the whisked eggs.

'In a bed and breakfast off the A406. It's not far, so I thought we could drive.'

'He's on a romantic weekend and he couldn't even stump up for a West End hotel? With the money they make? Your brother's always been a tight bastard. What about the twins?'

'Kayla's mum has them.'

Tony waves at the tap and I pour him some water, which he downs in one. 'Must be nice to have help with the kids.'

He's talking about the absence of my parents, who moved to Torremolinos just over a year ago, managing to time it perfectly with Riley's arrival. Tony doesn't speak to anyone in his family anymore.

'Dan and Kayla booked a table for six thirty, so we can still be back in time for you to get to work,' I explain.

'Why didn't you say anything earlier? I can't go.'

I put down the spatula and it falls to the floor with a clatter.

'Calm down, babe. Don't start,' Tony mumbles while using some bread to wipe up the grease on his plate. 'I told you yesterday. I'm going to the gym, then I have to get to work early because we have some new people starting. Someone has to make money around here.'

Yes. And what a great get-out clause that has become.

I used to love my job. I worked for a tour operator, a company that specialised in bespoke travel for the wealthy over-sixties. I was able to walk to the office from where we used to live, and although it didn't pay all that well, I'd get the odd freebie like hotel stays and weekends in Paris and Rome. I used to travel a lot before Tony and I got together. The girls I worked with were fun too. I miss it – the money, the friends, the freedom. All of it.

It's been a year since I earned my own money. The plan was to take six months' maternity leave and have my parents help out but then they emigrated, Tony got a new job, and we moved miles away from my office. Anyway, I earned less than the cost of full-time childcare, so it didn't make sense for me to go back to work. Tony acts like he got the shitty end of the stick, like I'm on a perpetual holiday. But the truth is that going to work is a lot less work than staying at home all day, every day, with a baby.

'How about I see my brother on my own and take the car?' I say. 'It will be quicker. Maybe you can look after Riley?'

Tony wipes his mouth with some kitchen roll. 'Sorry, babe, I need the car. I'm going to work straight after the gym. I'm not like other men, Lu. As soon as their wives get pregnant, they get fat too. That's not me, babe.' He pats his hard stomach. 'I look after myself. Healthy body, healthy mind. You should come on a jog with me some time.'

'How am I meant to exercise with a baby? How about *I* join a gym and *you* take Riley every afternoon?'

'Calm down. You're lovely as you are,' Tony says, kissing the top of my head. He's managed to defuse another argument, even though it feels like a dismissal. I blink back tears, but he doesn't notice. I've tried explaining to Tony how I feel, but it just sounds like I'm whining and ungrateful, when he already has so much on his plate.

Whoever is playing the awful music outside has turned it up so loud now that people walking past our house have stopped to see where it's coming from. I open the kitchen window and stick my head out to take a better look. Four guys in identical black puffer jackets are gathered around the neighbour's gate holding bottles of beer. The front garden is overgrown, with a mattress leaning up against the low wall and a skip full of pieces of wood and brick taking up two parking spaces. One man with a bald head has the bonnet of his car open – that must be my neighbour – while the other three are laughing about something as he revs the engine. Why are people like this? Why don't they care about their community?

'So you can't take Riley tonight?' I shout over the noise, shutting the window with a bang.

'Sorry, I can't make it work, babe,' Tony replies. 'Anyway, the train is faster and easier than driving, and it will give you a chance to get to know the area a bit better. Check out what there is to do locally with the baby. You'll be fine.'

Will I? I can't remember the last time I caught a train where I didn't get too close to the edge, imagining how easy it would be to jump or push someone in front of an oncoming train. I wouldn't do that, of course I wouldn't, but the urge to test my limits is always so strong I end up standing with my back against the wall. I don't want to have those kinds of thoughts when Riley's with me.

'Can't you skip the gym and take us?' I ask. 'We can leave earlier that way.' I nearly add that I'm tired, that I need an early night, but that won't help because I can see in his face that Tony is already in work mode.

He really does think we are both doing the 'right thing'. Him working because that's what good dads do. Me getting up every two hours at night and pretending to cherish every minute of my baby because that's what good mums do. I heard a man in an online video earnestly saying how his wife's life never truly began until she started a family. It got over 100,000 likes and lots of men agreed in the comments. So this is it, then? This is as good as it gets? I've reached the zenith of my existence and I didn't even realise. I can hardly remember who I was before –

the woman who travelled for work, and went out with friends on a whim, who spent the weekends doing whatever she wanted without having to check that it didn't inconvenience anyone else. I think I'd hate the pre-mum me if I saw her out there, untethered, having fun with no one but herself to think about.

'Sorry, babe. Next time,' he says. 'But I bet Dan and Kayla are excited to see you and Riley. You'll have a lovely time. You deserve a night off.'

A night off? I'm taking the baby with me. It doesn't matter, he's not listening. He never listens to me. I'm telling him I need him, that I don't want to do these things by myself, yet he still does what he wants to do while making it sound like he's the reasonable one.

I flip my omelette over because it's something to do with my hands and it stops me from clenching my fists and driving them through the window. Or Tony's face.

Of all the people I've imagined hurting, of all the people I've imagined dead, Tony is the one I've thought about the most. Which I know is unfair because he's the only person in my life I can rely on right now, the only one who thinks he's helping. Tony has no idea how bad my disturbing visions have got because he's never there at night when I wake myself up shouting, my duvet soaked through with sweat, wet and acrid like blood. His blood.

I've killed him in so many different ways.

I've strangled him, my thumbs pressing into the rough skin of his throat, his stubble prickling under my short nails as I restrict his airways. I've tied my dressing gown cord around his neck and watched as his eyes bulge and turn pink then red. I've stabbed him, the blade passing through his stomach more smoothly than our knives that can never cut through the cheap, tough steak I buy.

Most of the time I'm bludgeoning Tony to death with the Opti cast-iron dumbbells he bought online with the money my mum sent over for Riley. Our son wears size 12–18 months now but most of his sleepwear is for 6–9 months. Tony was really happy with himself when he saved us money with one snip by cutting off the feet from the Babygros.

'Problem solved,' he said.

'He needs new clothes more than you need exercise equipment,' I replied.

'The dumbbells are an investment. For both of us.'

So I pound them into his face, twenty kilos of metal crashing down on his jaw and his cheekbones and his eye sockets with a dull crack.

Tony plants a kiss on his son's head and takes his plate over to the sink.

'Have fun with your brother,' he says to me with a wink. 'Enjoy your time off while you can.'

He doesn't realise that although my body is standing next to his in the kitchen right now, I'm not really here. He has no idea that in my mind he's dead and I'm a lot calmer.

'Yeah,' I say, bending down to pick up the food Riley has been scattering on the floor like chicken feed.

'You want that?' he asks.

I don't know what he's talking about, so I answer no.

When I stand back up I have to blink three times to clear the stars, and Tony is spooning the freshly cooked omelette from the pan straight into his mouth.

'Thanks for the food, babe,' he says, his lips shiny with grease. 'You've always been a brilliant cook. See you in the morning.'

My fingers are curled around the handle of the frying pan, and I wonder how long it would take to beat him to death with it. But frying pans are not great weapons.

I look around me. Knives. Messy but effective. That heavy pestle and mortar Kayla bought me last Christmas for all those spices I'm never going to grind. It's heavy but not easy to wield. Can you strangle someone with apron ties?

I watch from the kitchen doorway as he pulls on his heavy boots in the hallway and grabs his leather jacket. He's going to be cold.

'I got you milk and the razors you asked for,' I shout out.

Silence. Then a jingle of keys and the slam of the door.

'Good chat,' I mumble as I pile up the dirty pan and plates into the sink and Riley starts to scream.

FOUR

Dan and Kayla are waiting for me outside the station. My brother messaged me while I was on the train to say he's booked a restaurant nearby. Something special, apparently. Maybe it will be worth the trip after all.

I give him a hug. His arms are chunky, and his hold is a little bit too tight, but I like it. My brother, my anchor. Kayla's already busy stroking Riley's downy head.

'Thanks for meeting us all the way out here,' she says without looking at me.

Riley's gone to sleep in his pushchair again, which means he'll be awake all night now.

'Kayla said we should have met more central and had dinner in Chinatown,' Dan says, rolling his eyes. 'I said who the hell wants to go all the way to Chinatown on a Friday night? It will be rammed. She doesn't get it.' He laughs. 'Bloody Northerners, eh, Lulu?'

I give him a weak smile. They have their car with them – they could have come to us and seen the new house. Bought us a housewarming gift. We could have got a takeaway and Tony could have said a quick hello. But I don't live in the kind of area that Kayla likes to spend her Friday nights in.

'I know London quite well, *actually*,' Kayla says. I've always liked her accent. They live over 200 miles away in Liverpool, in a four-bedroom house with a huge garden that costs the same as a studio flat would cost down south. But we've never been invited to stay with them. Tony says it's too far to drive anyway.

'Here we go, Miss La-di-da,' Dan says. 'Wait up, she's about to go off on one about how her important job takes her all over the world.'

It does though. Dan hates to admit it, but Kayla earns more than him with her corporate job in something to do with IT. She's always on work trips. My brother is a plumber. The money is good, but he doesn't get to go anywhere fancy. I don't say anything; instead I fuss around inside my nappy bag like I'm looking for something even though I'm not.

Dan nudges me, forcing me to look up.

'Honestly, Lulu, you'd think she was the first mum to go back to work after having kids. I bet you never get like this about your job.'

Does he think I've been working all this time? Who does he think is looking after the baby?

It takes us less than a minute to walk to the restaurant. It's an Italian called Giovanni's and it has a board outside advertising their specials, none of which sound very appealing. Or cheap. We go inside and are seated at a table laid out for four.

'Are you waiting for one more guest?' the waiter asks.

I shake my head and he hands us each a menu. It's A3 and laminated.

'I thought Tony was coming,' Dan says.

I shrug. 'Work.'

'Got to hand it to him, Lulu. That man of yours is a grafter!'

I don't reply and Kayla is staring at her phone, probably

checking the twins are OK. My brother has the type of toddlers who sit quietly colouring in all day, not the destructive kind who can't be left alone for two minutes. I doubt I'll be that lucky. Neither of them mentions Tony after that, which makes things a little less awkward.

I always feel so underdressed next to Kayla. She's wearing a beige sweater that I think is cashmere and cream trousers that no mother I know would ever dare to own. Her face is dewy and her hair always looks like it's been professionally blow-dried. Tony looked after Riley this afternoon for long enough that I could get ready, although no amount of make-up could hide the bags under my eyes.

'Bet it's nice to have a night off from cooking,' Dan says to me. 'How's the new place?'

'Lovely,' I lie. 'Really nice.'

I order the carbonara because it's the only dish I recognise and it's the cheapest. Tony and I haven't been out for dinner since before Riley was born, so it wouldn't be fair of me to be splashing our cash around when it's not even a special occasion. Kayla and Dan get a starter each, some wet mozzarella stuff for her and huge prawns with their heads still on for him. I nibble on a breadstick while I wait for them to finish, tucking two under my plate for when Riley wakes up.

'Happy anniversary for last week,' I add, holding my glass of water up, which they both clink with their wine. I sent them a card. I hope they didn't expect a gift as well.

'Five years,' Kayla says wistfully, holding my brother's hand. He looks at her with puppy-dog eyes but she's looking down, fiddling with her napkin.

Five years. That's five years since I met Tony at their wedding. Kayla worked with a girl called Kitty and invited her to the evening reception, and she brought her boyfriend along. That was Tony. Kitty and Tony didn't match... at all. Kitty was all woo-woo, wearing a big floaty kaftan in shades of pink and yellow with dangly earrings and sandals, even though it was early November. She was drunk and dancing with her arms up in the air like a hippy at Woodstock, golden hair sticking to her sweaty apple cheeks. And Tony, well, he looked like one of those sexy bad guys from an action movie, the kind that would shoot at you while hanging off a speeding motorcycle. He never got up to dance once, just sat there staring at his girlfriend as if he was at a show he didn't want to be at.

I was there on my own because an estate agent I was dating at the time had dumped me the week before. Kayla had chosen me to be one of her bridesmaids, probably because my brother had made her, and I was wearing a fifties-style dress the colour of duck eggs. I thought duck eggs were cream, but it turned out to be some kind of minty-blue number with a big sticky-out skirt like something Sandy from *Grease* would wear. I looked ridiculous and I know Kayla did it on purpose. She appears to be nice on the outside but deep down I'm convinced she gets a kick from making me feel like shit. Her other two bridesmaids were her sister, who was eighteen back then, and her best mate, who's a fitness instructor. Funnily enough their dresses didn't look that bad on them.

I was on the Prosecco and sitting on my own. Tony was nursing a pint at the other table, watching everyone watch his girlfriend, his face so blank I was desperate to know what he was thinking. After a while I sat at his table and said hello.

'You one of the bridesmaids?' he asked.

'No,' I replied. 'Dressing up like my nan's lampshade is one of my sexual kinks.'

Tony didn't even crack a smile. 'Some lampshades are very sexy, actually.'

I laughed so hard I snorted, which made him grin.

We talked and talked that night. He was funny back then. As we laughed at his girlfriend's increasingly erratic dance moves, he made a point of telling me that the two of them weren't that serious. I thought he was going to kiss me that night, but he didn't.

Tony and Kitty didn't last – in fact, she left Kayla's work a few weeks later and they didn't stay in touch, but Tony somehow became Dan's best friend so stayed around. Dan told me months later that Tony had asked for my number at the wedding, but he never called. I told myself that I didn't care, he wasn't my type anyway, but it wasn't that easy to avoid him. He was at my brother's thirtieth birthday party the following year and a New Year's Eve party Dan and Kayla threw the year after that. At every event, there was Tony, sitting at a table dressed in black and sipping a pint. Always with the same kind of woman – posh, blonde and well dressed. Women with clipped voices who called him 'Anthony' and never really wanted to be at these kinds of events but thought it was all 'rather fun'.

'Tony's girlfriends are so sophisticated,' Kayla would tell me, as if to say that I was wasting my time flirting with him. Men like Tony didn't like girls like me. Men like Tony aimed higher than that.

But I knew he liked me. I knew because at every party he'd hunt me out in the crowd, his dark eyes scanning everybody's faces until they landed on mine. Then he'd tip his chin up in a way that asked if I wanted a drink, and without saying a word we'd join the smokers outside even though neither of us smoked. He would do all of this with a straight face, serious, like it was business, until we'd find ourselves alone and he finally got to be himself.

'You're easy to talk to,' he'd say.

And I'd roll my eyes and reply with something stupid like, 'That's because your girlfriends only know how to talk about horses and skiing.'

We kissed twice. Once when he was dating a woman called Suzie who he didn't know how to get rid of, and once when I was dumped by a guy I met in the pub who owned his own snooker cue and hated going to the cinema because it was easier to watch a film at home. We called both kisses a drunken mistake and laughed it off, saying how we'd never be able to date properly because things would get messy. You don't risk friendship for a shag.

I never told him I was crazy about him because I believed him when he said I was like family to him. I liked that he would always be in my life, even if just as my brother's friend. I felt safe around him. Like everything would be OK.

Then Tony got engaged to Nadine, and I knew I'd lost him. She was a beautiful lawyer with a honey-coloured bob and a summer house on the Côte d'Azur. I knew all about the French Riviera because of my job, and I knew exactly the kind of people who could afford to have a holiday home there. Tony had hit the jackpot. It didn't matter what he did, he always seemed to land on his feet.

I think it's because men are better at being happy than women are. I'm sure of it. I look over at my brother now, at how content and at ease he looks with his perfect wife, his perfect kids safely tucked up in bed far away, and his overpriced wine that he can enjoy any day of the week if he wanted to, and I wonder how many crossroads we have in life where things can go a million different ways.

Like the night Tony turned up on my doorstep, his eyes rimmed red and his chin wobbling.

'Nadine wants us to move to New York and apparently never wants kids,' he'd said before I'd opened the door fully.

I didn't even know that Tony knew where I lived. Had he asked Dan for my address along with my number all those years ago? I opened the door fully, but instead of stepping inside he threw his arms around me and sobbed into my neck.

'I said England was better to raise children in than America and she said she never wanted a family. We'd never discussed it, Lu. I just presumed every woman wanted children.'

I wanted children. And I knew Tony did. It was something we talked about all the time, how we both wished we'd come from bigger families with raucous barbeques full of rowdy cousins and crazy Christmases like in the movie *The Family Stone*. How had he never told Nadine that? What did they even talk about?

Tony stayed at my house that night, a Friday, refusing to go back home to her. In the morning he called Nadine to break up with her, but she beat him to it. An hour later we were making love on my sofa, and it felt like the most natural thing in the world. He said so too. As we lay side by side in my bed, his stubbly jaw grazing my collarbone, his eyelids flickering in and out of sleep, he said this was 'it'. That I felt like home. That he'd only just realised that he'd always loved me, and he was sorry he'd wasted so much time. I was so happy in that moment I thought my chest was going to explode. I lay there stroking his hair, listening to our breaths in tandem, too scared to speak and shatter our bubble of perfection.

We saw one another every day after that until three months later I found out I was pregnant. He was elated. I was terrified. The world tilted on its axis that day and I've never been able to stand up straight since.

'The carbonara is for her,' Dan says. I snap my head up, pulled back to the present. Riley is still sleeping but my brother is looking at me like I have something on my face.

'Do I have something on my face?' I ask.

'You were mumbling,' he replies. I look at Kayla. She's folding and refolding her napkin.

'Sorry. I'm just really tired.' I take a deep breath. 'So, how are the twins?'

'Marigold and Petunia are doing wonderfully,' Kayla says.

I close my eyes at the sound of their names and will myself not to laugh. Tony and I weren't even a couple yet when my brother told me their names, but Tony was still the first person I told because I knew he'd find it as funny as I did. I wasn't wrong. We laughed so much he said he had tears running down his cheeks. I keep trying to call them 'Marie' and 'Niah' but Kayla gets angry... so now I just call them 'the twins'.

'They're so advanced for their age,' Kayla continues. 'We enrolled them in the local Montessori school. They have chickens there, you know.'

I move the gelatinous spaghetti around my plate, wondering whether Riley needs chickens in his life. Dan has ordered the steak and Kayla the seafood spaghetti marinara. I don't know why those two are so obsessed with having prawn eyes staring at them all evening.

Kayla picks her phone back up. 'The girls have such different personalities.' She shows me a photo on her phone. I've seen that exact photo three times already – once on Facebook, once on Instagram and once on the WhatsApp group we have that's just me, Kayla and Dan. Tony left the group a week after we added him, saying all the notifications were stressing him out. I wish I had the balls to leave a group chat with no prelude or fanfare, and no fear of being judged. He's not missing anything. The WhatsApp chat is just photos of our kids.

'Cute,' I say. Which is what I wrote on WhatsApp when she sent that photo last week. 'Are you both having a nice time away just the two of you?'

Dan nods, chewing his steak for ages. He likes his meat so overcooked he may as well be eating his shoes.

'Loving it,' he says. 'It's nice to see everything like a tourist, you know? Didn't bother with the London Dungeon or the London Eye, massive rip-off, but the M&M shop was fun. Eh, Kayla?'

She looks up from her phone and nods, but she doesn't eat sugar, so I doubt it's been the highlight of her trip. All these years and I'm not sure how I feel about my sister-in-law. I don't hate her, but I find it hard to get close to her. I think it's because she makes everything look easy when I find everything so difficult. She acts like she's too good for my brother and I hate that, even though she's probably right. Maybe she thought all of Tony's exes were too good for him too. I'm clearly not.

I watch my sister-in-law, so comfortable ignoring us while she flicks though her phone, confidently wearing tailored cream trousers while eating a plate of pasta soaked in red sauce. How is she always so clean and neat?

I imagine what Kayla would look like covered in blood, her cashmere jumper matted brown, her trousers bright red. I imagine her self-satisfied smirk turning slack, her skin waxy and sallow, her perfection reduced to nothing more than the thin skin and brittle bones we are all made of.

Kayla would probably be really hard to kill. She's strong in a lithe way. She's into her Pilates and does classes like 'kicksasize' and 'boxparty'. The only way to kill her would be from behind. In the dark. Maybe in a park or an unlit side street.

I'm not sure if a plastic bag would work best or wire around her throat. A bag would be quieter and easier to hook over her head. Then she'd go down quicker, and once she was down I could do whatever it took. Maybe a brick or stone to the head – the bag would contain the blood and keep me clean, although her face would be a right mess. A sense of calm washes over me as I imagine Kayla looking anything less than immaculate.

'And Riley is doing well, is he?' she asks.

I look up, blinking away the images of her brutal murder until her perfectly made-up face comes back into view.

This is what conversation looks like once you have kids – everything moves over to them. It's not 'How are you?' but 'How's your child?' Even when you're pregnant it's, 'Don't eat that. Don't do that. Don't go there... It's not good for the baby.' Mothers are conduits, not people.

'Riley? Oh, yes, he's great,' I reply.

'Is he walking yet?'

'Not yet.' I force a smile. Kayla already knows this because only yesterday I sent a video of my son staggering around the furniture. Which I think is really impressive for a child who turns one in seven weeks. She's told me more than once that the twins were walking by ten months. Of course they were.

'He'll get there,' Kayla says.

'Yeah.'

I wind the congealed spaghetti around my fork, my mouth filling up with saliva. I'm so hungry I'm not even hungry anymore. I reach for the wine, but the bottle is already empty. I take a sip of water instead.

I'm struggling to keep my eyes open, and this warm restaurant and mountain of carbs aren't helping. Jesus. I have to snap out of this fug. All I keep thinking is that Tony is out of the house and Riley is asleep, which means I could be sleeping myself right now. Instead, I'm here, and Riley will probably sleep all the way home, and then two hours after I get to bed he'll wake up and be up until four, and then Tony will get home at six and... More sleep maths. I'm so tired of the obsessive calculations. My mouth keeps filling with saliva and I swallow it down.

'You OK?' Dan asks.

He lays his heavy hand on my arm and for a short moment it stops the tide from washing me away.

'What? Yeah. Sorry. I'm just really tired.'

'Oh, we know what that's like,' Dan says, raising his eyebrows at Kayla. 'Remember what a nightmare it was with the girls?'

'Didn't you have one of those maternity nurses?' I ask.

'Only for the first eight weeks,' Kayla says.

'Then Mum came to stay with you.'

Kayla makes a face. I hate that she's always complaining about my mum, even though Dan and I are always moaning about her too. My parents visited the twins straight away when they were born as they were still in the UK. Then Mum stayed on longer to help out. She wasn't there for me when Riley was born though, and she's only seen him once this year. My parents say seeing their grandchildren is a lot harder now they're in Spain, and there's no one to look after the dog, plus there wasn't enough room for them at our old house. There wasn't, and there's even less in the new place, but that's not the point.

'Yes, Dawn was helpful but, you know, she can be a bit much.'

You got to sleep all night though, didn't you? You fucking slept.

I take another bite of my meal and swallow, forcing it down with a bubble of rage and the teary lump trying to fight their way up my throat.

'The twins are two and a half now. Surely they're sleeping better,' I say.

'Of course,' Kayla snaps, like I've buried an insult inside my innocuous comment. 'They sleep ten hours a night. But it's still hard, Louise.'

Yeah, must be so hard to sleep all night, and retain your career and your looks and your fancy wardrobe, and have your mum nearby to help out and babysit for you while you get to escape on sexy five-star weekends together.

'Sorry. I'm just really tired,' I mumble.

'We're all tired. At our age *everyone's* tired.' Dan laughs and looks at his wife like I'm his stupid little sister, even though they're both younger than me.

Kayla gives me a tight-lipped smile, which is hard to do with lips as plumped-up as hers.

'You'll be fine, Lu,' she says. 'Just sleep when the baby does.'

'Right.' I slurp up the spaghetti, flecks of white splattering over my cheeks. 'I'll sleep when he sleeps. I'll then clean when he cleans. Shop when he shops. Go out when he goes out. Screw when he screws. Make money when he makes money.

He's asleep now. Maybe I should crawl under the table and have a nap right here between courses?'

Kayla looks at Dan, who places his hand on my arm again. A little heavier this time.

'Take it easy, Lulu. Don't work yourself up. You need a day off.'

'Yeah, you're right.' I change the subject. 'So, what are your plans while you're here?'

'Having a quiet day tomorrow,' Dan replies.

'That's nice. So you have nothing planned?'

He shakes his head. Tomorrow is Saturday. They'll be in London until Monday. I wait, but the offer to look after Riley doesn't come.

'I'm having a "me" day,' Kayla adds. 'And Dan is going to catch up on the football in bed. You should try taking some time off for yourself once in a while.'

Everything on the table is beginning to double up, shift around, turn hazy. I screw up my eyes, but it doesn't help. I sip more water. I can't finish my dinner.

Kayla orders a gin and tonic instead of dessert and Dan has a cheeseboard. I ask the waiter to pack up my pasta for later. I'll have to put it inside a baby food box in the fridge so Tony doesn't see it when he gets in or he'll think it's for him.

By the time the bill arrives it's nearly nine o'clock and I'm doing the sleep maths again. I need to get home – which means leaving soon because trains are every thirty minutes after nine – and then hope Riley doesn't wake up while I put him down. How will I get his coat off him and change his nappy without waking him? There's no way I'm getting to bed before midnight tonight. I just hope that stupid git down the road isn't playing his music loudly again.

The waiter is standing over us holding a card reader. I put my card on the table and Dan hands it over with his own, saying something about splitting the bill, although I'm not really concentrating.

It's not until I'm on the train that I remember I forgot my spaghetti. I look at the receipt and my stomach dips. The waiter put fifty per cent on each card plus a tip. Shit! How am I going to explain to Tony that one bowl of pasta and a glass of tap water cost me sixty-five quid?

FIVE

I saw that selfish bastard again last night. The noisy neighbour. I recognised him and his stupid friends when Riley and I returned home from the train station. It was past ten o'clock and he was standing outside the King's Arms pub, a beer in his hand, laughing with the same men I saw him with before. I wonder if he has any idea how his actions affect everyone around him. I wonder if he cares.

I imagined approaching him, telling him that he's selfish and cruel for playing his music so loudly at night. Although it wouldn't have achieved anything. He'd probably have just laughed in my face, his friends joining in, a circle of drunk men braying at me like excitable donkeys. If life were like the movies, I'd have snatched the pint glass from his hand, smashed it against his bald head, held the glinting glass to his pale throat. I'd have put my face close to his and told him to watch it. To have some respect.

But this isn't the movies, it's real life, and women don't do things like that. We keep our heads low, and we walk fast. The men all glanced up as I passed them with the stroller then turned away again, none of them making space on the pavement for me. They probably don't think a mother should be out this late with her child because it's not safe. But it's not the night and the dark we fear, it's them, because women know all too well that men like that only have four categories for us – too young, fuckable, mum, too old – the boundaries for each blurring with every pint they drink. They want us, they hate us or they simply can't see us.

I knew Riley wouldn't settle after sleeping all evening, and sure enough, as soon as we got home, he wanted to eat and play, and he didn't get to sleep until an hour later. And sure enough, as soon as I got into bed, the pubs emptied, and the man down the road started playing his music loudly again.

It's now one o'clock in the morning and I'm staring up at the ceiling, thinking about everything I'll be too tired to do in the morning because one person has decided to keep the entire neighbourhood awake. The injustice of it is unbearable. *It's not fair*. There's so much rage building up inside of me that I don't know where to put it. It's white-hot, pushing up against my gums, scratching beneath the surface of my skin, bubbling up like vomit in my throat, making me want to scream. How does my body produce so much anger when I'm so tired I could weep?

I attempt to drown out the noise with my phone, playing 'relaxing meditation sounds' on Spotify while flicking through the pages of a book I've not managed to finish in four months, but nothing works. My body is too tense with impotent fury. I even contemplate getting up and unpacking the boxes, but I don't want to tire myself out even more when I'm going to be woken up by Riley at least once between now and daylight.

I don't understand how anyone else on the street is sleeping. They probably have earplugs in but I'm too scared to do that in case I don't hear my baby cry. And I can't walk down the street and ask my neighbour to turn his awful music down. No woman in her right mind would go out in the dead of night in her pyjamas and knock on the house of a drunk man. And I can't leave my baby home alone. Maybe Tony can go over there in the morning. No. He won't deem it worthy of starting a potential argument over. All that will do is cause a feud within a few weeks of having moved to the street. I contemplate calling the police, but the police aren't going to waste their time talking to a man playing crap techno too loudly – not when London is full of people getting beaten up, raped and murdered.

So I lie here, breaths coming in sharp pulls, skin prickling with frustration, imagining all the ways I want to kill the antisocial scumbag.

He must live alone to behave like that. I've never seen a woman or children near his house. That would make killing him easier. Men like him don't fear answering the door; he probably doesn't even lock it. It wouldn't be hard to take something from that full skip outside his house, sitting there like an eyesore, a gnarled chunk of stone or a heavy piece of wood studded with nails, and hit him. Drunk people don't have quick reactions. I can see it now, walking silently down his carpeted hallway, the back of his billiard-ball head shining in the moonlight as he nods along to his shitty music. He can't hear me as I raise my hands and bring the wood over his head. It cracks, like an egg, the yolk bright red as he collapses on to his filthy carpet. And I keep beating him. And I don't stop. Maybe he makes a sound, but if he does, it's drowned out by the incessant thump of the techno. And that's how I leave him, dead, crumpled up on his dirty floor, reduced to nothing but a pile of bloody, discarded clothes.

I don't know if the music is finally turned off or if my bloody visions lull me to sleep, but I eventually drift off until I'm woken by the piercing cries of my son and the scrape of the key in the lock. My day has begun.

SIX

It's a cold but sunny Saturday, so I decide to take Riley to the park because Tony has taken the weekend shift for extra money and has to rest beforehand. The park has a small children's play area and a café. Now Riley is old enough to sit up in a baby swing it's nice for him to join in with other children, although I take my own food and drink to save money.

He's calm in his pushchair as we make our way down the street, pointing at the birds and chewing on a rice cracker. The sun is warming my face, the sky the colour of washed-out denim, and for a split-second I'm happy. Not full of joy, and heavy with exhaustion, but the weather has lifted my spirits and I feel hopeful for the first time in a long time. Maybe everything *will* be OK here, in our new house; maybe I'll make friends and so will Riley and I'll create a nice home for us. I can do that. I *want* to do that.

As I near the end of our road I slow down to smile at two women talking over the low walls of their front gardens. One of them is holding gardening gloves and the other looks like she's been to the shops. They're saying something about techno, and I wonder if they're talking about the loud music last night.

'Hi?' I say.

Riley waves at them, which makes them both grin.

'You're the family that moved into number ten,' the one holding gardening gloves says to me.

I nod and introduce myself and my son. They wave back at Riley, and he gives them a big grin with his four teeth. They melt and make aww noises and it makes my chest ache.

'I'm Shona,' the one with the shopping says. She has a colourful scarf wrapped around her head, thick dark hair cascading from the top, her nails impossibly long.

'I'm Beth,' the other one says. Her hands are pink from the cold, and she rubs them together. 'Have you met your next-door neighbours yet?'

I shake my head.

'On your left, at number twelve, you have the Patel family. They're nice, but they're not around much. Then on the other side you have Jim at number eight. Lives on his own. He broke his leg a few weeks back and his sister, Maggie, has come to look after him. She lives in Devon. Not sure how long she's here for though.'

It's a lot to take in but I smile and nod. What they're telling me doesn't have to be fascinating, it's simply nice to talk to an adult beyond the usual 'hello' you give to shopkeepers and bus drivers.

'Sorry if I'm a bit of a zombie today,' I say. 'I'm really tired.'

Shona points at Riley. 'Not an easy age. How's it going?'

'Fine,' I say, because I'm scared if I say too much I'll either burst into tears or bore them to death.

'Mine are teens now,' Shona adds. 'And Beth's are all grown up with kids of their own. It goes quickly but when they're little like Riley days feel like months, and entire months feel like one long never-ending day. Right?'

'Yeah, he's not a great sleeper,' I say. 'I could have done without being kept awake by that music last night.'

The two women look at one another, their mouths set into straight lines.

'That's Dave,' Beth says under her breath, as if he can hear us from the other end of the street. 'Selfish wanker. We were just talking about him. That used to be his mum's house, Gladys, lovely woman. She died a few months back and he moved in. He got divorced recently and his mum must have left him some money because he's started doing up the house. It's taking forever and all he's managed to do is fill a skip, throw rubbish into his front garden and make our street look even worse than it did already. You'd think a man his age would know better than to act like a stupid teenager with all that noise and mess.'

Shona kisses her teeth and shakes her head. 'I told my husband we need to have a word with him, but he said it's not worth having beef with the neighbours.'

And that's exactly what men like Dave rely on: collective fear.

'Has anyone ever called the police?' I ask.

Shona snorts and Beth smiles. 'They don't care about us around these parts,' Beth says gently. 'We don't even have proper working streetlights or a regular bin collection. All the police around here do is stop and search young men in the street.'

'Tell me about it,' Shona adds. 'My boys never get any peace when all they're doing is walking to school with their friends. But Dave over there? He gets away with everything. All those men hanging about all the time? I wouldn't be surprised if he was dealing too.'

Beth nods and Shona says something about having to get inside before her frozen food melts, even though the air still has a bite to it regardless of the milky winter sun.

'Off anywhere nice?' Beth asks me, as if I'm not wearing

leggings and a cheap coat, my greasy hair tied up on top of my head.

'Thought I'd take Riley to the park,' I reply.

Beth shows me a shortcut, Shona dumps her heavy shopping in the house, and I thank them both, saying something generic about having a cup of tea together one day.

I don't know. Maybe I will. Maybe it's not so bad around here after all.

They both go inside, and I look over my shoulder at house number four. Dave's house, three doors down from mine. I imagine him inside sleeping off last night's drink, his mum's knick-knacks still on the mantelpiece beside his empty beer cans and old newspapers, his kitchen half-ripped out and in the skip outside. Then I see it all again, but with him dead in the middle of his living room, his face mangled and unrecognisable.

Would anyone miss him? Or would killing him be doing everyone a favour?

SEVEN

I can't see. My nostrils sting with each heaving breath, my lungs filling with the metallic scent of something hot, cloying, bad. I'm walking, even though everything is a blur. The ground is soft, then it's hard and sharp and cold. I stop, dropping whatever I'm holding in my hand, feeling it smash on the ground, shards showering my bare feet. Using both hands I rub at my sticky eyes, digging my knuckles into my wet sockets until I can see better.

It's dark and I'm on my street. The pavement is damp and full of crumbled concrete and glass, the gaps between my toes filling with debris as I stumble towards my house, each step falling in time to the distant thud of music. My jaw aches, my hands sting, my knees are sore.

I'm outside my front door now. It's too dark to see where I'm hurt. Most of the streetlights at my end of the road have been smashed, the few remaining too far away to illuminate where I'm standing.

I'm trapped in a nightmare. This isn't real. When I find myself caught inside a dream, the best thing to do is to move my body and step back inside of myself. I shake my head, willing myself to wake up, but I remain standing. I blink, my eyes still stinging. I rub them with my fists, but it only makes the pain worse. I peer closer at my black hands. It looks like oil, but it smells like blood. Where did that come from? Whose blood is that dripping from my fingers and soaking through my tartan pyjamas?

I pull at my hair and feel pain. This is not a nightmare. I jump once, noting the sharp bite of the doorstep against my toes and the heavy pull of my breasts as they bounce up and down. This is real. I don't want it to be real. I want to wake up!

I check the soles of my feet: they're black too and have turned numb from the cold. Maroon smears dry and flake at my wrists. I smell of hot pennies, of thick cuts of meat left out in the sun. There's a gash on the palm of my hand. Is all of this *my* blood? My skin is burning. I can feel the pain now.

I'm hurt and I'm not dreaming. I'm awake and I'm outside of my house. I try the door handle, but it doesn't open. Of course it doesn't. In this neighbourhood the front doors automatically lock when you shut them behind you; and still, everyone adds extra locks to the inside.

With bloody fists clenched, I bang on my door, leaving crimson splodges against the white wood.

'Let me in!' I shout.

I look around. The street is still and dark, the witching hour when the good are yet to wake and even the bad have had their fill. The in-between hours where anything can happen and nobody knows. A fox scampers past, the air ringing with the incessant beat of the neighbour's awful music. Is everyone wearing earplugs? Is that why no one is coming to my rescue?

I don't know why I'm banging on my front door when Tony is at work, like he is every night. There's nobody home.

My baby.

'Help!' I shout.

I don't know who I'm shouting to, who I expect to hear me

at this time of night, but all I can think about is Riley inside the house all alone. How long have I been wandering the streets? Did I hurt myself while I was sleepwalking? My hand is starting to throb; tears gather, making my eyes sting even further. I need to stay calm.

It's OK. I'm OK. My baby is OK.

I look around me, as if a passing stranger will run to my rescue. But this isn't a nice part of London; this isn't a Richard Curtis movie where couples go for romantic moonlit strolls and jolly policemen patrol the streets. Music and shouting in the early hours are nothing out of the ordinary here. Everyone minds their own business; that's what you do in this neighbourhood if you want to stay safe.

I try my kitchen window, but it doesn't budge because it's always kept locked so no dangerous crazy people break into my house in the middle of the night. Now I'm the crazy one everyone is ignoring. There's no point banging on the door again, I'll only wake Riley, so I ring Jim's doorbell next door. Surely he'll understand that it's an emergency and won't be angry with me. I don't know how broken his leg is, whether he can hobble to the door or if he's in a wheelchair. I knock three times. Three sharp raps. Then I instantly regret it. I shouldn't be introducing myself to my neighbours for the first time in the middle of the night wearing bloodstained pyjamas. But what choice do I have?

'It's me,' I shout out. 'Lu. Your neighbour. I'm in a spot of bother.'

The door opens an inch, the chain secured, and a woman is standing there. She's in her late forties, blonde hair in a neat bob, a fluffy dressing gown tied tightly around her middle. She looks like she's just got out of the shower.

Of course. Jim's sister.

'You must be Maggie,' I say.

She frowns at me, her eyes growing wider as she takes in the rest of me: the grisly pyjama top and dirty bare feet and my fingers covered in blood.

'Oh my God,' she says, hands flying to her mouth.

I start to cry, snot and blood and tears running into my mouth. 'I'm so sorry to bother you but I'm locked out and my baby is inside alone. I think I'm hurt.'

She's looking behind me, at the empty street, and to her right in the direction of the loud music.

'What happened to you?'

The relief of someone sharing a modicum of concern has me crying so hard I can hardly speak. My shoulders are shaking, and my mouth is wide open, a gaping maw of fear and confusion.

'I'm fine. I was sleepwalking, and I cut my hand and... my baby... please.'

She shuts the door and I crumple into myself. I don't blame her for being scared. For being wary of a bleeding, hysterical woman crying on her doorstep.

I need to try another neighbour. But who? Maybe the two women down the road – Shona and Beth. They seemed kind, both mums. They'll understand. Except I want them to like me, not think I'm a madwoman and a bad mother.

My heart is racing, breaths juddering in my chest, tears cutting streaks through the blood tightening on my face. I turn in the direction of the music still blaring from number four. Dave. Dave and his fucking music. He must still be awake, but I'm not going anywhere near him. Men like Dave don't help. They're the cause of people's pain.

Maggie opens the door again, this time with the latch no longer in place. She's holding up a set of keys. 'Jim still has these from when the Andrews family lived at yours.'

A wave of relief washes over me and I smile.

'He used to feed their cat,' Maggie continues. Is she talking about Shadow? 'Come along,' she says, jingling the keys in my face and shutting her front door quietly.

Maggie's dressing gown is white and fluffy, the expensive kind that smells like clean cotton, and beneath that I can see navy-blue silk pyjamas and velvety slippers that match. She's steering me to my door, her manicured hand on my stained sleeve, and I keep thinking of her fancy white dressing gown.

'I'm going to get you dirty,' I say.

'Don't worry about that.'

Her hair is so neat, like she's been out or on her way out, even though it's the middle of the night. She lets herself into my house and bustles me through the door. I've only just noticed she has a plastic box under her white fluffy arm.

'My baby,' I cry, running up the stairs two at a time, leaving more red streaks on the door of his nursery as I peer inside. I wait for my eyes to grow accustomed to the dark, watching Riley's chest rise up and down, listening to him breathe. At the sight of him safe and well, adrenaline pours out of me, my legs buckling and my shoulders shaking as I let out wracking sobs.

'Sorry,' I say to Maggie as I creep back downstairs. 'I'm so sorry. For all of this. I'm really sorry.'

I'm shaking all over now, either from the shock of finding myself locked outside, or the wet cold wind, or the sight of my nightclothes covered in so much blood now Maggie has switched the kitchen light on.

I glance up at the clock on the wall – 2.43am.

Maggie's lips are tight, but she stays quiet as she motions for me to sit at the small kitchen table on which she has laid out the medical contents of the box. Everything Maggie does is so precise that I find myself following instructions like a dirty rat dancing to the sweet sounds of the Pied Piper. Maggie doesn't look like someone who has ever made a mistake; she looks like the kind of woman who only shops organic, buys her clothes from boutiques and doesn't speak unless she's spoken to.

I haven't had a chance to unpack any of the moving boxes stacked in the corner, and my dinner plate is still in the sink. What must she think of me?

'Sorry about the mess,' I mumble.

'Let me look at that cut on your hand,' she replies. I hold out my hand and she takes it in her own, which is warm and clean. The shaking slows down a little at the touch of her.

'Are you a nurse?' I say, feeling like a wide-eyed child who knows she's safe now. 'You have a great bedside manner.'

She gives a slow nod and a small smile. She runs her thumb over the gash, and I flinch.

'It's not deep,' she says. 'It won't need stitches. That's a lot of blood you've produced for such a small injury.'

I look down at my nightclothes. They're ruined.

'What happened?' she asks.

'I don't remember. I went to bed a few hours ago and next thing I found myself a few doors down covered in blood and locked out of my house.'

'You don't remember anything?'

I shake my head.

'Do you live alone? Other than the baby?'

I shake my head again. 'My partner works nights.'

'I should call him.'

'No!' I shout. 'Sorry, I mean, no thank you. He'll only worry. I don't want him to think this kind of thing happens all the time.'

I don't even want to imagine how that conversation would go. How do you explain to your partner that your nightmare was so vivid you sleepwalked around the street at night and hurt yourself?

'Of course,' Maggie says gently. I'm sure in her line of work she sees all sorts of horrors. 'Go and have a shower. Leave your pjs outside the door and I'll see if I can get the stains out. You may need to throw them away, though. When you're done, I'll look at your hand again.'

I'm nodding, agreeing with everything she's saying, but I don't move. I can't.

'Everything is going to be all right.' She says it so gently, and so assuredly, I actually believe her.

'Don't leave me.'

Her gaze is soft and gentle. 'I won't. I'll stay here as long as you need me to.' She squeezes my uninjured hand and I breathe out. 'You've had a nasty shock, Lu, but you're going to be fine.'

I nod again, swallowing down more tears. Kindness always makes me cry. I can't remember the last time anyone was this nice to me. After a few deep breaths I get up slowly and do as I'm told, throwing my dirty pyjamas outside the bathroom door, gasping as the temperature of the shower goes from freezing cold to piping hot. The water turns pink from so much blood, it's even in my hair and up my nose. The cut on my hand stings from the pressure of the water and I pick the black out from under my torn fingernails, attempting to recall everything that happened last night.

There was an argument. Tony was in a bad mood when I got back from the park with Riley because he'd seen how much I'd paid for that meal with my brother.

'I'm working weekends so you can spend close to seventy quid on dinner for one? We can't afford that, Lu,' Tony shouted. 'The least Dan could have done was treat you, the tight bastard!'

He was right, we don't have spare money to throw away. I should have been concentrating when we paid the bill, but it's too awkward to bring it up now. I tried to explain this to Tony but everything that came out of my mouth sounded stupid and my head was swimming so much I felt like I was being held underwater. Tony left for work earlier than normal, muttering something about seeing the lads for a game of snooker, and I tried to unpack more boxes then gave up and put Riley to bed early. He fussed on and off until I finally fell asleep at eleven o'clock, covering my head with two pillows as the neighbour's music started up again.

That's all I remember. I was angry and exhausted, but I must have slept, or I wouldn't have been sleepwalking.

When I come downstairs, my hair wet and dressed in clean pyjamas, Maggie has already wiped the blood off the doors and made us some tea. My pyjamas have gone. Maybe she put them in the wash. She places a plaster over the cut on the palm of my hand and gives me that warm smile of hers.

'Better?'

I nod and take a sip of my tea. It's sweet and milky, exactly how I like it. 'Did you wash up?' I ask.

'Yes, I had a bit of a clean-up. I hope you don't mind. It's hard enough having a baby, let alone being kept awake all night with all that racket and no one to help you.'

I bite my lips together so I don't well up again.

'Thank you,' I say. 'You're very nice.'

She laughs softly. 'You don't know that,' she says. 'None of us are perfect, we just try our best. So you really don't remember anything at all about tonight?'

I shake my head and she looks at me with a mix of pity and confusion.

'That's good,' she says. 'Probably for the best.'

EIGHT

I'm already awake when Tony comes home a little later than normal. I'm in the kitchen allowing Riley to watch *Teletubbies* on my phone as I spoon porridge into his mouth because I've had three hours' sleep in total and I'm good for nothing.

Tony makes a face at my lazy parenting – no 'good morning' or 'how did you sleep?' or hello kiss. I half expect him to continue last night's argument about money or make a flippant remark about how the boxes in the kitchen still haven't been unpacked, but he's pointing out of the window saying something about yellow tape.

'What?' I say.

He throws his coat on the banister of the stairs and joins us in the kitchen.

'Hello, champ,' he says to Riley, ruffling his downy hair. The baby looks up, waving his hands about so fast he knocks the plastic bowl of porridge out of my hands; some of it lands in my lap.

I repress a sigh and wipe it up as Tony pulls the baby from his highchair and nuzzles his neck.

'The police,' he says to me. 'You not seen? They've cornered off the end of the street. Where the skip is.'

I put the bowl down and go to the window. I have to crane my neck all the way to the right to see the lights and yellow tape. That's weird. They're near number four. Surely they wouldn't be making so much fuss over a noisy neighbour. I think of my bloody pyjamas last night. What happened to them? Did I throw them away? So much blood from such a small cut...

'Is that number four?' I ask.

Tony shrugs. 'Looks like it.'

'I'm sure it's nothing serious,' I say.

If it's number four, then I bet that knobhead, Dave, has been busted for drugs. Shona and Beth said they thought he was dealing. Good. Hopefully the police will take him away and the music will finally stop.

'What you up to today?' Tony asks.

It takes a while to register that he's speaking to me. I'm not used to him asking me that. I'm not used to having an answer.

I stifle a yawn. 'Nothing. Unpacking a bit more, maybe take Riley for a walk. He liked the park yesterday. Are you working tonight?' I ask.

Tony looks distracted, like what I'm saying doesn't make sense.

'You know I am. I have that project, the German one. I'm going to be flat out.'

'I wasn't sure because you don't normally work on a Sunday. It is Sunday today, right?'

'Yeah, Lu. It's Sunday. You sure you're OK? You seem a bit spaced out.'

'What?' I blink hard, my eyes scratchy and sore. 'I'm fine!'

'What happened to your hand?'

I busy myself loading the washing machine. Where are my bloody pyjamas? They aren't in the washing machine or wash basket. Did I throw them away or did Maggie take them with her?

'I cut myself peeling potatoes,' I say.

'Potatoes? But you cooked pasta last night.'

I don't need to answer because Riley launches himself out of his father's arms and into mine and he smells so awful I have to go and change him right away.

'I have a lot on tonight so I'm leaving early,' Tony calls out as I head upstairs. 'Are you sure you're going to be OK? You look rough, Lu.'

He's been home ten minutes and all he's said is that he has a lot of work to do and that I look a mess.

'I'm fine,' I holler back.

Because what choice do I have? I can't imagine what he'd say if I begged him not to go to work this evening so I could sleep all day. The idea is so ridiculous I giggle to myself as I change Riley, and my son laughs along.

The high street is busy for a Sunday, then I see there's a market on. Nothing fancy, no fresh pastries or artisanal crafts, it's mainly fruit and vegetables and some jumble sale type stalls. I buy bananas for Riley and cheap gerberas in bright pinks and yellows. I think Maggie will like them. She strikes me as the type of woman who likes flowers, although I doubt she ever buys the cheap ones. It's not much, but it's the least I can do for her after the kindness she showed me last night.

But when I knock at number eight it's not her who answers but Jim. I've never met him before, and he's not what I expected. The way Shona and Beth talked about him I thought he'd be an old frail man, but he can't be much older than his sister with thick dark hair and bright blue eyes that crease with curiosity at the sight of us standing on his doorstep.

'I'm Lu,' I say. 'From next door.'

'Ah, the new family. Welcome.' Jim smiles and waves at Riley. He's balancing on crutches but doesn't seem too bad.

'How's your leg?'

'Getting better by the day,' he replies, looking at the flowers in my hand.

'These are for Maggie,' I say, holding them up. 'For her help last night.'

He grins down at Riley then gives me a concerned look. 'You all right, love? Maggie told me you got locked out.'

He doesn't mention the blood and doesn't look at my hand, so perhaps she didn't tell him everything. People are quick to judge others, especially mothers. I imagine Maggie knows that.

'Hope I didn't wake you last night. Silly me,' I say. 'Must have been sleepwalking. It happens, you know.'

He nods as if it's normal, when we both know it's not.

'Anyway,' I add, 'I wanted to give her some flowers for helping me out and give you back the spare keys. Thought it was safer if you had them. In case I get locked out again.'

I give a nervous laugh and he takes the keys off me but not the flowers.

'Maggie isn't here, love.'

Oh. He doesn't mention where she is or if she'll be back.

'Take the flowers anyway,' I say.

Jim grins, like he's not used to getting flowers. 'How lovely. Thank you. Settling in OK, are you? Probably not the best time to move here, what with all the drama going on. But don't worry, it's not like this all the time. Most of us are a decent lot.'

I don't know what he's talking about, then something catches the corner of my eye. Yellow tape and a white van. I hadn't realised the police were still here. Jim tips his head to the right, as if too scared to point.

'Number four. You not heard what happened?'

I didn't notice before, but now I have a better view I can

make out some white tarpaulin behind the skip. It looks like a little tent.

'I saw the police there this morning. I presumed it was drugs,' I say. 'Did they arrest him?'

'No. Dave's dead,' Jim says, his voice reduced to a grave whisper. 'He was found bludgeoned to death behind his skip at six o'clock this morning. Brian Humphries, from number thirteen, was walking his dog and told me he saw a pair of legs sticking out and thought Dave must have passed out or had a fall. Brian said he'll never be the same again. Awful business. His head was totally caved in. I know he was a selfish wanker with his music and all the mess, but no one deserves to be killed. And in such a violent way, too.'

Dave was *murdered*? A million images flash through my mind, none of them solid. None of them real. A scream is clawing itself up my throat, my mouth filling with saliva. I swallow it down, forcing myself to breathe properly. I grip on to Riley's pushchair to steady myself and attempt to take a deep breath, which shudders in my chest.

'I better be off,' I say, my voice too high and the words cracking around the edges.

'Sure you don't want to come in for a cup of tea?'

'No. I've left the oven on,' I lie. I've got to get out of here. I need to go home.

I wave goodbye before stumbling away.

My mouth is dry and acrid, my hands sweating so much I can hardly grip the pushchair. I manage to get the key in the lock and throw myself through the door before I vomit all over the hall floor.

NINE

I shut the front door behind me, but I can't move. I'm stuck, flesh turned to stone, concrete for brains, standing in a puddle of my own sick. I'm reminded of a documentary I once saw about Michelangelo, how he carved statues from lumps of marble and some of them he left encased in the stone. That's how I am right now: encased in a prison of solid fear and confusion.

Dave was murdered in exactly the same way I'd imagined killing him. And it happened on the night I found myself locked outside my house covered in blood with no recollection of how I got there or what I'd done. That's more than a coincidence. That's horrifying.

It's not until Riley starts to whine that I realise he's still in his pushchair and it's his naptime. I wipe the mess off the floor then take the baby upstairs to bed. Once he's settled, I stand between his bedroom and mine, balancing on the top step of the stairs. For a moment I consider joining Tony in bed or lying down on the sofa, but I can't. All I can do is stand there, staring down the stairs at the front door, at the floor I'll have to properly mop later, and into the kitchen, where the tower of boxes still hasn't been unpacked, my mind completely blank as to what I should do next.

Every inch of me is aching and I'm wondering if it's from last night. Why do my arms hurt? Why are my knees sore? How did I pull a muscle in my back? Did I do something to myself last night or is it simply from hauling a baby about day and night? Grasping the banister tightly, I slowly head downstairs and into my ugly neon-green kitchen. I take a mug off the sideboard and fill it from the tap. The water doesn't help my nausea, so I make some tea and take a paracetamol. All that blood from a small cut? So much blood. Where did it all come from?

I trace a finger over the plaster on the palm of my hand, running it along the jagged edges of my broken nails. I wish I could remember what happened. I pull at the memories from last night – Tony left for work. I put the baby to bed. I went to sleep. I woke up covered in blood outside my front door. Did I murder the neighbour? Did I go to Dave's house to tell him to turn his music off and kill him? *Kill him?* No. I wouldn't do that. I've never been in a physical fight in my life, not even as a child, so why the hell would I hurt someone? Anyway, I'm not big or strong enough to beat someone to death. Am I? How hard is it to strike someone on the back of the head enough times to bring them down? I've thought about it, of course I have, but I've never actually hit anyone. I wouldn't. I hated that man so much my skin burned with fury. I was desperate for him to stop keeping me awake and being a stupid fucking selfish bastard. But hate him enough to kill him? No.

I can't stop shaking so I add more sugar to my tea and sit at the kitchen table, arms resting on the surface, remembering the soft touch of Maggie's hand in mine. I should talk to her. Maybe she will remember something I said or did that will explain how I hurt myself and why even my pyjama bottoms were soaked with blood. I wonder where she is and when she'll be back.

My sweet tea isn't as good as Maggie's was. I drag my mind

back to last night. Maggie took my nightclothes away. What did she do with them?

Every time I blink my head lolls forward. Maybe if I rest it on my arms right here, I can sleep for a little while. But as soon as I close my eyes, my mind goes red, and I sit back up with a start. All I can see is blood. So much blood.

Tony finds me in the kitchen an hour later, head on the table, eyes staring at nothing.

'You OK, Lu?'

That's all he ever says to me. *Are you OK? Are you OK? Are you OK?* He can see the kitchen is a mess, he can see I need to sleep, but all he does is ask if I'm OK so that I will tell him I am and he can get on with his day unencumbered. I look at the clock on the wall.

'You're up early. You've slept seven hours,' I say, doing the maths. Always with the sleep maths. Seven is good. Will Tony be happy with seven? I'd be happy with seven. 'Riley is having a nap.'

'I have to head out shortly.'

I stare at him blankly.

'I told you – I'm leaving for work a bit earlier today. Got to take the car for its MOT first, then I have to sort out the Germany thing because...'

His voice is hollow, a *wa wa wa* of a distant echo, like I'm in a tunnel and he's somewhere outside. He's talking about work but all I can think about is the feel of rough brick in my hand and blood under my fingernails. Who killed Dave? Was I there?

Tony makes himself a ham sandwich and asks me if I want one and I say yes, but it sticks to the roof of my mouth and swallowing it is like masticating wet cardboard. As he talks about work, I open a few boxes, taking pots and pans out and nodding to words I'm not hearing, seeing nothing but visions of something I imagined that now feel like memories, until eventually a scream cuts through the thick treacle-like images sticking to the inside of my mind. Riley.

'I'll get him,' Tony says, but I tell him it's fine because he has to take the car for the MOT soon. He looks relieved, as I knew he would. I push past him and head upstairs.

Riley's face is creased from his sheets, his hot face searing my neck as he clings to me. I hold him tight and breathe him in. My boy. The only thing that feels real right now.

I can't believe I left him alone last night. What if something had happened to me and he'd been in the house by himself all night? What if I'd been run over or bled to death or passed out on someone's doorstep? I can't ever tell anyone what I did, or they'll take him away from me. Even if the blood was all mine and I had nothing to do with the neighbour's murder, sleep-walking the streets at night and leaving your baby alone is criminal. I can't let them take my son from me.

There's nothing I won't do to protect my boy.

TEN

I've not kept still since Tony left for work. I've scrubbed every surface in my house until my chipped fingernails broke entirely and my hands grew dry and sore from the bleach, but no matter how hard I clean all I can think about is blood.

My mother calls while I'm preparing dinner. I consider ignoring her, but she'll only keep calling until I pick up. I can tell she's been drinking from the first word she utters.

'Darling!'

It's six o'clock here which means it's seven o'clock in Spain. She'll have been drinking since lunchtime because it's Sunday, and although every day of her sunny retirement on the Costa del Sol is the same, she and Dad always make a big deal about going out for a nice lunch on a Sunday. And by 'nice' they mean 'boozy'.

'Twenty-five today,' she says by way of greeting. She's talking about the weather. My parents have lived in Torremolinos for over a year yet every time I speak to them, they have to tell me how hot it is for the month we're in.

'Hi,' I say. 'How are you?'

'Living the *vida loca, chiquita*,' she says with a laugh. 'What are you up to?'

'Peeling potatoes.'

'Tell Lu about the paella we had and those lovely padrón peppers,' Dad is shouting out.

They always call on WhatsApp, because it's free, and they always put me on loudspeaker so they can both speak at once. That, coupled with their bad WiFi, means I can never hear them clearly.

'How's my beautiful boy?' Mum asks, her words slurred and running into one another like water on ink. 'He's such a clever little soul. Let me talk to him. Let him say hello to his granny.'

I'm clasping the phone between my ear and my shoulder as I hold the potato with one hand and the knife with the other. I stop what I'm doing so I can hold the phone up to my eleven-month-old baby's ear. He was perfectly content in the living room, in his playpen, banging two wooden blocks together, but as soon as he sees me he starts whimpering and holding his hands up to be picked up.

'Say hello to Granny,' I say through gritted teeth.

He starts to cry, and I can hear my parents telling one another that he's sad because he misses them. He's met them once.

'When are you coming over?' I ask. 'Have you decided what you're doing for Christmas yet?'

Christmas is seven weeks away and Riley turns one five days later. They promised they'd make it over for the summer and that never happened. Surely they're not going to skip Christmas too?

'We still don't know,' Mum says. 'We're looking at flights.'

They haven't seen the new house. The only time they've met Riley was when he was three months old, and they came over for his christening.

'You need to be here for Riley's first birthday,' I say. 'It's the thirtieth of December.'

Mum gives an exaggerated sigh. 'I know when my only grandson's birthday is, Louise! But it's not that simple,' she says. 'Your new place is smaller than the last one, you have nowhere for us to sleep, and you know your dad isn't good in strange beds with that back of his.'

My brother has a big house. They didn't mind coming over when the twins turned two because they got an en-suite bedroom and a pretty country pub next door. They didn't even manage to come and see us, said it was too far. I could remind them that there are hotels in this part of London, but I don't have the energy to listen to them tell me, yet again, that moving to a rough part of London means we've exposed our boy to gangs and knife crime.

'Why won't you come out to the Costa del Sol?' Mum adds. 'The sunshine will do you a world of good.'

I don't need sunshine. I need sleep.

'We don't have the money right now,' I say, cradling the phone on my shoulder again and jiggling Riley on my hip while I attempt to slice a carrot.

'Oh, don't you worry about the money,' Dad is hollering in the background again. 'I've told you before, sweetheart. You get the tickets, and we'll pay you back.'

That's what they said last time, and they never did pay me back. I was nearly six months pregnant with Riley, and Tony convinced me to go and see my parents in Spain for a week while he painted the nursery. It was September, the temperature was still in the high thirties in Torremolinos, and my mum and dad went out with their bridge friends all day every day, everyone smoking and drinking. They called me a party pooper for going to bed before midnight, told me that sunbathing would be good for the baby, and insisted that there was nothing wrong with me eating cured meats and stinky cheese. I spent the entire week listening to them tell me how women complain too much nowadays, and no pregnant woman made such a fuss back in the early nineties.

I can't go to Spain. I need my parents *here*. I want them cooking for me, and helping me get the new house ready, and bonding with their grandson. All I need is to be able to switch off for a day or two knowing everything is under control.

'Maybe I'll come over in the new year,' I say, placing Riley in the highchair and handing him a cold carrot stick to chew on for his sore gums. 'I'm really busy at the moment with all the unpacking.'

'Still unpacking?' Mum cries. 'You moved last month. Honestly, Lu, with all that time you have on your hands now, I thought you'd have got on top of it all. Make the most of your maternity leave, get that place in order, and you'll stop feeling so miserable. Get it all out of the way then you can go out with your friends.'

'What maternity leave?' I say. And what spare time? I don't have a job, I don't get a minute to myself, and I certainly don't have any friends to have fun with. 'Also, it's really hard moving to a new place. I'm struggling a bit, to be honest.'

'I bet it's freezing over there,' Mum says, ignoring everything I just said. I can hear laughter in the background and the sound of drinks being poured. Why are they calling me when they're not even listening?

Mum is saying something to her friends and Dad is ordering another beer.

'Got to go,' she says. 'Glad everything is going well.'

It's not, Mum. Nothing is going well.

'We'll transfer you some money,' Dad shouts out.

Tony and I share a bank account. Any money my parents send us simply gets swallowed up by bills and grocery shopping. I thank them anyway and they hang up before I have a chance to say goodbye.

I wonder what my mother would have said had I told her that I really needed her. Would she have told me to get a grip, that new mums in her day didn't complain so much? Or would she have flown over the next day, sent me to bed and made a fuss of her only grandson? I wonder if she calls my brother more often than me. I wonder whether she has long calls with Kayla about the twins.

'Sorry you have such shit grandparents,' I sing-song to Riley. 'And I'm sorry your mum isn't much better.'

He gives me a goofy grin, which makes a lump form in my throat. I chop up some ham and cheese, add it to his plate, and test the softness of the potatoes and carrots I'm boiling for him. I then drain them, mash them up and place them on the side to cool down. Riley is babbling to himself, and for a moment everything feels normal. I keep getting little lulls of normality before flashes of blood flood my mind. I glance out of the window and see the police tape and vans and I know nothing is normal anymore. I know it's just a matter of time before the police start questioning everyone on the street, and then what? Did anyone see me last night? What will I say?

I may well imagine bad things, and I feel the urge to *do* things, but I never would. I'm not violent. I don't choose to envisage bloodshed, and I can't control my nightmares. They are just a release valve for all the stress I'm under. That's what I read online when I looked it up. It's normal, when sleep-deprived after having a baby, to sleepwalk and have an overactive imagination. Normal. And my getting locked out on the same night Dave was killed is simply a coincidence.

My hand shakes as I feed Riley his mashed vegetables, but I keep smiling and pulling funny faces as I try to clear my mind of the bloody images. My son doesn't notice that I'm not in a good place. He only sees his mama.

'Here comes the choo-choo train,' I trill.

Everything I've given him to eat on his highchair tray is now on the floor. With a sigh I put the empty plate of mash in the sink and scoop the mess up. It's dark outside but in the pale moonlight I can make out shifting shapes. I wonder if Shadow is out there prowling. I open the window and leave him the ham from the floor.

My hands are still trembling as I clear up the cooking utensils, the handle of the vegetable knife smooth in my hand. I grip it tightly, trying to control my breaths and clear my mind. Then I stop. Something is moving at the kitchen window. I peer closer, calling out for the cat, but it's not there. The movement is coming from a group of men outside. They aren't as old as Dave's friends, yet not teenagers either. They're laughing and kicking at something, their white trainers glowing through the darkness.

'Don't let it get away,' one of them cries out, his hood obscuring his face and a spliff glowing in his hand.

'Get it!' another shouts.

Shadow. My cat. They're terrorising my cat.

I run to the door. I don't mean to, I don't plan to, but before I know it I'm outside, a knife in my hand and four men surrounding me.

ELEVEN

'Leave my cat alone!' I shout.

One of the men laughs, a low, guttural rumble. 'Chill, lady. Get back in your kitchen.'

I glance behind me. I've left the front door open, and through the window I can see Riley strapped into his highchair. What am I doing? The police tape is still flapping a few doors down. I shouldn't be drawing attention to myself like this. What if there's a police officer nearby, watching us? There *should* be a police officer nearby. A man was murdered and now these men are terrorising an animal.

'Stop hurting my cat,' I say calmly.

One of the men is tall with bright red hair. He has to stoop low to talk to me. 'There ain't no cat here,' he says, his face so close to mine that the peak of his baseball cap beneath his hood nearly touches my forehead.

I glance behind him. There are no other people and no police around. There's no one here to protect me.

I grip the knife harder. It's only a cheap vegetable knife, the handle bright orange and the metal so thin the tip is chipped. But it's sharp. It's not illegal in the UK to carry a knife with a blade under three inches, if you have a good reason to have it on your person. That's because you can't fatally stab anyone with a blade that short.

'Leave her. She's just some pathetic mum with nothing better to do,' another one says, turning his back to me. 'Stupid bitch.'

The knife I'm holding wouldn't kill these men, but it could hurt them. Really hurt them. I see it now. I see myself pulling on the back of the ginger guy's hoodie and throwing him to the ground, slitting his neck open, his eyes growing wide and glowing white in the dark. I see myself punching the air, puncturing whatever comes into contact with the blade – his friends' outstretched hands, their legs, their eyes, hot blood splattering all our faces and running into my screaming mouth.

Would they fight or would they run? Would they call out for their mums? Men. Boys. All babies, really. How tough would they be if, instead of them hurting my cat, it was me terrorising them?

'She's got a knife,' a man with a gold tooth says, stepping back and pointing at my hand.

'What the fuck, man,' the ginger one says, shaking his head. 'I told you this street was trouble.'

The four of them walk away in the opposite direction to the police tape, shoulders hunched against the cold, not running yet taking nervous glances behind them until they melt into the shadows. There's a crushed can of Coke on the floor. Is that what they were kicking? I move it with my foot. My bare foot. I'm back out in the street with no shoes on. Again. What was I thinking?

I look around me at all the empty windows on the street. A curtain twitches. Something moves behind the blinds of the house next door to mine. Is that Maggie, watching me? Oh my God, what the hell is the matter with me?

I run back inside my house and slam the door shut, dropping the knife on the hall floor with a clatter. Riley points at me and laughs, waving his half-chewed carrot stick in the air. I scoop him up and hold him to me. What did I do? What was I thinking?

I saw them hurting my cat. I thought that's what they were doing, kicking Shadow, and I went out there with a knife. *A knife.* I went outside with no shoes on, left my baby alone and confronted four men who, for all I know, are the ones who killed Dave. But what if I don't need to be scared of them? What if they're the ones who should be scared of me? Maybe I do have the capacity to be a killer.

I hold Riley to me, and I sing him a song – 'Summertime'. I sing to him not to cry as tears roll down my cheeks. I tell him his daddy is rich and his mother's good-looking and I tell him other lies like the living is easy when it's not. Nothing is easy. Everything is hard.

I switch on the TV, another game show like all the others, and watch my son play with his toy car, moving it back and forth over my dirty bare feet. I'm too nauseous to prepare dinner for myself. My stomach has been aching for a few weeks now and every inch of me is heavy with exhaustion and confusion.

Why am I so angry all the time? Why do I keep putting myself in danger? Why do I want to hurt people?

I stumble into the kitchen and survey the mess. I blink as I stack the dishwasher, the dirty plates swimming before my eyes like a photograph double exposed. I can't do it. I'll clean the kitchen later. I need to get Riley down then I can go to bed myself.

I change and bathe him, then read him three picture books that he insists on chewing, the words on autopilot while my mind flickers with images of blood and dirty feet and snarling faces.

Riley finally falls asleep and I take the opportunity to go to bed early, but I can't rest. I toss and turn, clutching the duvet in my sweaty fists, my breaths hard to pull from my lungs. I have so many feelings scrunched up into a ball lying heavy on my chest, a boulder crushing my ribs and pressing against my throat. I want to cry but my invisible tears turn to concrete, adding to the ball growing hard in my gut. My body is buzzing, my teeth aching as I grind my molars together.

The street is empty, the house is silent, yet I can't sleep. No one is stopping me this time except myself because I can't trust myself. What if I go out there at night again, but this time with a knife? What if I hurt someone in my sleep? What if I kill?

TWELVE

I stayed awake all night watching the shadows from the moon against our flimsy curtains making shapes on the ceiling, like claws reaching out at me. I'm not a good person. I'm impulsive and erratic and dangerous. I wanted to kill those guys yesterday for hurting my cat, but now I'm not even sure there was a cat. I'm not sure about anything anymore.

This rage, this anger, it clouds my vision. It's cliché to call it a red mist but whatever it is, it's real and tangible and takes me over, pulls me forward, shows me things I don't want to see. If I was angry enough to run outside with a knife, to confront four grown men in the street and leave my baby unattended at home – was I angry enough to kill a man simply because he was keeping me awake at night? And would I do it again?

This isn't right but who can I talk to about it? Who is going to tell me it's normal, that I'm not an unfit mother, that it will pass? Not a doctor or my partner or my mother or the police. They will say it's my fault. They will take Riley away from me.

Tony hardly says two words to me when he gets in from work, says he's too tired and that he'll see me when he's up, and I'm happy about that. I'm too scared to open my mouth in case everything comes pouring out. You can't undo that. You can't tell someone you're a vicious psycho then take it all back.

I'm exhausted and I get nothing done all morning because Riley keeps whinging, but I can't leave him alone for a second. Even in his highchair, in front of the TV with some chopped-up banana, he's screaming and trying to clamber out. His right cheek is bright red. I've given him Calpol, but he keeps rubbing at his nose, so I decide to take him for a walk to distract him from the discomfort. Maybe I'll feel better too once the sharp slap of winter bites into me and I'll be able to breathe properly again.

I bundle Riley up into his pushchair and wrap a scarf around my throat, wondering how tightly I would have to pull until I stopped breathing. How easy is it to strangle someone? Is it easier to kill yourself or someone else?

You're OK, I tell myself. *Everything is going to be OK.*

I open the door and instantly close it again. The police are outside. Not just one van this time, but three cop cars and seven officers in uniform. Shona is talking to one of them, pointing at Dave's house. I can't hear what she's saying from here, but I don't want her to see me.

Maybe Shona saw me shouting at those men last night? Maybe someone told the police that I'm neglectful, dangerous, mad.

'It's going to be OK,' I say to Riley, who pulls his mitten off and throws it to the floor. I take a deep breath and pick it up. As I bend down, Riley grabs a handful of my hair and I shout out in pain then burst into tears, crumbling to the hall floor. The baby starts to cry, and this time I let him because I'm crying too, and his wails will drown out mine.

I never used to be this pathetic, this crumpled and weak. Things didn't used to split me open like a wet paper bag. I was the sturdy one, the hard one, the one made of something pliable but solid, the one who bounced back. Now I'm brittle, every part of me cracking, too afraid to sleep, to talk, to leave my house.

But even broken things don't stay on the floor forever.

'Come on,' I say to my son, clearing my throat and using the cuffs of my jumper to wipe my face. I scramble to my feet and do up my coat. 'Let's go and feed the squirrels.'

I have nothing to fear, I tell myself. *I've done nothing wrong.*

I hand Riley a breadstick and he looks up at me, his big navy-blue eyes making my heart ache. His cheeks are wet. When a baby is first born, they scream and bunch their fists together but there are no tears. It's just noise. The first time you see a tear roll down your baby's face is the first time you feel like a monster. Even if it's not you who made them cry.

'I didn't do it,' I say to him, catching his tears on the side of my finger. 'I didn't kill him. Mummy isn't bad.'

An hour later I'm on a park bench crying again. I went the long way around so I didn't have to walk past the police outside Dave's house. No one so much as looked at me but my heart was still racing as I imagined them arresting me, ripping my son from my arms, telling me they know everything.

The park is empty; there's never anyone near the ponds. Sometimes there's the odd mum at the playground, but on a bitterly cold Monday morning like today everyone is staying in the warmth. I'm doing my best, holding it together, not letting my baby see my fear. Riley and I have fed the squirrels and the ducks, and now he's babbling at the seagulls while I sit on the bench behind him with tears running silently down my cold, numb cheeks.

'Good boy,' I say, as Riley throws more bread at the birds gathering at his feet.

He squeals in delight as I wipe my face with the back of my hand. I want my mum. Why is it that as soon as we feel ill or scared or alone, we instantly want our mothers? Even if they are useless and no help, like mine yesterday. I can't confide in her. If I tell her about the neighbour being killed, she'll say we need to move house again. And if I tell her I've been sleepwalking, locking myself out, accidentally hurting myself, she'll tell Tony and he'll worry about Riley. I need to forget about it all. No one can help me.

'Lu?'

A woman sits down beside me, her blonde bob shining in the weak November light. She looks so put together in her matching white woollen coat and scarf, her hands in suede gloves and her handbag the type most people would deem too nice for the park. I hide my muddy trainers beneath the bench and pull my polyester puffer jacket shut, although it's got a bit tight around my chest lately. She smiles at me and it's so real, so warm, I start to cry again.

'Hey,' she says, rubbing my arm. 'Are you OK?'

I've just realised who she is. It's Maggie, my neighbour's sister. The one who was so kind to me Saturday night. She's wearing white again. It takes a certain kind of woman, the kind like Maggie and Kayla, to wear so much white. I wish I had the confidence.

'What's the matter?' she asks.

I try to answer but all I manage to do is open and close my mouth like a landed fish.

'You must be exhausted,' she whispers. 'You poor soul. What a fright you had Saturday night. Where's your husband?'

'We're not married,' I say, as if that matters. 'Tony's at home, asleep, he works nights. I'm just...'

Riley starts to cry, and I trail off, staring into the distance. I rock his pushchair, but I feel too heavy to stand, to lift him, to hold him. I try to give him more bread for the ducks, but he wants to get out of the pushchair.

'And who's this little one?' Maggie says, crouching down beside him. 'Is this Riley?'

Did I tell her his name when we were sitting in my kitchen together? I must have done.

Riley strains against the straps, his face going from fresh-air pink to angry puce. Maggie takes his squidgy little hand, like she took my injured one, and rubs it between her soft suede gloves.

'Aren't you a handsome fellow? Have you been feeding the birdies?'

Riley's cries fade to faint hiccups and he points at the seagulls with a 'Ma'.

Maggie unclips his straps and lifts him up. She doesn't ask permission and normally that would annoy me, but this feels like a relief. Like someone has taken the reins and I can rest for a moment.

'What a lovely little boy you have here,' she says. 'Absolutely gorgeous.'

He rests his head on her shoulder and all I can do is stare. He's never done that with anyone else before, only me and his dad. I sniff and smile and nod, still unable to speak.

Maggie has her back to me, pointing at the ducks and rocking Riley back and forth as anyone who is used to holding children does without thinking.

'You're really good with him,' I say. She stays silent, swaying back and forth. 'And thank you,' I add. 'For helping me the other night.'

When she turns around her eyes are so full of concern I have to swallow down the pain in my throat so I don't cry again.

'Don't be so hard on yourself,' she says. 'You're tired. You can't do it all alone.'

'I have no choice.'

'Yes, you do,' she replies. 'I'm right next door. I can help whenever you need me.'

I give a little polite laugh, as if that's far too much to ask of anyone.

'You've done more than enough,' I say.

Riley's eyes are drooping, his head growing heavy on her shoulder. I imagine what that would look like in my own living room, Maggie on the sofa cradling my son while I get things done or shower or take a nap myself. Other women, people like Kayla, have this – they have sisters and mothers and friends nearby who will scoop up everything that's too heavy to carry and tell you it's all being taken care of.

'The offer is there,' she says, gently placing Riley back in the pushchair and tucking his bobbly blue blanket from the nappy bag beside him. She does all of this like she already knows him, like she's been looking after him forever. When she turns to me, she looks too bright for this dingy park with its brown leaves and misty grass. Too clean and calm to be part of our lives.

'Thank you,' I say again, smiling at the image of my sleeping baby with his puckered lips sucking on an invisible dummy. 'You've been very kind.'

She rests her hand on my arm and leaves it there for a moment, the scent of her delicate perfume filling the air.

'And thank you for my flowers,' she says. 'You're a good person, Lu. A good mother. You need to accept help. Let people in.'

Without another word she turns on her heel and I watch her walk away, her white coat flapping like a feather floating across the green of the park until she turns the corner and she's gone. I take a deep breath and rub the tears out of my eyes. Maybe this is how you make friends. Maybe all I need is a friend.

THIRTEEN

Riley sleeps on the way home and I make the most of it, stopping on the high street to buy toilet roll and bread. The sun is fading already although it's only three thirty. There's no point going home yet, not if I'm only rushing back so Tony can wake up and ask me to make him food. It's cold but dry, the air crisp and the sky clear, and I'm enjoying window-shopping in silence. The stores are already decked out for Christmas and a little jolt of excitement runs through me when I think about it being Riley's first Christmas. I need to make it special and start planning, whether or not my parents will join us.

I close my eyes and breathe, the cold air filling my lungs and clearing my head, hoping it will wash away all my thoughts. I'm not a bad person. Anyone would have gone out and confronted those young men yesterday and sleepwalking isn't unusual. I'm having a hard time right now, that's all. I'm a bit stressed. I'll be OK soon.

The high street is so quiet I can hear music coming from the church hall on the other side of the road. There's a new sign, bright pink this time and not so wet, advertising the free playgroup on Mondays, Wednesdays and Fridays from 2 to 5pm.

I stare across the road, contemplating going in. Maybe my problem is that I'm not part of a community. Of course I'm going to struggle if I'm alone. Doesn't it take a village to raise a child? I'll feel calmer and stop having all these crazy thoughts once I get into a routine and surround myself with people I like and trust. I lost touch with my old friends from work. They all live too far away now and we didn't have as much in common once Riley was born anyway because they were all younger than me without kids.

'They were just drinking buddies,' Tony always says. 'They were never your real friends.' Maybe he's right. I need to know my neighbours and make more mum friends... other women who will understand what I'm going through.

I cross the road and wheel Riley inside. It looks the same as last time except there's a woman dressed like a bear reading from a book, a group of mothers sitting cross-legged at her feet with disinterested babies on their laps. I take a flimsy cup of weak orange juice and avoid the biscuits this time.

'Hi, Lu. Nice to see you back,' a woman whispers over my shoulder.

I recognise her daughter before I recognise her. The child has a large pink bow on her bald head and she's wearing a pink cardigan and a long floral dress she keeps tripping over.

'Daisy?'

The woman beams at me, overjoyed I've remembered her name. She ushers me over to the back of the room where she has her pushchair, a thick anorak slung over the back and a collection of shopping bags.

'Started the Christmas shopping early,' she says with a guilty grin. 'Bebe Tu has a sale on.'

I've seen that shop. It smells expensive, everything in muted shades of ivory, powder blue and blush pink. I've never been inside, though. I'm never dressed nice enough to shop there.

'How have you been?' she asks.

Don't say 'tired', I tell myself.

'Good. You?'

'Oh, I'm great. We had a lovely weekend. Mark, Tilly and I went to a farm and Tilly rode a pony for the first time and we picked pumpkins. What did you do this weekend?'

I'm smiling so hard my cheeks ache. What did I do this weekend? I got locked out of my house, found myself covered in blood and discovered my neighbour has been murdered. Then I realised no one gives a shit about me, not even my parents.

'Not much,' I say. 'Went to the market, bought some flowers, still unpacking.'

'It takes ages to settle into a new home, doesn't it?'

'Yes.'

We sit in silence, listening to the dulcet tones of the bear woman reading a story about rabbits that won't go to sleep. I'm trying to politely focus on the story the lady is reading but every time she mentions the word 'sleep' I think of bloody pyjamas, and torn nails, and how I was too scared to close my eyes last night because I don't know who I am anymore. I signal for Daisy to move to the back of the hall so we can talk without interrupting the woman reading.

'Do you ever feel angry?' I say.

She looks up, a tiny line etched between her light green eyes. 'When?'

'Always,' I say. 'Like, when you were pregnant were you filled with uncontrollable rage?'

She gives a little titter. She thinks I'm joking, then realises I'm not. 'No. I loved being pregnant.' She looks down at her flat stomach, like she misses having a bump. 'I felt so serene. So whole. It put everything into perspective, you know? I went to prenatal yoga, and Mark and I had a babymoon in Santorini. It was a special time.'

So she didn't walk down the street wanting to gouge everyone's eyes out with her bare fingers? She didn't hate every man who would never know what having a period was like, or what it felt like watching their body stretch and change against their will, or having to consider giving up their job in order to have a baby? She wasn't scared or nervous or furiously indignant that in order to continue the human race women have to lose everything that makes them who they are?

I'm waiting for her to ask how it was for me. How I'm feeling. Why I'm asking her these questions. But she doesn't.

'What about now?' I ask after a long silence. 'Do you lose your temper more than you used to?' She widens her eyes and I hold both hands up. 'I don't mean with Tilly, of course,' I quickly add. 'I mean in general. With adults. Does everyone irritate you?'

'Oh, yes.'

I close my eyes and let out a long breath. *OK. Good. I'm not a freak.*

'I get very ticked off with Mark sometimes,' she says. 'I even used the F-word last week because it was bin day and I asked him three times to put the bins out and he forgot. Luckily I heard the binmen and ran out just in time and did it myself. It was a close call, and of course he was ever so sorry, but I wasn't happy.'

'Did you want to kill him?' I ask, thinking of Dave and Tony and those men outside my house and all the ways I've wanted to kill all those people who simply don't care.

I need her to say yes. I need to know it's normal to have these thoughts and visions. It doesn't make us bad people, bad mothers; it's not like we would act on them. Daisy laughs so loudly that some of the mums listening to story time turn their heads sharply in our direction.

'Not quite,' Daisy says. 'But I did give him less dessert than normal that evening.'

She chuckles and I join in, so she thinks I'm just like her. But I'm not. I'm bad.

'Men, eh?' she says, rolling her eyes. 'Can't live with them, can't live without them.'

'Many do,' I say. 'Live without them, I mean.'

'Oh, I know. I have so many single friends. Poor things. Some are in their early thirties and it's all quite desperate. One of them said she never even wants children. Imagine that.'

We both look over at Tilly as she says it. Her daughter is sucking on a wooden cube, two trails of snot glistening on her top lip. Riley is still sleeping, but I can smell that one of them needs changing.

'Good for them,' I say. 'I love my son, but I don't blame women for wanting to remain childless.'

Daisy sits there in silence, staring at me, waiting for me to elaborate. This is good. We're bonding over shared struggles. This is how women make new friends.

'I mean... don't you think it's unfair?' I say. 'All of it? How much our lives change when we become mothers? Our bodies, our careers, our social lives, money, how we spend our time, what we talk about and think about and dream about and focus on? Everything changes. All of it. Forever.'

I feel my eyes filling up with tears and I blink them back. Maybe I've gone too far. It's clear Daisy doesn't feel the same way as me and now she's going to think I'm a terrible mother. Neglectful. Selfish. Ungrateful.

'It's a blessing,' she says quietly, wiping her daughter's nose. 'I wouldn't change it for the world.'

'No, of course not,' I say, thinking back to how much I wanted Riley. But would I still have wanted him if I'd known what I'd have to go through to be here? The monster I'd turn into? 'We're so blessed.'

Daisy gives me a tight smile and pats my knee. 'You need a day off. You'll feel better after a day to yourself. Get your mum or a friend to have Riley and splash out on a pamper day. You can get a spa pass for about ninety quid these days. It's so worth it.'

'Yeah,' I say. 'Bargain. That would sort me right out.'

I spend less than that a week on my grocery shopping. I drain my juice, the two of us staring at the woman dressed as a teddy bear as she puts on a puppet show with marionettes. I glance at Daisy, and I remember how pretty she would look as a corpse. Delicate white limbs, twisted into dainty shapes, her hair fanned out like Ophelia singing her last note before crumbling elegantly before death. Daisy is the kind of woman the media would have a field day over if she were murdered. Innocent, blonde, skinny, white Daisy. Such a good mother. Such a wonderful wife. She never did anything wrong and didn't deserve to die like other women do. Daisy would accept death the same way she accepts every other injustice in life: with grace and humility.

'Riley is waking up,' she says to me. 'I think he needs changing.'

'Yes,' I say. 'I'll be back in a minute.'

But I don't go back. I change him and leave.

Tony has left for work by the time I get home and I'm thankful for that. I've done a lot of crying already today and I don't need him to set me off again. He wouldn't even do anything on purpose; maybe he'd sit down while something needs doing around the house, or he'd make a comment about the baby sick stain on my top, or he'd ask me what I'm planning to cook for dinner so I can save him some, and it would be the last straw. And then I'd have to choose between being irrationally angry or collapsing into a ball on the ground and sobbing uncontrollably. And I wouldn't be able to explain either of those things, so I'm simply glad to be alone with Riley. It's easier that way.

I feed him, and bathe him, and as I rock him to sleep, I think about Maggie in the park and how put together she was and Daisy at the playgroup and how serene and at peace she is, and I wonder where I went wrong. Why can't I sail through life unruffled? I have the baby I wanted and the man I longed after, and I don't have to go to work and leave Riley with strangers. Tony's right, I need to know when to rest and go easy on myself. My stomach has been aching lately and I'm so exhausted, I really need to slow down. I don't need anyone's help, I just need to have one good night's sleep. I'll make sure everything's locked up then I'll go to bed. I've got nothing to be scared of. I'm not a midnight murderer. The sleepwalking won't happen again. Everything will be OK in the morning.

All is dark as I head back downstairs. I don't need to put the lights on to see as I scan the dark shapes in the living room and kitchen, checking windows are shut and all is safe. Although I can't deadbolt the front door because Tony is due home in eight or nine hours. I enter the kitchen to get a glass of water and a shadow moves. There's somebody in here.

'Hello?' I call out into the darkness.

A woman steps forward, the faint light from the moon outside illuminating her face.

'Maggie?'

FOURTEEN

'Hello, Lu. I knew you were home so I knocked but there was no answer. I figured you were putting the baby to bed.'

'How did you get in?'

She jangles my spare door keys in the air. 'Jim said you'd dropped these at his house, so I let myself in. I know I should have waited to bump into you again, but you looked so distressed in the park today I thought it best I come over and see how you're doing.'

I'm too shocked to say anything. Who the hell lets themselves into a virtual stranger's house at night? Although Maggie doesn't appear bothered by my silence or shock. I clasp my stomach as another jab has me wincing. All this stress is giving me a tummy ache. Maggie rushes over and motions for me to sit down at the kitchen table.

'Here,' she says, pouring me a glass of water as if I'm the guest in her house. I thank her, sipping it, sighing as the cool liquid travels down my gullet. The pain subsides but I don't move or talk; instead I watch as she takes a dishcloth and starts to dry the plates on the draining board, putting them away like she already knows where everything goes.

She's wearing smart black trousers, a gold heart pendant at her neck and pearl earrings in her ears. She looks like she's returned from dinner at a posh restaurant, or a funeral.

'I enjoy helping,' she says, even though I haven't spoken yet.

The vegetable knife is still on the draining board.

'I saw you yesterday, with those hooligans,' she says, picking up the knife and with a deft swoop slicing open the tape on one of the many cardboard packing boxes towering against the wall. 'Serves them right. I'm sick of men like them terrorising our streets.'

Our streets? She doesn't even live here.

I watch her as she places the knife on the table and begins to unpack the large cardboard box, one item at a time, studying each thing with curiosity. A sieve, a wooden salad bowl, a framed picture of me and Tony the day Riley was born. I look pale and bloated in the photo, but his smile is radiant. My Tony has a great smile.

'This must be Tony,' Maggie says, peering closer at the picture. 'My, my, I see where Riley gets his looks from. You have a very handsome man there, Lu.'

What is this woman doing in my house, going through my things?

I take the photo from her and study the two people staring back at me, trying to remember how I felt that day. Relief, exhaustion, happiness. I really did think everything was going to get easier. I really did think I had it all.

'He's a good father,' I say to Maggie, even though it's Tony's eyes I'm staring into.

'Is he?' she says. There's no emotion in her voice, no judgement. She doesn't know him. 'How?'

And I realise I don't know the answer. He earns all of the money right now – that matters, although it wouldn't matter as much if I were able to contribute. And he plays with Riley sometimes. They love a cuddle. So is that it? Money and cuddles. Is that how low the bar is? I wonder if anyone is calling me a good mother for simply keeping my son alive. They wouldn't say that if they could see inside my mind. If they had seen me on Saturday night. Whose blood was it drying on my skin? I don't think it was mine anymore. What did I do? Maggie was there, she saw the state I was in, but like some unsaid agreement neither of us mentions it.

The light in the kitchen is fading, the neighbours' windows clicking to black one by one as they go to bed, but I don't get up and Maggie doesn't move to put on the light. She works in the pale glow of the moon while I sit and watch.

'And this?' she says with each item she pulls out of the boxes.

'In the living room.'

It's nice deciding where all your things will live when you move house. I've always liked new beginnings – the chance to do things differently, be different, start again. Maybe I'll give away some of my things, or put them in different rooms, or buy other things that are different to the old things. This new home of ours can be better than the previous one. Tony and I can be better.

As it nears ten o'clock my eyelids start to grow heavy and ache. I rest my head in my arms and close my eyes, telling myself I'm not sleeping but resting. I breathe out one long breath at the touch of Maggie's hand stroking my hair.

'You poor love,' she coos. 'You just need someone who cares. Someone you can rely on.'

I want to tell her how scared I am, how my mind is always filling with terrible thoughts: things that I might have done, or things I might do. I'm not safe to be around. What if I start to sleepwalk again? What if I lose my temper with her, like I did with those men in the street?

'I'm bad,' I mumble. 'I have bad thoughts.'

'Shhh.' She keeps stroking my head, her other hand heavy on my shoulder. I like it. It's like she's keeping me inside my own body, her hand stopping me from floating away. 'All you need is rest.'

'No. You don't understand,' I say, my words slow and far away. 'The man at number four is dead.'

She keeps stroking my head. 'I know, my love. It was a big shock. Did you know him well?'

My head is in my arms, my left ear flat against my elbow. She's sitting beside me, her face on its side from this angle.

'No. He died Saturday night, around the time I locked myself out,' I say quietly, even though Riley can't hear us from upstairs. 'The night you found me covered in blood.'

She doesn't answer. We both stay silent. She's waiting for me to say it.

'What if I...'

No. I can't do it. I can't finish the sentence.

'You had nothing to do with that,' she says.

I didn't realise how much I needed to hear those words until I find my entire body turning to liquid with relief. I'm not a bad person. I'm not. With each stroke of her hand on my head I feel myself slipping under, like I'm sinking into a hot bath. Sounds are growing distant, my body weighs nothing, yet I'm sinking fast. She's right. I was sleeping. I had a nightmare. I lift my head up a little and stare at the palm of my hand, my fingers swimming in and out of my vision like hundreds of stubby little worms. I cut my hand falling over in the street. That's all it was.

My eyes flicker open. I didn't realise how close Maggie's face is to mine.

'Who do you think could do such a thing?' I ask, imagining what Dave's face looked like as he died.

Maggie's gaze rests on me for a long time, her brow creased, as if wondering how best to form the next sentence.

'It doesn't take a monster to do a monstrous thing.'

I must have fallen asleep after our chat last night because when I open my eyes again the light in the kitchen has changed and Maggie is standing before me holding Riley. He's wearing a different Babygro to the one I put him in last night. I glance up at the clock on the wall. It's ten past six in the morning.

'You've been here all night?' I say, blinking up at her.

Every inch of me aches. I've been asleep for eight hours, face down on the table. I should feel a little more refreshed, shouldn't I? So why do I feel so awful?

She sits beside me and Riley clambers into my arms.

'Are you going to be OK?' she asks. 'I'm worried about you now. You know, after what you told me last night.'

What I told her last night? What did I tell her?

'Told you about what?'

She tips her head to one side, assessing me, her brow a little furrowed.

'Hormones and sleep-deprivation can do strange things to women. That anger you feel, the visions, you shouldn't take any notice of them. You have nothing to worry about.'

I told her about all of that? Why can't I remember? I want to hide my face in shame, but I also want her to stay beside me all day so I can tell her everything, spill out all my fears and dark thoughts at her feet like an offering.

'Thanks,' I mumble. 'I'm sorry.'

'For what?'

'For saying too much.'

She places her hand over mine and leaves it there. 'We're friends,' she says. 'You can tell me anything.'

We're friends? Something warm travels over my chest and I find myself able to breathe again.

'I better go,' she adds. 'We don't want Tony coming home and wondering what I'm doing in his kitchen at this hour.'

She squeezes my hand then leaves the house with a wave goodbye to Riley.

Riley wraps his hands around my hair and tugs it with a yelp. I untangle his hand and kiss the top of his head. It's still dark outside so I get to my feet and put on the light, making us both blink. My hand flies to my mouth. What on earth has Maggie done?

The kitchen is immaculate. All the boxes have been unpacked, folded and stacked neatly beside the door. There are cookery books on the shelf, displayed in size order. All the cupboards have been cleaned, the tins and jars positioned with labels facing out, pots and pans piled one on top of the other like a homeware magazine, and even the inside of the fridge has been cleaned.

Did Maggie do all of this while I slept? I wander upstairs to Riley's room. Everything is how I left it, except his nightclothes are in the wash basket and the bin contains a plastic bag with his wet nappy inside.

I don't understand. Why is Maggie being so kind to me? She hardly knows me.

My eyes are aching and so is every inch of my body. Sleeping at the kitchen table wasn't the best idea.

I pop Riley in his crib and as I'm stretching and contemplating my first cup of coffee, I hear the key in the lock. My first thought is that Maggie has returned, and I'm surprised by the light flip in my stomach. I want her back. But then I hear Tony throwing his work boots to the floor with a thud and I leave Riley playing with his board books in his crib to say hello.

'Where's my boy?' Tony says.

'Asleep.' I'm lying because I want to talk to him and have a sliver of his attention before my son does. How pathetic of me.

Tony looks at my crumpled pyjamas and the way they're

straining over my stomach. These are the ones I wore before I was pregnant. I was so pleased they fit me last month. They're tight now because the move has made my healthy eating habits go out of the window. Did I eat dinner last night? I think I did. I can't remember. There are a lot of things I don't remember.

I pull my top down and wave at the kitchen.

'Ta-da!'

Tony scans the room and nods appreciatively with both eyebrows raised.

'Looks great. Better late than never.'

And just like that my exhaustion is replaced with something hot and thick. My body prickles like a million ants marching beneath my skin, my teeth clenched so tight my cheeks ache.

That's it? Twelve boxes unpacked and the kitchen sparkling and the baby in his crib, clean and ready for cuddles before the sun is even up, and that's all he can say about my efforts? Well, not *my* efforts, Maggie did it all... but he doesn't know that. He should be impressed. Appreciative. Grateful that I do so much for him and our family.

He pushes past me and heads upstairs to his son's room, but all I see is the father of my child tripping on the stairs and falling. I see his hand clasping for the handrail and missing, his thick body cracking against the banister, his head bouncing off every step. I see his body falling to the bottom of the stairs, his arms twisted behind him, a bone jutting out of his right thigh. But I don't see myself helping him or calling an ambulance; I see myself putting on Tony's steel-capped work boots and stamping on his stupid, smug face.

'Lu?' he calls down to me as I'm flicking on the kettle for a coffee. 'Lu!'

I rub my eyes and take a deep breath, waiting for my heartbeat to slow down before trudging upstairs to Riley's room. Will Tony know what I was thinking just by looking at me? Can he tell how much I hate him? He's standing by the cot, our perfect little cherub in his arms.

'Thank you for sorting the kitchen out,' he says, kissing me lightly on the lips. He turns to Riley and nuzzles his neck, making him laugh. 'Hasn't Mummy done a wonderful job? Isn't your mummy beautiful and clever and hard-working?'

I bite down on my bottom lip, thankful the light in this room is dim and Tony can't see the tears swimming in my eyes. Why am I so hateful?

He holds out his arm and I nestle into him until the three of us form a whole. The perfect family. Mummy Bear, Daddy Bear and Baby Bear.

I think of Maggie and her honeyed Goldilocks hair. Maggie in our house. In our kitchen. Who's been sitting in my chair?

FIFTEEN

Seeing the kitchen so clean and organised has inspired me to keep going. The police vans are still there, outside Dave's house, but I can't see any police talking to the neighbours and they haven't knocked on my door yet. Is that it? Will they leave soon?

While Tony sleeps I fold down the empty boxes and put them in the recycling bin, I sort through Riley's baby clothes and put aside the items that are too small for him so I can take them to the charity shop, and I even manage to have a shower during his naptime. As the water runs over my face, I imagine it washing away all the fatigue and the doubt and the fear I've been harbouring lately.

Clearly, all I needed was that head start, one tidy room in the house that I can feel proud of, feel calm in – as for the rest, I'll find the energy to do those myself later in the week. Yet as I look down at the plug hole I see the water turning pink like it did the night Maggie found me on my doorstep. The cut on my hand is healing, but it itches and aches, reminding me that I'm not OK. That I did something wrong. As the water flickers from clear to red to clear to red, Maggie's words swirl around in my mind.

It doesn't take a monster to do a monstrous thing.

But Maggie knows me now, she knows all my weird thoughts and she still likes me. I think. She said I shouldn't worry about it.

Riley is still sleeping when Tony's alarm goes off at three thirty in the afternoon. He's waiting to use the bathroom, and when I step out in nothing but a towel, his pupils dilate and he gives me a crooked smile.

'What?' I say. But I know what.

He steps towards me, circling my waist with his strong hands.

'You're beautiful,' he says, kissing my neck.

I close my eyes. When was the last time he kissed me, long and hard like he always did the first few weeks we got together? When was the last time he held me all night? I press myself against him, enjoying the touch of his lips brushing along my jawline, making their way to my lips, and I realise that I've missed my man. Tony is a good person. He's trying. This hasn't been easy for either of us. I love him.

I run my fingers through his hair, tugging at the back of his head, and he groans as his kisses get more urgent.

'Let me go for a quick wee first,' he says, breaking away. 'Wait for me in bed.'

I go to our room, drying my hair with the towel along the way, hoping Riley won't wake up soon. Then in a flash I'm bent double, a shooting pain gripping my insides.

'You OK?' Tony asks, already by my side.

I can't talk. My stomach is a tight knot, twinges jabbing into my back, my uterus pulling down like a clenched fist.

'I think I'm due on,' I say.

Tony waits for me to continue, unsure whether this means

I've gone off the idea of sex or whether it might help me take my mind off the pain.

'Can I do anything?' he asks, running his hand beneath my towel and stroking my thigh.

'Yeah,' I shout. 'You can stop expecting sex the one time I get ten minutes to myself.'

He jumps back at my outburst, hurt flashing in his eyes. He probably didn't deserve that, but I don't deserve to get only one hour out of my entire day to myself. Then, even though I'm aching all over and have stomach pains, I'm still expected to put his pleasure before my own. I don't have the chance to explain myself because Riley has woken up crying. I head for the bedroom door, but Tony puts a hand out to stop me.

'You're not even dressed,' he mutters. 'Let me go. I'd like to see my son before I go to work.'

Another thud hits my stomach, but this time I don't know if it's my impending period or all the feelings I've been trying to deny curling up and settling in my guts for the day.

Tony hardly says two words to me while he gets ready for work, the spark between us gone, replaced with something heavy and unspoken. I busy myself with the baby, tidying and making another grocery list that I'll forget to take with me, and he says he has to leave at five for a reason I neither listen to nor care about. As soon as the front door slams behind him, a wave of exhaustion hits me, and I stumble against the wall.

I should have slept when Riley slept. No shower, no sex, no housework. I should have slipped in beside Tony, cuddled up to him and rested. Instead, I tried to do too much and now Tony and I are having one of those arguments where no one says anything because neither of us knows how we ended up where we are.

I hear a sound in the hallway. Has Tony come back? Maybe

I should confess what happened Saturday night, explain why I'm acting so strange, and remind him that I love him. I see his silhouette at the door. He's always forgetting his keys. I open the door but it's not Tony, it's Maggie, my spare keys in her hand.

'I hope you don't mind my coming around so soon,' she hisses. She looks agitated. 'I just thought you should know that the police are questioning everyone on the street again, this time more thoroughly. Have you already spoken to them?'

I shake my head. 'Not at all. I didn't know they were knocking on doors.'

I should have thought of that. I should be more prepared. I peer behind her. Three police vehicles are lined up along the kerb. I pull Maggie into the house and shut the door quietly behind her.

'Sit down,' I say, pulling out a chair for her at the kitchen table. 'I'll make us some tea.'

She's wearing a skirt like she's off somewhere nice, not merely popping over to a neighbour's house in dank grey London in the drizzling rain.

I check the milk in the fridge. It's empty. Tony has used the last of it and put an empty carton back.

'Coffee OK?' I ask. 'Do you like it black? If not, I have water. Tap water.'

She nods like she doesn't care so I flick the kettle on and take two mugs off the draining board. I don't like coffee all that much, but I need the kick right now. No matter how much I push it down, my brain keeps reminding me that whatever happened on Saturday night, it wasn't normal. And now the police are about to know that I was on the street that night... covered in blood.

Maggie hasn't said another word, just sitting there demure and silent. I check on Riley in his playpen. He's hitting a xylophone over and over with a plastic car. He's fine.

'Thank you, again, for everything you did for me last night,'

I say to Maggie. 'And this morning. The kitchen looks great, and I really needed the rest.'

I would probably feel less sore and tired today had I slept in a bed and not at the table all night, but I rested. And that's what matters.

She gives me a small smile, her head tipped to one side.

'You look better,' she says, leaving her coffee untouched. 'No more bad thoughts?'

'None,' I lie. 'I feel a lot better. So, what were you saying about the police?'

I'm trying to keep the panic out of my voice but failing. Maggie remains unruffled, though. For someone who has been up all night unpacking boxes for me, she looks immaculate.

She leans forward and for a moment I think she's going to take my hand again, like she did last time we sat at this table together, but she doesn't. 'The police are interviewing everyone on the street. I spoke to them this afternoon, so no doubt they'll knock on your door tonight or tomorrow.'

My heart starts to thunder in my chest. Why am I nervous? I've done nothing wrong.

'You might want to get your story straight,' she adds.

I swallow. 'I'll tell them the truth.'

'No. You don't want to do that,' she says. 'Tell them you were sleeping Saturday night and that your partner was at work.'

'But that *is* the truth.'

She tilts her head again as if to say there's a lot more to it than that. I guess there is.

'What have you told them so far?'

She purses her lips. 'Nothing much.'

What does she mean by that? What's 'nothing much'? I've been so worried about whether or not I had anything to do with the murder that it didn't occur to me that even if I didn't, the neighbours may have seen me outside, covered in blood, and now suspect my involvement. What if they've all told the police that and then I don't mention it, and it makes me look even guiltier?

I stroke the cut on my hand, wincing at the sharp sting. A constant reminder that I'm not OK, and neither is any of this.

'They won't ask about your hand,' Maggie says, as if reading my mind. 'Stick to the story and they won't suspect you.'

Suspect me? Why is she saying it like that?

'You think I killed him?' I ask.

She doesn't answer.

SIXTEEN

Maggie was right. The police make it to us the next day. I'm thankful it's the afternoon and Tony is awake and already dressed, so I won't be doing all the talking alone. He's washing the plate he used for his bacon sandwich when I spot two police officers through the kitchen window, but I don't say anything. There are three sharp raps at the door and I let Tony answer it. I don't want my face to be the first thing they see: my nervous, guilty, culpable face. Tony's working hours mean he doesn't speak to any of the neighbours, and each time he's asked me what's going on out there, I've acted like I have no idea. I was worried about appearing like I know something, worried he would ask me a million questions until I confessed about my night wanderings, making everything worse. All of this means I'm going to have to pretend I still don't know anything.

'Come in,' Tony says to the two police officers on the doorstep. They look like a couple of university students on their way to a fancy dress party. I'm not old, I'm not one of those people who thinks doctors are getting younger every day, but this is ridiculous.

They introduce themselves. I don't catch their names. The

man is short and blond with the kind of hair you can see the scalp through. The woman is willowy with dark features and has a tiny tattoo of a pink flower on the inside of her wrist.

The dull whine of Riley's cry floats down the stairs.

'Excuse me,' I say as Tony leads them into the living room. Oh God, I forgot how messy the house is. I still haven't unpacked the boxes in the other rooms and Riley's highchair is dirty with food from his lunch. Tony gives me a strange look as I head to the stairs to get the baby from his nap.

'What? You want me to ignore him?' I hiss.

He joins the police in the living room while I climb the stairs slowly, trying to regulate my breaths, telling myself the police don't know anything about me, what I did, what I might have done. Maybe I can keep out of it all by looking after Riley, only speak when spoken to. But when I reach the top of the stairs, Riley isn't standing in his cot crying out for me. He's fast asleep. I could have sworn he was crying.

I come back downstairs and find the three of them sitting in the living room – Tony in the armchair and the two police officers on the main sofa. There's nowhere for me to sit, so I stand.

'Tea? Coffee?' I ask them, thankful I went to the shops this morning.

This will be my fourth coffee already. I don't think caffeine works on me anymore. They all smile and say no, so I stay standing, covering the cut on my palm with my other hand.

'How can we help you?' Tony asks with a leisurely smile. So confident. So self-assured. So innocent.

'We're speaking to everyone who lives on your street following the incident at number four.'

'Oh right, yeah. I've been dying to know what happened,' Tony says. 'I saw the tents and the police the other day, but I work nights so I've not spoken to anyone. Lu said she didn't know either so I figured it can't have been that bad.'

He looks at me and I shrug lightly like I've been totally in the dark all this time too. The room is spinning and I'm not sure if I'm swaying, so I sit on the hard, wooden floor. It's not fancy wood, just the cheap stuff from Ikea, cold and slippery through my leggings. The black fabric is instantly covered in dust, which I subtly brush off.

The male police officer is doing most of the talking. 'The body of Mr David Hardcastle was discovered in the early hours of Sunday the twelfth of November and we believe he was bludgeoned to death. We're speaking to all possible eyewitnesses who may have noticed any unusual activity in the day leading up to his death or the night in question.'

The line is rehearsed; he's probably said it a dozen times already. Maybe more. I wonder who else he needs to speak to after us.

The female officer has a tiny notebook, so tiny I can't imagine how minuscule her handwriting has to be. I understand that those little pads have to be small enough to carry on their person but surely they can't fit that much information in them. She's writing something down even though we haven't spoken yet. Has she noticed anything about me that she doesn't like? Am I fidgeting? Do I look guilty? Is it my dirty leggings?

'Would anyone like a tea or coffee?' I ask. They shake their heads and Tony looks at me strangely again.

'You already asked them, babe.'

No, I didn't. I hear Riley crying again so I excuse myself. I look at the kitchen clock as I head to the stairs. He's only been asleep forty minutes – surely he's not awake already. When I go upstairs, he's still fast asleep. I have to stop doing this. I'm acting like a weirdo.

'Sorry,' I say when I get back to the living room.

Tony is talking and the officer with the pretty tattoo is writing.

I rub my eyes but the scene before me is still fuzzy. I must get my eyes tested.

'I thought it was drugs,' Tony is saying. 'There was always a lot of noise over there and shady-looking blokes hanging about; one guy was always coming and going with one of those annoying scooters that don't go that fast but make a lot of noise.'

'And how do you know this?' the male officer asks.

Tony yawns and sits back, like he's having a chat with his mates. Why is he so comfortable? Why isn't he finding any of this excruciating?

'Like I said, I work nights, so they kept me awake during the day. Selfish bastards. You know that old mattress has been in his front garden for weeks. Inconsiderate. He must have been on something because he never slept. Lu said he played music all night too.'

Why is he telling them that we hated him? Why is he talking so much?

At the mention of my name the two police officers turn to me sitting on the floor cross-legged like I'm in assembly. They are forced to look down at me and I instantly feel like a naughty child.

'Lu. That's your name, right? Lu Baker?'

I shake my head. 'Lu Smith. Tony and I aren't married.'

'Right,' the woman says. 'I understand that while your husband is at work during the afternoon and at night, you are home with your son, Riley. Is that correct?'

She's not listening. I swallow. 'Yes.'

'There's nothing to be nervous about,' she says with a smile. 'These are routine questions.'

'I'm just really tired,' I say. 'Sorry. The baby doesn't sleep well at night.'

I see Tony out of the corner of my eye looking at me like I'm stupid, like I'm wasting their time talking about my boring issues. He's probably getting twitchy because he likes to get to the gym before he leaves for work, and it's already gone four.

'And did you see anything strange on the day or evening of Saturday the eleventh of November?' she asks me.

I shake my head. 'All my days are the same,' I say with a small laugh. No one smiles. 'I've been unpacking and looking after the baby. Boring stuff. We moved here a couple of weeks ago. End of October.'

'We moved here on the twentieth of October. It's been nearly a month,' Tony says.

'Right, yes.' I give a nervous little giggle. 'He's so much better at dates than I am. I lose track of time.'

God, everything I say makes me sound so suspicious. I look at the boxes still stacked against the wall. How have we been here nearly a month? A month is a long time. I need to sort out another room, probably this one as it's the most crowded. Maybe Maggie will help again like she did in the kitchen. My back is aching from sitting on the floor and my stomach is still twinging. I stopped breastfeeding two months ago but my periods still haven't come back. I didn't come on yesterday so maybe it will be today.

'Sorry? Pardon?' I say. The policeman was asking me something, but his voice is low and measured and sounds so far away.

'I was asking if you saw anything strange on the night of the eleventh of November. This past Saturday.'

'No. Just the usual. Like Tony said, Dave always had friends around and played really loud music at night.'

'Dave? Did you know him? Had you ever spoken to him?' the man asks.

Oh, shit. Why did I call Dave by his name? 'No, I mean, the neighbours talked about him. You know, moaned that Dave at number four was being antisocial again. That kind of thing. But I never spoke to him and I didn't see anything strange that night. I don't really know any of the neighbours, only Jim next door.'

'Ah, yes,' the male officer says. 'Mr Jim Daniels at number eight. He mentioned you'd been locked out that night.'

Oh, fuck. Jim told them that? Jim knew I was locked out, but how much more did Maggie tell him? Did she mention I was covered in blood? What has he said to the police? Fuck!

Tony is sitting forward, waiting for me to answer, but neither officer has noticed his change in body language. He's wondering why I didn't tell him I was locked out that night when I should have been looking after his son. I can feel it – frustration, irritation, embarrassment, all of it – emanating off him in waves.

'Oh, yeah,' I say. 'I was locked out for a minute, but it was nothing. I was taking the rubbish to the bins and the door shut behind me.' I give a little laugh and a light shrug of my shoulders. 'I was in my pyjamas. Very embarrassing. But luckily Jim had a spare key.'

'The neighbours have keys to our house?' Tony shouts.

Maybe he's not shouting, but it sounds loud to me.

'Yeah. How lucky was that, eh?' I say, forcing my face into a smile. See, police officers, see how we're just an average family with an average life? See how happy we are? Nothing to worry about here. Move along. All perfectly normal.

Tony sits back with an exasperated wave of his hands. 'Yeah, bloody lucky. Told you to leave the bins to me, Lu. What if you'd not been able to get in with Riley in the house alone?'

Why is he doing this now, in front of the police? Why is he telling me off?

'Do they still have our keys?' he asks.

I don't know what answer he wants me to give. Does he want them to have them or not? I'm not going to tell him the truth, that Jim's sister Maggie comes and goes as she pleases and how she spent the whole of Monday night in our home doing my job for me while I slept like a drunk with my head on the kitchen table.

'No, I took them back,' I say. 'But maybe our neighbours should have a set just in case.'

Oh God, I sound like a victim. This looks like I have a mean husband. The female officer is smiling at me kindly again, which makes the tears in my eyes grow heavier.

'What time was this?' she asks me. 'When you got locked out?'

'I don't know,' I lie. I can't say two o'clock in the morning. No one normal takes their bins out at two o'clock in the morning. Tony shuffles on the sofa. He thinks I'm wasting their time and his. He has somewhere urgent to be – somewhere more important and interesting than here. This shouldn't be taking so long.

'I can't remember what time it was. Riley was asleep, so maybe... ten o'clock?'

Did Jim tell them the truth? Is this a trap?

'And you didn't see anything unusual?' the policewoman asks me.

I shake my head. 'Dave... I mean... the guy at number four... he was playing his music really loudly again.'

The policewoman frowns. 'I understand he was at the pub, the King's Arms, until gone eleven. Are you sure you heard his music at ten o'clock?'

'Oh, maybe I took the rubbish out later, then. I don't know. As I said, every day is the same for me.'

I've messed up. They know it. They can tell I'm hiding something.

The male officer clears his throat and leans forward, as if he has to explain something very simple to a very stupid child. 'This may seem excessive to you, Ms Smith, but it's important we get an accurate account of everyone's comings and goings on this street that night.'

'Don't any of the neighbours have those Ring doorbells?' Tony asks. 'You know, the ones with the cameras?'

There are doorbells with cameras? My heart starts to thud, and I surreptitiously wipe my hands on my dusty leggings.

What if someone's fancy doorbell picked up images of me wandering the street barefoot and bloody that night? What if there's footage of me leaving Dave's house at two in the morning with a brick in my hand? I don't remember anything except shuffling to my front door in a daze, but I've thought about beating his head in a million times. I've imagined it in so much detail it's starting to feel like a memory.

'No one has a Ring doorbell on this street, unfortunately,' the policeman says. 'It was the first thing we checked. They are very expensive, so I'm not surprised.'

Of course, why would poor people worry about their safety? He probably doesn't think any of us have anything worth stealing, and that anyone on this street who gets hurt had it coming to them. He must hate his job.

'Should *we* get a doorbell camera?' Tony asks.

'If it makes you feel safer, it's not a bad idea,' the male officer replies, standing up and shaking his hand. 'We have many people to talk to, so we won't take up any more of your time.'

I get on my feet and the female police officer smiles at me. 'Thank you for your help. If either of you have any questions or remember anything that you think may help proceedings, please do get in touch with your local police station.'

I presume she means calling them because there's only one police station in the area and it's closed. I know it's closed because one of the windows is smashed and there's graffiti all over the walls. Maybe people would behave themselves, not play loud music at night and not wind their neighbours up so much that they resort to bludgeoning them to death, if police still patrolled the streets.

Tony continues talking to the male officer as I go to open the front door for them. We're all crammed in the hallway, nodding and smiling and nodding until the police leave and Tony shuts the door behind them. I wait for the questions: Why was I taking the bins out so late? How did I get locked out? Why am I such a shit mum? And why the hell was I acting so weird? But Tony doesn't say anything at all.

I follow him upstairs to our room, where he stuffs his gym bag with a clean t-shirt and socks.

'I really wanted to get a run in today before work,' he says. 'Bloody police, wasting everyone's time. That guy down the road was a selfish knob. Whoever killed him did us all a favour. He probably deserved it.'

That's it. That's all Tony's going to say?

He kisses me on the lips, and I hold him to me a few seconds longer than normal.

He gives me a lopsided smile, his hand moving down to my bottom. 'Yeah? I mean, Riley's sleeping and I guess I can cut my run in half.'

I let out a laugh of relief and for a moment I even consider lying down beside him, his warm hands on me, feeling desired and not like a machine who gives and gives and gives. I wasn't fair on him yesterday. I can't remember the last time we had sex. Definitely before the house move. Maybe even the summer. But then Riley cries out and I know he's definitely awake this time because Tony gives a heavy sigh and lets me go.

'Try and take it easy tonight, babe,' he says. 'You've been a bit out of it lately.' He makes his way downstairs and puts his boots on by the door as I stand on the top step watching him. 'And I'll fit us one of those Ring doorbells, yeah? I'll feel better knowing you're both safe while I'm away.'

I nod and smile and head for Riley's room. Poor Tony, wanting me to feel safe when the only thing I fear is the one thing I can't escape. Myself.

SEVENTEEN

I'm at the kitchen window with Riley, waving goodbye to his daddy, when Shadow appears on the ledge, making me jump. He's staring right at me, eyes an unnatural yellow like two amber marbles. Maybe he's hungry. I go to the fridge and see what I have in terms of food, ripping a slice of ham into shreds and placing it before him.

Looks like we have a cat now. I guess the 'they choose you' thing is real. I'll buy some cat biscuits. They don't cost much. Not as much as ham. I won't let Shadow in the house, though. Tony would have a fit, saying it's unhygienic with a baby crawling around. He's probably right. And we certainly can't afford the vet's bills that come with a pet.

'Say "cat",' I say to Riley, who's still waving out of the window even though Tony has already driven away.

'What can you see?' I say, jiggling him on my hip.

It's only five o'clock and already the light has faded. I hate this time of year when winter is fast approaching and all you have to look forward to is the dark and the cold and everything on TV being about family and Christmas.

I think I can see Maggie for a moment but I'm not sure as

the windows have fogged up from our breath. There's a click in the hallway and a rustling sound in the living room. I hold on to Riley tightly as I go to investigate.

'It's only me, Lu.'

Maggie is standing in the middle of my living room, a knife in one hand, a smile on her perfectly lipsticked lips.

'I waited until Tony left,' she says, smiling at Riley and waving.

I blink three times and try to clear my head, but I still feel like I'm trying to walk underwater. The police being here has really rattled me. I need to snap out of it. Everything is going to be fine.

'Would you like some tea?' I ask Maggie.

She thanks me and I place Riley in his playpen and go to make tea. I blink and I'm already dunking the teabags in. I don't remember switching the kettle on. I shake my head. Is that my knife Maggie was holding or did she bring one with her? Wait, where's Riley?

I walk so fast into the living room tea slops over the side of the mugs, scalding my hand. Maggie is there bending over a box, slitting the tape open, Riley looking up at me with a dribbly smile.

'Leave mine over there, my love,' she says.

I fuss over Riley for a while, showing him toys, while Maggie says something about cooling down the drinks while she stirs both our teas.

'Why don't you sit down and have a rest?' she says, passing me my mug. 'I can do all the heavy lifting.'

I do as I'm told and sit on the sofa, sipping my tasteless tea, watching her bend back and forth over the boxes, unwrapping each item she takes out, examining them one at a time. A vase. Books I'll never have time to read. A fruit bowl for all the fruit I never buy. Another photo frame, this one of me as a child on a beach somewhere in Cornwall. We never went abroad as children, my brother and I, so it came as a shock when our parents chose to retire in Spain. Maybe that's why I got a job in travel, to make up for all the places I never got to see. I can't imagine having that freedom again. There's still so much I want to do with my life, but my wings are clipped now. For how long, I don't know.

'The police came,' I say to Maggie.

She doesn't react.

'I had to tell them I was locked out the night Dave was murdered.'

'You were,' she says.

'Exactly. And they said your brother had told them, so I confirmed it. The problem is I lied about the time as I said I was taking the bins out. Do you think anyone saw me?'

'No. It's too dark out there without the streetlights working.'

'But if they did, I had blood all over me. How would I explain that? That's strange, isn't it? Walking around at night in your pyjamas covered in blood?'

Maggie crosses the room to me, bending down so her face is so close I can smell her floral perfume. 'It gets very dark on this street.'

I nod. She's right. It's hard to see anything out there at night.

'It *was* a lot of blood, though,' she adds.

I look up so fast I nearly spill my tea again. She's ripping the knife along another box in one swift motion, the blade glinting in the light of a lamp she's found in one of the other boxes. Everything Maggie does is so meticulous and measured. No rush. No mess. No fuss.

'A lot of blood for such a small cut on your hand,' she adds.

I think about my pyjamas. She took them away. What did she do with them? She said they might need throwing away, but I'm too scared to ask. I don't like the way she's looking at me.

'Do you think I did it?' I ask in a small voice.

She turns to me, eyes wide in surprise, her golden bob perfect – not a hair out of place.

'Do *you?*'

I really don't know. I was angry enough. I've been so tired, and his music was so loud, and I'd thought about it in great detail. I'd imagined exactly how I'd do it. Exactly like that.

'I don't think so,' I say.

Maggie smiles and sits next to me, tucking my greasy hair behind my ear.

'Then you have nothing to worry about,' she says. 'Your night wanderings are our little secret, yours and mine. Forget it ever happened. You look tired, my love. Are you tired?'

I nod and she takes the tea out of my hand as I sit back on the sofa. She plumps one of the cushions and I rest my head against it. It's completely dark outside now although it's not yet dinnertime. Riley is babbling to one of the teddies in his playpen, the TV on so low the voices are nothing but a murmur, the soft glow of the small lamp in the corner making the room warm and orange.

I have time to close my eyes, just for a moment. Five minutes. Maggie won't mind.

'I defrosted some sausages,' I mumble as everything turns into a haze and I'm gone.

I don't so much wake up as come to. I'm no longer lying on the sofa but sitting on the floor with my back against it, Riley's playpen beside me. All the boxes have been unpacked, folded up and stacked beside the door. The highchair is out, even though I'm certain I folded it up this morning, but it looks cleaner than I remember it being.

The living room looks like a different place, everything unpacked, put away or neatly on display. I squint at the old carriage clock that used to belong to my nan, now on a fully stocked bookshelf. The clock says it's nearly nine o'clock. That can't be right.

I scramble to my feet, pulling myself up by the playpen and peering inside it. Riley isn't there.

I swivel my head from side to side, looking under the table and chairs as if he would have been able to climb out on his own and crawl away.

'Riley!' I call out. 'Maggie?'

Silence.

I race upstairs two steps at a time, using the banister to haul myself up, and run into his nursery. It takes a while for my eyes to adjust to the dark and I blink and blink and blink until I see my baby curled up in his cot, fast asleep. Something fizzy and liquid rushes out of me with relief and I gently place a hand on his back, making sure he's breathing, smelling his freshly washed hair. He's in a clean Babygro, his room is tidy, the nappy bin has been emptied.

I go downstairs in a haze. In the kitchen plates have been washed up, a frying pan on the side, the sausages and pureed vegetables I'd defrosted no longer in the fridge. I don't understand. Tony left for work around five o'clock and then Maggie came, and what did I do for four hours? Did I really sleep through her unpacking, looking after the baby, feeding him and bathing him then putting him to bed? I'm a light sleeper – I wake at every small sound. I don't understand.

Yet, everything is good. Everything is perfect. I should be happy.

I sit on the sofa and look around, taking it all in. My empty mug of tea is still on the table, although hers remains untouched. Other than that the house is immaculate. I'm not, though. I smell of sweat, my hair is lank and every inch of me aches. How has Maggie achieved all of this in such little time? She must think I'm such a failure.

I want to call her and thank her, but I don't have her telephone number. And I can't go next door, not at this time of night with Riley asleep.

I rub my back, my head pounding. I need to eat something, yet I don't feel hungry, just tired. How could I have slept for four solid hours yet feel worse than I did this morning?

My mobile phone rings and I snatch it up, expecting it to be Maggie... even though I've never given her my number.

It's not. Of course it's not.

'Why are you like this, Lulu?'

It's my brother. Dan never starts with 'hello' or 'how are you?' – as soon as I answer his calls, he immediately starts talking as if we're already halfway through a conversation.

'Like what?' I say with a sigh.

'Like *this*! All moody and miserable.'

I go to tell him about my dead neighbour, but he keeps talking, his voice rising with every word.

'Mum said you gave her a huge guilt trip on Sunday when she called. She was all happy about being out to lunch, they were good enough to call and see how you were, and you laid into them. She said you kept pestering her about coming over to help you.'

How many days ago was Sunday? I have no idea what day it is today.

'I didn't pester them,' I say, standing up so I don't get too comfortable on the sofa and fall asleep again. 'I was only asking about Christmas.'

'All you do is moan,' he says. 'You know Kayla went back to work six weeks after giving birth to twins. Twins!'

He's shouting now. Dan loves to shout. Even when he's not angry he's shouting. He also loves to show off about Kayla like she's an extension of him, as though the prettier she gets and the more she earns, the more respected he will be. I can't compete with the Kaylas of the world because she has money and a family to help her and doesn't get phone calls from her brother shouting at her for asking for help.

I want to explain this to him, to stay calm and rational. That's how women are told to talk to men so that they listen – don't be emotional, or shrill, or hysterical. But I can't. I know if I open my mouth, my voice will be too high and too fast, and he'll be on the other end of the phone rolling his eyes not listening to what I'm saying, only *how* I'm saying it.

So instead, I imagine Dan choking. I imagine every one of my brother's words being lumps of grisly fat that he's stuffing into his flabby gob and the gelatinous words are getting lodged in his windpipe. I imagine him staggering to his feet, pointing at his throat, clawing at his neck with no sound coming out. I see him drop to the floor, his face puce, his eyes bulging, his legs kicking out like a cockroach being sprayed with repellent. And then he goes slack, and still, and silent.

He's still talking.

'What was that?' I say, my hand trembling, my fingers aching from the grip on my phone.

'You've changed,' Dan replies. 'You used to be fun to be around, Lulu. No wonder Mum and Dad prefer to come to our house rather than yours. Maybe think about that next time you give them a hard time.'

I hang up on him and switch my phone to silent. My brother is the only family I have in this country, but he may as well be on another continent for the good he is. I have no one. None of my old friends have children, they all petered out as soon as Riley was born, and I don't think I can count the overeager woman from playgroup or a few random neighbours as my friends. All I have is Tony, who is never awake when I am, and Maggie.

I sit back down, my breaths ragged and my chest tight. Why would he call me to shout at me? Why would my mother tell him I was being mean? I'm not going to cry, there's no point, I just need to sleep.

I sit back down on the sofa and press the heels of my hands against my aching eyes, making the cut on my palm sting. What if Dan is right, though? What if I'm turning into a boring nag? Or a dangerous bitch. I saw the way the policewoman looked at me. I wonder if she told her colleague that I'm not right in the head. What if they come back? What if they've pieced it all together?

I don't understand what's happening to me. I've not been myself lately, my brother's not wrong about that. And I've been feeling a lot worse since the sleepwalking incident when I first met Maggie. But is it any wonder I've been a little out of sorts with a restless baby and a house move and no sleep and the fact that *my fucking neighbour was murdered*?

I yawn and wince as a shot of pain blooms across my breasts. I stopped breastfeeding after the summer, yet they still feel so heavy and painful. I'm sitting here bone-tired yet trembling with rage, my chest aching and my stomach bloated and my bones so heavy they feel like they're made of iron. The last time I felt like this was...

Oh. Oh, shit.

Well. That explains a lot.

EIGHTEEN

Tony woke me up coming home earlier than normal. Five in the morning. By the time he'd finished brushing his teeth and switching on every light in the house, I couldn't get back to sleep so I lay awake thinking about the fact I'm probably pregnant.

My periods never came back after Riley was born. There was some faint spotting – I've never been heavy – but when I looked it up online, it said it can take up to six months if I exclusively breastfed and I did for at least six months. Then we moved house, and I was so tired that every day blended into one and I didn't even notice. And it wasn't as if Tony and I were having that much sex, so it never occurred to me that I was taking any risks when we didn't use protection.

Oh God. I can't do this. Not now.

I lie in bed, Tony snoring beside me, and watch the shadows of the trees against the ceiling. For a street with hardly any working streetlights, our bedroom is never dark enough.

When was the last time Tony and I had sex? I think back to our previous home, with its high ceilings, bigger rooms and pretty window boxes. I think we last had sex in August. I know it was a hot day because we laughed about it. No. July. Jesus, that's a really long time. Tony had just found out he'd got the new job he has now, and we were celebrating. He'd bought a bottle of Prosecco and we drank it on the balcony. Riley was sleeping but it was still light outside, and Tony kissed me. We used to kiss so much before I got pregnant. Even when we'd bump into one another at family events and have too much to drink and vow we'd never do it again, it was the kissing I liked the most. That man can kiss. But it has been such a long time since I've felt sexy and irresistible, even though he doesn't seem to want me any less. I'm not that girl anymore. As soon as I told him I was pregnant I went from being someone he'd been secretly pining for to something he had to protect and provide for. And that's not very sexy.

The day he'd been offered the job we'd got drunk and laughed and stumbled inside, kissing on the sofa like a couple of teenagers. We then made love there and then, and it was more intense and intimate than normal. We stopped laughing and he looked at me, really looked at me, and I felt seen. And for a fleeting moment we were invincible, united, bonded forever. He told me he loved me and that this new job would change everything for the better, and I believed him.

I look at Tony snoring beside me and wonder where it all went wrong. I shouldn't have believed him when he said things would get better.

As soon as Riley wakes up, I get him dressed and fed and into his pushchair, and I'm on the high street by six thirty. I can't stay in that house, listening to Tony sleep soundly, for a second longer. Not until I know for certain how much worse my life is about to get.

The nearest supermarket to me opens at seven. It's only a small express store, but at least I won't have to wait long by the time we walk there.

I feel sick but I don't know if that's because I'm pregnant or nervous or because I never get enough sleep. I'm doing the maths in my head, and if I'm pregnant then I must be beyond twelve weeks. How is that possible? How can I be that pregnant and not know?

I've been trying to lose the weight I gained after Riley was born for ages. I've been so confused because I never slow down, and I hardly have time to eat, yet my tracksuit bottoms have been getting tighter. Tony said I had two options: embrace my bigger size and be confident or do something about it. So I stopped eating so much and went on longer walks. Yet I should have been eating more not less, taking it easy not upping my exercise.

I'm outside the supermarket entrance ten minutes before the doors open but I'm not alone. There's a woman dressed in a smart shift dress, maybe on her way to work or a job interview, and she has a long ladder in her shiny black tights. That's probably why she's looking at the time on her phone impatiently. The other people are mostly old or mums with kids like me who have been awake for hours already. Riley is fussing so as soon as the doors are opened I race to the baby aisle and get him a packet of those expensive but tasteless organic crisps for babies. The kind that melt in his mouth and turn to mush, which he then spreads everywhere. I don't care if he eats them now, I'll pay for the empty packet at the till.

While there I grab some nappies, a couple of things for dinner and some more milk. Then, finally, I find myself standing before the pregnancy tests, my stomach twisting like it did nearly two years ago when I last took a test. Back then I'd known I was pregnant within a few weeks. I was certain and I so wanted to be right because I longed for that baby so much. Now... now I don't know what having two babies will be like. I don't know if I will survive it.

I pick the cheapest one that comes with two in the pack, just in case, and go to the only open till, beating a middle-aged woman who scowls at me and huffs even though she has a full basket of food and I only have six items.

'Ah, how old is your little boy?' the cashier asks me as she scans my items.

'Nearly one,' I say.

'He's lovely. I remember when mine were that little.'

I smile at her. I miss talking to new people. At work I used to speak to dozens of people every day.

'Oh, I need to pay for the crisps he was eating,' I say as I bag up my six items.

I try to prise the empty packet out of Riley's hand, but he starts to scream.

'Please, sweetheart,' I say, looking up so the woman behind me knows I'm trying to move things along as fast as possible. She sighs, making my skin prickle. The more I tug, the more Riley screams. Someone else has joined the woman in the queue and the two of them are saying something about 'common decency' and how 'she literally has all day to shop'. The manager comes over and I realise the woman behind me has fetched her.

'She's holding up the whole queue,' she says loudly, nodding her head at me. 'The two of them have been chatting for ages and I'm in a hurry.'

We haven't been chatting for ages! I blink back tears as I try to get the crisp packet out of Riley's bunched fists, but the more I pull, the louder he screams.

'I'll open up another till, madam,' the manager says to the woman behind me.

'I don't want to go to another till,' she replies. 'I've already put all my shopping on *this* conveyor belt.'

The manager turns to the cashier. 'Go and get another packet off the shelf, Lisa. You can scan that instead.'

The cashier gives me an apologetic smile and walks off, leaving me alone with the manager, the angry woman and my screaming child who won't let go of his crisps. The other customers in the queue have moved to the second till, now manned by a surly teen boy, but the old woman behind me is too busy glaring at me, creases forming like dead spiders at the edges of her eyes and her lipstick bleeding into the cracks around her mouth. She rolls her eyes at the manager and mutters, 'Mothers knew how to control their children in my day.'

I picture her dead. I imagine what it would be like to take the plastic bag I'm holding, empty it and wrap it over her head. To pull the handles together tightly while she thrashes and flails around, her knees buckling beneath her purple anorak as I sit astride her, every one of her frantic breaths sucking the bag tighter around her haggard face.

Riley's cries have reached a crescendo, his face bright red, snot and saliva coating his mouth and chin. The cashier has come back and tells the manager there are no more packets left on the shelf. The manager is saying something about searching for the code on the till screen. Riley is waving his arms in the air, the packet still in his tight fists, crisp crumbs flying through the air like sand. His screaming is so loud my ears are ringing.

'Aren't you going to do something?' the woman shouts at me.

In my mind I'm pinning her hands to her side with my knees and wrapping my hands around her throat. Her legs kick at nothing, my knees aching from the bones in her arms, and on and on I push my thumbs into her gullet until she stills beneath me and the bag stops rustling.

'Here's your change,' the cashier says to me with a shaky smile. I didn't realise I'd paid her. Or that I'd bagged everything up. Or that Riley had finally stopped screaming.

I smile back at her and ignore the mutterings of 'finally' from the woman behind me.

I look at my receipt. The cashier didn't charge me for Riley's crisps. I hook my carrier bag over the pushchair handle and step outside, where the cold air calms my beating heart and cools my searing veins. I want to hit something. I want to scream. I want to cry. But I can't do that on the high street at seven twenty-four on a weekday morning because I'm a woman and a mother and a respectable customer who stays calm when her child has a tantrum and a stranger is mean to her.

And I did. I did keep it together. I didn't kill her… I only thought about it.

NINETEEN

Tony is asleep when I pee on the stick. I'm definitely pregnant. I'm having a baby. I pee on the second stick, and that one is positive too.

I stay seated because if I get up, I fear I'm going to faint. I place my head in my hands, still holding the pee stick, and all I can do is wail. *What am I going to do? What am I going to do?*

So I do what I've been doing for a year. I don't think about my feelings, I just go into autopilot.

Tony stays sleeping while I clean up the mess he left from the omelette he made when he got home this morning. He's still asleep as I break down what's left of the empty packing boxes and add them to the recycling. And he sleeps while I give Riley his lunch and cuddle up with him while we watch old re-runs of *In the Night Garden*. And as my son grows limp in my arms, secure and safe and warm, I try not to fall asleep myself for fear of dropping him, or losing him, or something terrible happening.

And the entire time that Tony sleeps, I feel dead inside.

Two babies. By when? What the fuck are we going to do with two babies? My days are already exhausting and empty and mind-numbing with one child... What the hell will they look like with two? And my nights? I'll never sleep. Not ever. I'm already losing my mind, imagining awful, violent things. What if having a second baby turns me into a real monster?

Riley is having his nap in his room by the time Tony wakes up and asks if I bought any more milk today. I nod. What's he doing with all this milk? Bathing in it?

'What about bread?' he asks.

'I didn't remember the bread.'

He gives me a look that's not quite disappointment or anger. Incredulousness. Incomprehension. *God, Lu. Why didn't you remember the bread? It's not like you have a lot to think about in your mundane little life,* I imagine him thinking. *You're so stupid, Lu. Stupid and useless.*

He doesn't say any of that, of course he doesn't, but I can see it in his eyes and the tension around his mouth.

'Sorry,' I mumble.

'It doesn't matter.' Except it does. I know it does because of the way he's putting the butter he no longer needs back in the fridge and pouring so much cereal out there's no room for the milk, so it splashes over my clean surfaces and some drips on to the floor.

'I'm just really—'

'Tired?' he says in one outward breath. 'All you ever talk about is being tired. Lu, please. I'm working seven days a week, not one day off, taking all the overtime I can get to make up for what we spent on the deposit for this place. I bust a gut for you and Riley. I'm on my feet, my job is physical, I work with some right dickheads in those warehouses – Steve, Greg, Ian. I never get a moment's peace. Do you ever hear me complain that I'm tired? We're all fucking tired!'

I thought he drove a lorry all day, quietly, sitting down, no one climbing on him or screaming in his face or getting sick and shit and snot on him. I thought he got to go to the pub with other adults he likes, play snooker and work out at the gym because he cares about his mental and physical health. And when he *does* sleep, I thought he actually *got* to sleep.

He's waiting for me to say something but I'm still asking all these questions in my head. Doing the maths. Wondering if it's me. If I'm missing something.

'I don't get it, Lu,' he says, shaking his head. I'm such an enigma to him. Such a letdown. 'You're home all day. How can you be so tired all the time when you can literally watch a movie whenever you want and chill with the baby?'

Chill? How can I relax when my mind keeps screaming at me, *You're pregnant, Lu! You're a killer, Lu! What are you going to do?*

Riley still has me up in the night, but even when he doesn't it's not like I'm sleeping because when I *do* close my eyes all I see is blood and what I might have done and what I want to do, and what the hell am I going to do? Every waking moment is like being on red alert. Even when I'm doing nothing I'm completely exhausted by the very essence of existing.

I wish I could go back and be tired simply because I didn't get my eight hours of sleep. I could cope with that. I could. But this? Questioning myself, what I'm doing, what I'm capable of doing? Tony has no idea the effort it's taking me to simply drag myself from one day to the next.

'I've not been feeling right lately,' I say.

'Have you been to the doctors? Did you get the supplements we talked about? Have you tried getting some exercise?'

And that's when the flame ignites, and I want to kill him. Just like I wanted to kill the woman in the supermarket. I want to watch the life ebb away from Tony's eyes, like a dimmer switch slowly being turned down to black. What do other couples do? Are we the only ones, or is every couple like this – stuck in a perpetual cycle of who's the most tired and who does the most, and whether making money or raising a child is the more important role? It's so dull and tiring. All of it. I never used to be this goddamn boring!

Maybe he'll understand if I tell him about the baby. Maybe he'll finally realise I can't do it all alone and work fewer hours and be at home more.

'Riley turns one next month and... well, you still want a big family, right?' I ask tentatively.

Tony's slurping his cereal from his spoon and the noise is making my eye twitch. I want to knock the spoon out of his hand, or better yet stab it repeatedly in his eyes, handle first. Just stab it and stab it and stab it, the splashes of blood making his milk pink.

'Yeah,' he says. 'You know I love kids.'

He says it in all seriousness even though Tony hasn't mentioned Riley once since he got up and he hasn't been into his room to see him yet.

'I was wondering... should we have the chat? You know? About having a second?'

'Another baby?' he says.

I nod and he laughs, more milk speckling the table.

'You have to be kidding, babe. I love you and I love our little family, and I'm not saying never, but... I mean... look at you. You've been wearing the same tracksuit bottoms for four days now. Let's face it, you're struggling with one baby – two would be too much. Let's talk about it when you're less tired. Yeah?'

He gets up and heads for the bathroom, and as he passes me, he drops a kiss on the crown of my head, but all I see is red. I could have killed today. I could have killed that bitch in the supermarket, and I want to strangle Tony right now. Which makes me wonder... is it really that inconceivable that I bludgeoned Dave to death?

TWENTY

Over the last few days Maggie and I have got into a routine of sorts.

She waits for Tony to leave for work then lets herself into my house and starts helping me. With what, I'm not sure seeing as all the unpacking is done, but I often find myself snoozing and waking up on the sofa or at the table or on the floor, noticing that everything looks better than it did before I blanked out.

'I don't know what I'd do without you,' I tell her as she passes me a cheese sandwich and a glass of juice. When did I buy bread? I don't remember. I'm not even sure when I last left the house.

Riley loves her too. There are some mothers who would be jealous of their baby feeling so comfortable around another woman, but I like to see him nestle his warm little head in the crook of her neck like he does with me. He always says 'Ma' when he's with her. Is he saying Maggie? I don't know.

She switches on the TV. It's the local news and a woman is at the end of our street talking about crime rates soaring, and that they are still seeking leads for Dave's murder. The white tent has gone but the police are still there in the day, one or two of them milling around. I wish they would go. I don't want to think about it anymore.

'We don't need any of that,' Maggie says, switching the TV back off again.

I'm not sure what the time is. It's dark outside but that could mean late afternoon or the middle of the night. During this time of year, home alone, day after identical day, every hour feels and looks the same. Most of the time I'm barely even here, suspended a few inches out of my body, as if I'm the dream and it's reality that I'm watching from afar. A little bit like being intoxicated. Or high. Or dead.

I chew my cheese sandwich slowly, Riley sitting on the floor beside me, occasionally pulling himself up and standing like a little drunk man contemplating his first steps. Maggie appears and disappears out of my peripheral and I don't really care what she's doing in my house, busying herself, it's just nice to not be alone. This is what it must be like to have a sister or a mum living nearby. Someone you can depend on, who makes sure you're eating and getting enough rest, who cares about your baby as much as you do.

Maggie is in her forties, I think. I've never asked. Closer to Tony's age than mine. She reminds me of some of his ex-girl-friends – graceful, smart, like she has her shit together. Everything I'm not. I'm trying not to feel guilty about taking up her time when it's her brother and his broken leg that she's meant to be looking after, but she seems to be enjoying herself. Must be because she's a nurse. I'm sure she told me she was a nurse. Nurses are kind like that.

She smiles at me, and I smile back.

I like to watch how she moves, marvelling at how well presented she is, always dressed nicely with jewellery and make-up. Maybe I need to start doing that, wear earrings again now that Riley doesn't grab at them as much. Or maybe not. What's the point of looking pretty now I'm pregnant again? I'm not a woman anymore, simply a vessel housing a parasite. That's what babies are, parasites. No one likes to admit it, but it's true. They only thrive as long as their host does. But I don't know if I have enough left of me to give this time.

Instinctively I lay my hand on my stomach, rubbing it in large slow circles. Then I stop. This isn't my baby yet. I haven't decided. Nobody knows I'm pregnant.

I can't feel it moving yet, and my bump isn't noticeable. It's easy to pretend something isn't happening if you can't see it. If you don't tell anyone. If you don't give it any attention.

I don't know what it's like to be pregnant and not be excited about it. Even though Riley came unexpectedly, he was wanted. I was prepared to do it all alone, with or without Tony; I didn't want to wait any longer to be a mother. But that was before I truly understood what being a mother meant. And I don't think I can be a good mother to a second while failing to be a good mother to the first.

I contemplated calling my own mum and telling her about the positive test, but I couldn't bear it if she continued to tell me how busy she is, and how useless I am, and how inconvenient coming to visit would be for her especially with an extra baby in the house. It's my fault she can't help me because I don't live in a mansion. And I'm definitely not telling Dan and Kayla. My brother can fuck right off after the way he spoke to me the other day. How long ago was that? Was it this week or last? I don't know.

I sigh and rub my eyes, running my fingers through my greasy hair.

I'm going to have to tell Tony eventually, though. But not yet. I want to get used to the idea myself first. Unless it doesn't happen. I shudder at the thought of losing a baby I don't even want and shake my head as dark, uninvited images start to invade my mind.

'Are you OK?' Maggie says.

'I'm fine.'

She strokes my hair the way she does, the way my mum used to do when I was little and scared, and I bat at the tears in my eyes. Riley lifts his hands up to me and I pull him up, holding him close, just the three of us.

'Is it the baby?' Maggie says, sitting on the sofa beside me.

I shake my head. 'Riley's fine.'

'Not Riley.' Maggie gives me a gentle smile and moves her hand from my head to my stomach. 'The other baby.'

I tense, the three of us frozen like a sculpture. Madonna and child. But which one is the holy mother?

'How did you know?' I ask quietly.

There's that benevolent smile again. 'I know you.'

No, she doesn't.

'You're a nurse,' I say. 'I guess you can tell these things.'

She hums in agreement.

'Do you have children?' I ask her.

Maggie stands up and takes Riley from me. He coos, his head growing heavy on her shoulder. It's close to his naptime. Maggie knows that and got to him before I did.

She rarely talks about herself and her life. I know she lives in Devon – the neighbours told me before I met her – but beyond that all she's said is that her brother hardly needs her help anymore.

'I don't have children,' she says. 'Free and single. I nearly did once... but...'

She stops there and I don't say anything further. She would have made an excellent mother.

'You have a good thing here,' she says. 'Tony's a good man.'

She doesn't know that. I never mention him. She's basing that comment on nothing more than a few photos I have scattered around the house that she helped me unpack. I suppose we do look happy in those pictures. We were. We *are*. I think back to the way he spoke to me this morning. No, wait, was that yesterday? When he told me I wasn't coping. I am, I'm doing fine. Look at the house. Look at my baby. I'm fine. Totally fine.

'I'll take him,' Maggie says, nodding to Riley on my lap, his head lolling from side to side. I thought she'd already picked him up. I hadn't noticed the weight of him on me. It's perpetual, first with him growing inside of me, then being in my arms, then sitting on me all the time and wanting to be carried. Now another one is starting the cycle all over again. So much weight, pushing down on me and out of me, taking and taking and taking.

It's dark outside. It must be the evening already, which means this isn't his naptime but his bedtime. Did we feed him already? He's in his nightclothes, so Maggie must have. I'm glad it's night-time... that means I survived another day.

I thank her. She says something about taking the bins out for me on her way out. My eyes grow heavy. I'm gone.

'Lu!'

Tony is standing over me, concern etched like black pen over his shadowy features.

'Why are you sleeping on the sofa?'

I'm cold and curled up in such a tight ball my legs ache.

'It's still dark,' I mumble, glancing at the carriage clock. Six thirty.

'Riley!' I say, jumping up. Something pulls at my stomach, and I sit back down. I'd forgotten about the baby. The new one.

'The baby's asleep,' he says.

He knows about the baby? My baby? It takes me a while to realise he's talking about our son.

I stare at Tony and take a deep breath. Six thirty is too late for Riley to be having a nap – he won't sleep tonight.

'Are you off to work, then?' I say, getting up slowly. 'You normally leave earlier than this.'

Tony rubs the back of his neck, like he's trying to pull the right words to the front of his head. 'Lu, it's six thirty in the morning, I just got home. Did you spend the night sleeping on the sofa in your trainers?'

In my trainers? I look and he's right: my grubby, no-longer-white trainers are caked in mud, and I've left marks on the grey sofa. I brush at them, and they flake off. Why do I have my shoes on?

Tony looks tired. I haven't properly looked at his face for a long time, not this close up. He looks grey. Or maybe it's this pre-dawn light. He sits down beside me with a heavy exhale of air as if the effort of talking to me is too much for him.

'You're not right, Lu.'

What?

'Maybe we should look at getting you some help.'

You're meant to be my help! I want to scream. *You! The other half of this parental unit.*

'I already have help,' I say, although the words come out as one long drunken slur.

He rubs his face with both hands like he's washing it.

'Who?'

'Maggie.'

'Who's Maggie?'

Haven't I mentioned Maggie to him before?

'Jim's sister.'

'Jim?'

He's looking at me as if I'm making these people up. As if I'm completely mental. If he thinks I've lost my mind, then how is he still so comfortable going to work every evening and leaving me alone with his son? He can't be that worried about me if he's not stepping in to take over.

'Jim is our neighbour, the one who broke his leg,' I explain. 'You know this. Jim at number eight. I've got to know his sister, who's been staying with him. She's popped around a few times and helped me unpack.'

His shoulders visibly lower. 'That's good. OK. So you're making new friends?'

'Huh?' I say.

His voice has floated away again, distant and hollow. Sometimes, when he's talking, his words are nothing but echoing sounds.

'Did you have a good sleep?' I ask. 'Don't you have to leave for work in a minute?'

He looks at me again, this time his head tilted to one side. 'See a doctor, Lu.'

'I'm fine.'

'Seriously.' He gets up with a sigh and heads for the bathroom. 'See a doctor today. I'm worried about you.'

He shuts the bathroom door and flashes of him in the shower appear before me. Slipping. Cracking his head on the tiles. Blood circling the plug hole. His feeble voice calling out for me. In my mind's eye I imagine putting music on and turning it up loud, as loud as Dave used to play his awful techno, drowning out Tony's voice.

I don't want to see a doctor. I don't want Tony looking at me like I'm mad. And I'm not sure if I even want to bring this child into such a cruel world. A child deserves a good mother... and I'm not even a good person. I look down at my muddy trainers and I want to be sick. Where did I go last night? What have I done?

TWENTY-ONE

I go to the doctors, but only because Maggie told me to.

'I'm fine,' I told her.

'You're losing the plot,' she said.

It took three phone calls to get through to the GP's office, then I had to wait two days because I'm new to the area, and I had to fill in forms, and then the only appointment they had was eight o'clock in the morning. So here I am looking like death warmed up, trying to calm a grizzly baby.

'Mrs Smith?' the doctor calls out.

'Ms,' I say. He doesn't hear me.

His office is so clean and white it hurts my eyes. There are two chairs in front of his desk and for a second I stand there, unsure which to sit in.

'Please,' he says, signalling at the one nearest to me. I hand Riley a cracker and hope it's enough to keep him quiet.

'How can I help you?' he asks.

He's old but not too old. He looks interested but not really, more in an 'it's my job to look interested' way.

'I don't think anyone can help me,' I say.

It was meant to come out light and jokey; instead I sound

seriously unhinged. My voice is hoarse, each word having to be dragged out of my throat. It's an effort. Everything is an effort. Even talking and blinking feel impossible. The doctor has a play area at the back of the room with a soft rug and it takes all my willpower not to crawl over to it, curl up like a kitten and close my eyes.

I wonder how Shadow is. I haven't seen that cat in a while.

The doctor leans forward, his hands steepled in that professional doctor way they all have.

'This is a safe space,' he says. 'Anything you say will be dealt with in the strictest confidence.'

'I'm exhausted,' I say. 'Like, really, *really* tired.'

He leans back again, as if my issues are not exciting enough for him.

'How old is your son?'

'He turns one at the end of December.'

The doctor types something up on his screen.

'And is he your only child?'

I nod.

'Are you working at the moment?'

I shake my head. I know what he's doing: he's deciding whether it's normal for me to be this tired. If I tell him I work nights as a surgeon and spend my days volunteering for the animal sanctuary while caring for my elderly parents and triplets, then he'll nod sagely and tell me that I should try doing less and that will solve my exhaustion. Except he can't tell me to do less because I don't really do anything.

'How much exercise do you get, Mrs Smith?'

Really? I shake my head. Tears are gathering in my eyes, and I try to blink them away, but they fall regardless. I don't even have the energy to lift my hand up to wipe them away, let alone go for a run. I open my mouth to answer and release a sob.

'And how is your mental health?' he asks gently, pushing a

box of tissues towards me. 'Do you often feel hopeless and desperate?'

Yes. Doesn't everyone? I'm not sure if I think that or say it out loud. He nudges the tissues closer to me and I take one.

'Is there anything else you wish to tell me?' he says without looking at me, his fingers punching out words on his keyboard.

I want to tell him about the things I see: the horrible visions that flash through my mind in a matter of seconds which feel like hours. Images I know aren't real but feel so real it's like I'm living in that world more than this one. I want to tell him about the things I see happening to people, the blood and the accidents and all that violent rage simmering beneath the surface of my skin. Behind my lips. On the tips of my fingers.

'No,' I say. 'I'm tired. That's it, really.'

He doesn't ask me how much sleep I'm getting, or whether I have any support at home, or whether anything dangerous has happened due to my lack of sleep. He doesn't ask me anything, which is a shame because I've started recording the sleep maths on my phone. Last night I slept for four hours, but in small increments. I didn't drop off until 11.57pm because I couldn't stop thinking about the second police car I saw outside, then Riley woke up at 1.03am and needed feeding. The next batch of sleep was 1.41am until 3.56am. Then I woke up because I thought I heard Riley crying, but he wasn't. Then it took a while to get back to sleep so I googled whether you can kill people in your sleep. The answer is yes, you can, there's an entire article in *The Guardian* about it, so that didn't make me feel any better. Then I slept from 4.30am until 5.18am, when I woke up to use the toilet, but I was worried about Riley not having woken for a while so I went in to check on him. He was fine. Then I figured he'd be awake soon anyway, so I didn't get back to sleep. How many hours is that? Four. Four hours and nine minutes. That was a good night.

But the doctor doesn't want to see my maths.

He prints something out and hands it to me. 'Take sixty milligrams once a day, in the morning,' he says.

I stare at the piece of paper, the writing blurry and swimming black across the thin page.

'What's this?'

'Fluoxetine. An antidepressant.'

I hear the words he's saying but I can't get them in straight in my head.

'Antidepressants?'

But I'm not depressed; I'm exhausted and terrified. I keep imagining what Tony will say when I tell him what the doctor prescribed me. Maybe this is what it will take for him to realise how much I'm struggling and he'll step up. Or not. Maybe he'll be relieved because then the pressure is off him; it was me all along, I was the unreasonable one, he didn't do anything wrong. Either way, pills won't change anything. They won't stop my baby crying all night, or my partner having to work around the clock, or my loneliness, or me being a stone-cold killer.

'We take postnatal depression very seriously nowadays,' the doctor says. 'I'm pleased you came to see me. Let's make a follow-up appointment for eight weeks' time. See how you're feeling then.'

'I can't take these,' I say. 'I'm pregnant.'

He finally looks up from his screen and stares at my stomach.

'You should have said. How far along?'

I shrug. 'A few weeks. Months. I'm not sure. I only found out last week.'

How long ago was it that I wanted to kill the woman in the supermarket? Five days? Something like that.

His face is set stern, as if I've been wasting his time for the last ten minutes.

'That will explain why you're so tired. We'll need to arrange a blood test and I'll call you with the results in a week or so. In the meantime, you can still take the medication. There's no evidence that it will do any harm to the foetus.'

Riley has started to struggle against his pushchair straps, his face turning a dark shade of red from either exertion or the strain of crapping while sitting down. I should have let Maggie look after him like she suggested.

'I'm not sure I want to take meds,' I say.

'See how you get on with the dose I suggested and—'

'The baby,' I cut in. 'Not that one.' I point to Riley. 'This one.' I point to my stomach. 'I'm not a good mum.'

He nods, like he agrees with me. 'Let's arrange the blood test and take it from there.'

I didn't know for sure I didn't want the baby until I was at the GP's, wishing I had someone to look after Riley, wondering how it would have been sitting there with him in the pushchair and a baby in my arms. And all the way home, battling my way down the busy high street, the tears kept on falling, my stomach contracting into a gnarly fist so sharp I could feel it pushing against my ribs.

If I don't have this baby, then I don't have to tell Tony anything. I can tell myself it didn't happen either. That it was one of those things. It was simply not meant to be. This isn't a selfish decision, it's the opposite of that – I'm doing the right thing. It wouldn't be fair on the baby either. Who wants a batshit crazy psycho for a mum? A woman who doesn't know what day of the week it is and can't even find the time to wash her hair. A woman who finds herself in the street covered in blood with no idea how she got there. A murderer. I'm not taking those pills and I'm not having the baby.

. . .

The doctor calls me three days later. Maggie is with me, holding her fingers crossed in the air as if I'm waiting to find out something exciting like my exam results or if I got a job.

The doctor tells me I'm around twenty weeks pregnant. I do the maths. That's halfway to birth. I can't get rid of it now, not this far along. I'm having this baby, whether I like it or not, and if my maths is correct, it will be here early April.

'Don't forget to pick up your prescription and some folic acid,' the doctor says. 'And try to get some rest.'

How am I meant to get some rest? Why does he think I came to his surgery with extreme sleep-deprivation if I was able to rest in the first place? Everyone wants me to lie down, be quiet, numb myself, be easier. And I want that. Of course I want that too. I want to switch off and not be here anymore, but I have a baby to look after. Two now. They don't care how tired I am; all they care about is that I stop complaining and that my babies are OK. It's not about me. It's always about everyone else.

I hang up the phone and stare into space. It's fine. I can do this. I simply need to get to April without doing something really stupid. Something dangerous... to myself or others.

TWENTY-TWO

I wake up drenched, my hair clinging to the nape of my neck, pools of sweat collecting between my swollen breasts. I was having a nightmare and I was killing Dave. I was in his house, and I was telling him to turn the music down and he was laughing at me.

I can still see it. His pallid face made of shadows, dark rings beneath his eyes, a cigarette burning to cinders cupped in his yellow hand. He takes a drag and blows the smoke in my face, telling me to go home.

I go to his old-fashioned stereo system, made of three layers, a pile of opened CDs stacked beside it. His hand darts out as I try to turn down the volume dial.

'Get out!' he shouts in my face, his breath rancid with stale beer and nicotine.

I can't hear him over the music throbbing dully in my ears like a heartbeat, but I know what he's saying because I can read his spit-encrusted lips inches from my face.

'Your music is too loud!' I'm shouting. 'It's two in the morning. This isn't fair on the rest of us.'

He pushes me aside and I stumble, my bare feet stepping on

something soft. A polystyrene box containing the remnants of a kebab. The carpet, once grey, is now various shades of brown and black, smudges of mud and cigarette ash and something greasy. I think of his mother, how she probably vacuumed that carpet every day, looking around her living room smiling because every item in there meant something to her. Because that's what mothers do with their houses, they make them more than a practical place to live... they make them into a safe home. And *my* home, my community, isn't safe as long as people like Dave take up so much space with their noise and their bodies and their power.

'Turn it down!' I'm screaming, and he pushes me. He keeps pushing my shoulder, making me stumble backwards, pushing and pushing until I reach the door, which he yanks open, spilling the music out into the night. And that's where I slap him. In the dark, on his doorstep, against the soundtrack of his techno beat. I hit him harder than I thought I could.

I storm off, walking quickly down his garden path towards his broken gate set into a crumbling wall. The skip is in front of his house, taking up the space of three cars. It's full but Dave's clearly too tight or too lazy to get it emptied so the debris continues to pile high, pieces of brick and tiles and glass littering the floor around it. I'm careful not to step on anything but Dave does as he marches behind me, his thick boots crunching glass underfoot as he closes the distance between us.

He grabs my shoulder beneath the broken lamp post and spins me around. His face is contorted, scrunched up tight like a paper ball.

'You little bitch,' he growls, speckles of saliva landing on my cheek. His mouth looks black in the dim light, his teeth grey and crooked.

It may be dark out here, but I can still make out the mark I left on his cheek, the mark shaped like a hand. Then he shoves me strong enough that I fall forward on to the hard ground on all fours, my hand landing on something glinting and jagged that cuts through my skin. Sharp. Sweet. The jolt I need.

On the pavement, next to my hand, is half a breezeblock. It's heavy but I can fit all my fingers through the hole which was once an ornamental shape. Perhaps once part of his mother's garden wall. Now it's the weapon I'm going to use to kill him.

I swing out and he falls. I swing again at his face, and he hits the ground hard with a crack, glass cutting his skin, something piercing his eye, his hand coming up but unable to predict where the next blow will be. And I don't stop, and I don't stop, until there's nothing left to hit.

I'm wet but it's not blood, it's sweat. And I'm not standing on the pavement in my pyjamas but lying in bed, in my home, safe and silent. So silent my ears are ringing, and my clean, unbloodied hands are trembling.

'It was a nightmare,' I tell myself out loud, throwing the damp duvet off me. 'Just a silly nightmare.'

But I'm not so sure anymore. It didn't feel like one. All those details, all that blood. It felt like a memory.

My stomach twinges and I sit up with a start. Then another one. My baby. My baby is punching and kicking me from the inside because it knows who and what its mother is. It can feel everything I feel. Which means it felt everything I felt on the night I murdered Dave. I was carrying one life while ending another.

TWENTY-THREE

I'm in the kitchen when Tony comes home at six in the morning. The house is dark and silent and I'm sitting at the table, sipping a mug of cold tea, staring at my hand.

'Are you OK?' he asks me. Does he ever say anything else? 'Where's Riley?'

'Sleeping.'

I wasn't able to go back to sleep. Every time I closed my eyes, I saw split skin and congealed kebab and a pavement soaked red. I pick at my thumbnail even though there's no dry blood trapped beneath it anymore. But the cut on my hand is still there. The scar that remains to show me that I did it. That I'm a killer.

'Is there anything to eat?' Tony asks, opening the fridge and peering inside as if the food will magically jump out, shouting, *Pick me, pick me.*

I look up. 'What?'

'Sometimes there are leftovers, like pasta or something. I'm starving.'

I can't stop staring at him, his perfect hair and broad shoulders silhouetted in the white glow of the fridge light. That's all he can think about? Food?

He notices my silence and turns around. 'I need a shower. If the baby is still sleeping, maybe you can rustle something up for me. A quick omelette or a cheese toastie would be nice.'

'What did you say?'

He's squinting at me through the dark, trying to read the expression on my face. 'I was just saying—'

There's a crash and he ducks, and I don't realise I've thrown the mug of cold tea at the wall until shards of ceramic are skittering along the tiled floor and liquid is dripping off the cabinets.

'Don't you fucking care?' I scream. 'You never think about me! It's always what you want and what I can do for you and what you can stuff into your fucking gob!'

My breaths are coming in large gulps, my chest heaving, my entire body shaking. I lean on the table for support. I'm going to vomit. I'm going to pass out. I'm going to kill him. I am. I'm going to kill him.

Tony has his back to me, peering into the fridge, the light shining around him like he's the messiah. He's offering to make me poached eggs. I'm sitting down, the mug of tea still in my hand. I look at the floor. It's clean. Of course it's clean, Maggie mops it every day. The rage is still coursing through me, but I haven't said anything. I haven't done anything. I imagined throwing the mug and screaming. Tony has no idea what I'm feeling right now.

'Thank you. Poached eggs would be lovely,' I say with a smile. 'Would you mind if I take a quick shower while you fix us something to eat?'

'Of course.'

He gives me a wink and I blow him a kiss and I stagger out of the kitchen and into the bathroom to cry.

. . .

We ate the breakfast Tony cooked and he went to bed. Then Riley woke up and I've spent the day playing with my son while holding back yet more tears. Do they never run out?

I really didn't think I'd hurt Dave, but now I know I did. I'd imagined doing it, but I didn't think I was that evil, that dangerous. People sleepwalk, especially sleep-deprived mothers, but I didn't realise it was possible to kill while asleep until I read it online. I knew, deep down, that a small cut on my hand could never have produced so much blood. And Maggie knew it too. That's why I can't find my pyjamas. She must have disposed of them – burned them, buried them, thrown them away. All this time she's been protecting me.

That wasn't a nightmare I had last night, that was a repressed memory. And now I have to decide whether to keep playing dumb or tell the truth. I need to talk to her.

'Look at you both,' Tony says, walking into the living room. I glance at the carriage clock. Three o'clock. He leans down and kisses me on the lips, planting another on the crown of our boy sleeping on my chest. 'I love you so much,' he says. 'Both of you.'

He thinks he's looking at two people right now, not three. He's not seen me naked for such a long time, and every time I see him, I'm in a baggy jumper or a thick dressing gown or I have Riley in my arms. Imagine living such a peaceful life, so self-assured in your own little bubble, that you have no idea your wife is pregnant.

I smile up at him, blinking hard so he can't see the tears in my eyes.

'Have a nice day at work,' I say.

'Everything I do, I do for my family.'

'I know. I love you.'

He likes that. He leaves the house smiling while my own

smile drops as soon as I hear the front door click shut behind him. I start to count. She never takes more than three minutes.

I stay on the sofa, Riley in my arms, and wait as I hear the key in the lock and the door shut, and Maggie steps into the room.

'He left early today,' she says.

This time my smile is genuine. I'm so happy to see her. We need to talk.

'Sit down,' I say.

'Hey, what's the matter?'

I'm crying now – heaving, wracking sobs that make my shoulders shake and my lip tremble. She takes Riley out of my arms and places him in his playpen and holds me. It's so good to be held by someone who isn't going to ask me if I've bought milk or if I fancy a quick shag.

'It's OK,' she says, even though she doesn't know what she's comforting me about. 'It's OK.'

'It's not,' I say, pulling back. 'I've done something really bad.'

She strokes my cheek and I take a deep breath, attempting to regulate my breathing. She waits, my hand in hers.

'It's about Dave,' I say.

She nods encouragingly. The words are caught in my mouth, like a fat, hairy insect trying to climb up my oesophagus. I part my lips, cough, try to spit it out.

'I killed him,' I whisper.

The room is vibrating, undulating, the walls closing in. Everything is fuzzy. Maggie's hand is still in mine; she hasn't pulled away.

'Are you sure?' she asks.

I nod. 'I had a dream, like a repressed memory. Should I tell someone?'

'You just did.'

'No, I mean...' I swallow. 'Should I tell the police?'
'No!'
'But...'
Maggie sits up, squeezing my hand tighter.

'Keep your mouth shut and so will I. No one suspects you; no one saw anything, or you'd have had the police here already. You don't even know it was definitely you. If you confess, they'll take everything away from you.' She places her hand on my hard stomach. 'Everything.'

'I don't think they will,' I argue. 'I've been doing some research. I might not even get in trouble; they may just treat me for psychosis. That's what they'll say it is. Postnatal or pregnancy psychosis or... What was it called again? Parasomnia. Extreme sleepwalking. It wasn't premeditated; it was out of my control. Even if I get put in a ward, I'll get to rest, *to sleep*. I'll be looked after. Riley will be fine with Tony for a few months. Everything will be fine.'

Even hearing myself say those words, I know I'm wrong. I did a bad thing and nothing I do will turn back the clocks. Attempting to right my wrongs will only take me away from my babies, and I can't let that happen. They are all I have.

'You need a nice cup of tea and to calm down,' Maggie says, getting up and heading for the kitchen. I follow her.

Calm down. Yes. I think about the pills the doctor prescribed me. Maybe that's all I need. Maybe everything is in my head, and I simply need to erase it.

'The doctor gave me a prescription for some tablets,' I say. 'He says I have postnatal depression.'

Maggie laughs. 'Well, isn't that convenient for the men, to sedate the mothers so we accept our sorry lot. We are all a lot easier to manage when every one of our senses is switched off. No. Stay present, stay sharp, feel it all.'

But I don't want to feel it all. I don't want any of this.

'Maybe I should pick up the prescription,' I say. 'I need to take them. Everything will make a lot more sense once I clear my head.'

She swings around, her eyes flashing. 'It's gone.'

Did I miss some of her sentence?

'What's gone?' I ask.

'I saw the prescription and I threw it away,' she says, opening up the dishwasher I keep forgetting to use and unloading the plates.

'You went through my things?' I exclaim.

She keeps her back to me, her perfect blonde bob swaying as she unloads the plates one by one.

'I picked you up some folic acid but you don't need antidepressants. Trust me. I'm here to help you. Not only with the housework but to help *you*. And those pills won't do you any favours.'

'But you can't do that,' I say. I pull at her shoulder, and she swings around. 'You can't throw people's things away!'

'Like your pyjamas?' she replies. Her eyes are usually a periwinkle blue but now they're icy and cold. 'The evidence that I destroyed? You don't think I should have done that? What should I have done, then? Gone to the police, told them that the pregnant woman next door is a murderer, a dangerous, unfit mother? Is that how I should be looking out for you?'

'No... I...'

Maggie goes back to unloading the dishwasher and I remain standing, swaying, unsure what to think. Nothing makes sense. Everything is a blurry mess of colours and smells and sounds in my mind.

'Think of your children, Lu!' Maggie suddenly cries out, spinning on her heel to face me. 'You can't crumble now, you have to stay strong for them. Say nothing. Do nothing. Get through each day, one at a time, and keep your mouth shut.'

'But I can't bear it,' I protest, my voice rising so high the last word is like a musical note. 'I can't sleep, I can't function, I can't do anything. All I can think about is the night you found me on the doorstep with blood all over me, and my cut hand, and my bare feet. I killed a man, Maggie. I killed him!'

The slap comes out of nowhere and has me staggering backwards against the doorframe. I instinctively look on the ground to make sure I've not stepped on Riley, even though he's still sleeping in the playpen. I hold my hand up to my face. It's warm and wet beneath my touch and I'm not sure if it's from my tears or the plates she's unloading.

'I said keep your mouth shut!' Maggie hisses.

I back away as she steps closer until I find myself up against the hallway wall.

'If you do anything or tell anyone, you will go to prison,' she says, each word like the rasp of a snake. 'And they will take your babies off you. Forever.'

I slump down to the floor, my knees instinctively raised to my chest. A protective wall between her and my unborn baby. She's looming over me, her beautiful face no longer so soft and light. She's angry but it's not at me, it's at them. All the people who are making everything so difficult for me.

She crouches down so she's eye-level with me. 'Do you want to give birth in prison? Have someone else raise your children? Because Tony could never cope alone, and his family isn't on the scene, and your family couldn't give a damn. I'm saying this because I care about you and the children, Lu. Why would you risk it?'

I don't remember telling her any of that about my family or Tony's but she's right. If I say anything, my life will be ruined before it's had a chance to get better. I peer around the doorframe and watch Riley sleeping soundly in his playpen surrounded by his favourite toys. My baby. My boy. I feel another kick, another life. No one is taking them from me.

'Come on,' Maggie says, holding out a hand to me and getting me back on my feet. 'Let's go.'

'Where?' I say, rubbing my cheek. I can no longer feel where she hit me. Maybe she didn't.

'We're going to the park,' she says. 'There's something we have to do.'

TWENTY-FOUR

'The police haven't stopped their surveillance, you know.'

What's Maggie talking about? She's handing me coats and shoes and gloves. Riley is standing up in his playpen, grinning over at us. Did I wake him with my shouting?

'The police?' I echo back at her.

'Of course. They're watching us. The whole street.'

I look around the room, thinking back to the day the police were here, unable to recall the things they told me. I was in the kitchen making them tea, wasn't I? I know I was out of the room. Maybe I was upstairs tending to a crying Riley. What were they doing down here with Tony? Did they suspect anything? Did they say anything to him?

'Do you think they bugged my house?'

Maggie laughs. 'Don't be silly, that's just in the movies. But they may be monitoring your phone calls or listening to you via your phone. You know all phones have a mic that picks up what we say. They can even check your search history, you know.'

I gave the police my phone number. I'm sure I did. What if they've been listening to me? Watching me through my camera? Seeing the things I've been typing into Google. Can they do that? I pull on my trainers and my coat, plucking Riley out of the playpen and bundling him into his coat. He screams and goes ramrod-straight, arching his back, making it impossible to get him into the chair. I only manage to clip one of the straps up. I'm on autopilot. I'm not sure what's going on, but the urgency in Maggie's voice has my entire body buzzing.

She's right, I need to listen to her. I need to stay alert and sharp and quiet. I'm not alone anymore. She's here and she can help me get through this.

'My keys,' I say.

Where are my keys? I look in my bag and in the tray beneath the pushchair and the changing bag and the hook where they should be. Maggie stays calmly waiting by the door. I yank open cupboards and drawers in the kitchen, then open the fridge door and there they are. With the eggs. What are they doing in the fridge? I didn't put them there. Did I?

'Let's go,' Maggie says, following behind as I open the door and step out into the cold. She's wearing a woollen coat and leather boots instead of muddy trainers. I should start making more of an effort, style my hair nice, get out of my tracksuit bottoms. I don't want her to be embarrassed by me.

Maggie turns right instead of left. It's quicker to get to the park this way but I don't like it as it means going past number four.

'Let's go via the high street,' I say, sidestepping the dog muck and a bag of chips five pigeons are fighting over. She ignores me so I follow her.

There are no more police vans outside Dave's house, but it's all boarded up and the yellow tape is flapping loose in the wind. This is the first time I've walked past the crime scene and I can't help but glance at the pavement where they found him. The skip is still there, although it's been emptied of debris, no doubt looking for a murder weapon. There's still glass on the ground though, and my stomach contracts at the dark mark on the concrete. It could be car oil. It could be blood.

The wind is cutting, and I zip up my coat so it covers my mouth, leaning down to check Riley is covered up enough. He gives me a gummy grin and my heart expands three sizes. We turn at the end of the road and spot a couple of the neighbours with shopping bags. They smile and say hello. I wave and so does Maggie.

After a few minutes we follow the hedge that surrounds the park, and as soon as Riley recognises where we are, he starts to clap his hands and bounce up and down in his seat. There's no one around. I'm not sure of the time but it's already getting dark. I suppose all the other parents have rushed their kids home for their dinner. I don't slow down for the swings or give Riley nuts for the squirrels; I keep going until we reach the pond and the bench, sitting down on it with a long sigh. This area is empty too. I sometimes wonder whether I'm the only person who knows about this corner of the park. Riley is amused by the ducks, waving at them and making quacking sounds. I knew he'd be fine once we got some fresh air.

'I'm sorry,' Maggie says.

'For what?'

'For getting angry with you earlier. I worry about you.'

I nod and give her a small smile. 'I know.'

'I'm just trying to keep you and Riley safe.'

She takes my hand and I let her. I can't quite remember what happened in the kitchen earlier. I think she pushed me. She definitely shouted. But I was being silly, unreasonable. I scared her.

'What you said about the police,' I say. 'Do you think they suspect me?'

'Not yet. But they may do if you start acting unusual.'

'But the phones,' I venture. 'You said they listen in on phone calls and can hear us through the mics. What if they're listening now?'

Maggie shrugs and I unravel my fingers from hers.

'I need to be careful,' I say.

I take my phone out of my pocket and look at it. I have to get rid of it. I have photos on there, photos of my precious boy, and important telephone numbers, but it's all backed up on the cloud. I'm not losing anything, not really. Not if it's being used as a tracking device.

'I need to throw my phone away,' I tell Maggie.

She stays silent, staring out over the water.

'For my babies,' I add.

She turns to me and nods. 'Do it.'

This must be why she brought us to the park because she knows this is something I have to do. I stand up slowly and she does too, matching every one of my steps one by one until we reach the water's edge. I take out the battery from my phone – I've seen in the movies that it's what you have to do – and hold both of the black plastic squares in my hand.

'You're so brave,' Maggie says, her hand on the top of my arm. 'And such a good mother. Dave's murder has helped everyone in the community. He deserved it. Every brave decision you make now, you are doing for your babies. Don't forget that. You are saving lives.'

She's right. Everything I do, I do for my family. Sometimes you have to do bad things for a good reason. Nobody else knows about that night, nobody suspects me, and now I can keep us all safe.

I take one final look around me, pull my arm back, and throw the phone battery and handset as far as I can, grinning as they plop into the water. I'm free. I can feel it. Untethered.

I turn to Maggie and she's smiling, her eyes kind again, her face so close to mine I can smell peppermint on her warm breath.

'Well done,' she says, stroking my cheek. 'You're such a good girl, Lu.'

I close my eyes at the touch of her fingers on my skin, breathing in the faint rose scent of her perfume. I turn my face a fraction, making her knuckles glide across my lips. I part them a little, wanting to know what her skin tastes like, then close them again.

When I open my eyes, she's already walking away.

TWENTY-FIVE

I'm out of bed before my eyes are open. I know that because I've slammed into a wall, Riley's wails still drilling into my head like a police siren. I stumble blindly into his room, reach for him, hold him to me. This is the fifth time he's cried tonight. He's not hot, he's not wet or hungry or teething. He won't stop. I don't understand why he won't stop.

'Please,' I say to him. 'Please, stop crying.'

He throws his head back, arching his back, his clammy hands pulling at my hair and clawing at my face. He digs one of his fingers in my eye, causing tears to stream down my face. It hurts. No one tells you your own children can physically hurt you, yet it's them you need to comfort when what you really want to do is scream and shout and get angry. If anyone else pulled your hair and poked you in the eye, you'd react, but when it's your child you can't. So I try to stay calm, I really do, even though my eye is throbbing and my head is stinging and he's kicking my pregnant stomach, and... no, I can't do this anymore.

For a moment I contemplate putting him down and going

outside, barefoot and in my pyjamas, and knocking on Maggie's door. That's crazy. I can't wake her brother up; he'd think I was mad. And I can't phone anyone, not now I threw mine away.

Fucking Tony and his fucking night shifts!

I hold Riley up to my face, nose to nose. He's crying so hard now he's started to wretch, his tiny fists pummelling my sore, swollen breasts. I want to put him down and walk away. That's what they say, isn't it? That it's OK to put them back in their crib, safe and sound, and take a moment to breathe. But I *can't* breathe. I'm in a fog, caught in an autopilot time loop, where all I can do is bounce him up and down making shushing noises and hoping he's not keeping the neighbours awake.

'Why do you hate me so much?' I whisper.

He can't hear me; my baby, lost in his own little world of fury and rage.

'Is it because you know I'm a bad mum?' I say. 'Because I did a bad thing?'

He keeps screaming so I take him to our bedroom. They say not to sleep with your baby, that it's dangerous, but neither of us is doing much sleeping tonight. I have no idea what the time is. It's still dark outside but it's nearing the end of November, so it's always dark outside.

'Do you want more milk?' I say, offering him the bottle I tried to give him twenty minutes ago. He throws it out of my hands, sending it flying through the air and on to the bed. The plastic teat pops out of the front, milk drenching my bedsheets.

It's a futile thing to cry over, spilled milk, but it's everywhere. On the duvet cover and the pillows and soaking through to the mattress. I try to remove the sheets with one hand while balancing him on my hip but it's impossible. He's still crying, throwing himself backwards with no sense of danger. I put him down on my bed but he's trying to stand, screaming, clawing at me. He's going to fall off the bed. I lift him up again and hold him to me, his hot little body tense and damp. I throw the duvet to the floor, pull half of the sheet to one side, making the bottle roll on to the carpet.

He's still crying but it's now become a wall of sound. I can hear it but it's far away, background noise, a constant that no longer buries into my mind. I close my eyes and when I open them again Tony is standing in the bedroom doorway in his winter coat. The room is still dark, but at least it's silent now. Did I fall asleep?

'Take him,' I say quietly. 'I'm going to drop him.'

Tony remains standing, filling the entire doorframe, not moving. My face stings. I think of Maggie helping me yesterday, remembering how soft her fingers were against my cheek. Against my lips.

'What's going on?' Tony says.

I'm huddled in a ball on the bed, our duvet on the floor, my nightclothes wet and sour-smelling, the sheets half hanging off the bed, my face tender and swollen. Did Maggie hurt me... or did I?

'Take him,' I say. I'm slurring. I sound drunk.

'The baby's asleep,' Tony says.

'I know,' I say, nodding at Riley in my arms. 'Take him.'

'He's in his cot.'

I look down at my empty arms. I can still feel Riley's weight, heavy against my chest. I've been rocking him. Telling him everything will be all right. When did I put him back in his bed?

'Did you see a doctor?' Tony says. I know he means well but it sounds accusatory, like he's trying to catch me out.

'Yeah, I went to the doctors.'

He doesn't sit beside me; he doesn't reach out or hold me or tell me how well I'm doing. Because I'm doing so well. I really am. Some people get angry and shake their babies, or they give up and neglect them. Not me. I hold my babies. Both of them. So tightly.

'What did the doctor say?' Tony asks.

'The baby is crying.' I try to stand but he puts a hand on my shoulder. Heavy. Why is everything always so heavy?

'No, he's not.'

He is. I can hear him. Then I can't. It sounds like a cat. Shadow? Maybe it's birds. What time is it?

'What did the doctor say?' Tony asks again, this time slower and gentler.

'I'm fine,' I reply. 'I just need more rest. I had a bad night.'

'What happened to your face?'

He reaches out to touch me and I bat him away. His touch is too hard and rough.

'Get some sleep,' he says. 'If Riley cries again, I'll go.'

'But you have—'

'Lu. Let me...' he says.

And I'm asleep before he finishes his sentence.

When I get up it's gone nine and I panic until I go into the kitchen and see everything is tidy, Riley's breakfast bowl washed up and on the side. In the living room Tony is on the floor playing with his son, making choo-choo noises with a toy train.

'Thank you,' I say. 'Do you want to eat before you go to bed?'

Tony looks up. 'You look a bit better,' he says, getting to his feet. Riley stays on the playmat, chewing on the train. Tony holds the back of his hand against my cheek, and I flinch. 'What happened?' he asks.

I touch the tender spot, trying to remember how I hurt myself. Didn't Maggie hit me? No. It was Riley headbutting me. Wait, maybe I ran into a wall? Or am I imagining that too?

'Nothing,' I say. 'I'm just clumsy.'

'Put ice on it.'

'Are you hungry?' I ask again.

'I've already eaten.' Tony kisses my forehead and for a second I want to tell him everything: Dave and the baby and everything about Maggie. How beautiful she is, and how much Riley likes her, and how I wouldn't have managed without her. Everything she's been doing has been to help me, protect me. Us.

'Have your shower now then I'll go to bed,' he says.

I take full advantage of my baby-free luxury, I even use conditioner on my hair, and when I get out of the bathroom I feel like a different woman. I've slept a bit and I've washed my hair and styled it with a hairdryer. I even put on a bit of mascara.

I walk into the living room, smiling shyly at Tony, hoping he notices.

Sometimes I look at him as if I don't know him; pretend I've walked into a bar and seen him at the other side of the room. And I ask myself whether I'd still find him hot, and I would. Maggie is right, he's attractive. And he's kind. And he's a good father. I need to make more of an effort, because I don't have that many people left in my life... not many who actually care. Tony and I are having another baby. We're going to be a family of four. I need to remember how much I love him.

'Tony,' I say, running my finger down his thick, hard arm.

He doesn't look at me; he's too busy frowning at his phone.

'Why does your mum keep messaging me?'

'What?'

I don't seem to be able to hear people very clearly lately. I can hear Maggie, no problem, but with other people it's like their words are sewn together. Maybe I still have water in my ears from my shower.

'Your mum.' He holds out his phone. 'She says she can't get hold of you. I tried calling you last night too. Is your phone on silent? You always have it on silent.'

I was waiting for this. I'm prepared.

'I lost it,' I say.

'Jesus, Lu! You've lost your phone?' I expected him to be annoyed but not this angry. 'How the fuck does someone lose their phone?'

People lose things all the time. I found my door keys in the fridge the other day. It's normal to lose things.

'I don't know.'

'Where did you lose it?'

I hate it when people ask that. If I knew where I'd lost something, then I'd be able to go back and find it.

'We were in the park, and it must have fallen out of the buggy tray.'

Tony rakes his fingers through his hair with both hands. 'Why the hell would you put your phone under the buggy?' My man is so sensible. So practical. He really does have all the answers. 'Why wouldn't you put it in your pocket or your bag like a normal person?' he shouts.

Normal person. Why can't I be a normal person and not throw my phone in a pond because my new best friend told me the police are watching me? Because I'm a killer, Tony. A cold-blooded killer. And I'm scared, and confused, and I don't want to get caught.

Tony breathes out in a way that feels far too aggressive for breathing. He's tired. His eyes are skull holes, his face patches of grey. He's getting old, I can see specks of white in his stubble. Maybe I wouldn't find him so hot in a club after all. Maybe he has the face of a man I'd avoid for my own safety.

'You need to get a bloody grip,' he mutters, nodding at my face. Oh yes, my injury.

I hold my hand up to my sore cheek. Last night is a blur. Riley cried so much, and I ran into the wall, I'm sure of it. But he was also punching and kicking me, he wouldn't be calmed, and I was worried about the neighbours hearing. Isn't that what happened?

'We haven't got contents or phone insurance, you know,' he continues. 'You told me you'd sort it, after we moved house. Along with everything else you said you'd do.'

'I've been busy,' I say. But have I? I look around. Maggie did all of this. What have I been doing?

'So where do you expect us to find the cash to buy you a new handset? We weren't even on a contract. Have you blocked it? Everything was on that phone – banking apps, Google Pay, photos of our son... Jesus, Lu!'

I'm not listening anymore. His voice has turned into another wall of sound like Riley's wails do after a time. *Waa waa waa.* Like the teacher in the old Snoopy cartoons. I watch his face move, the lines so deep it's like someone has sliced into his flesh.

I hate him. I actually hate him. I feel the baby moving inside of me, clawing at the inside of my skin, fists pounding. If I hate Tony, does that mean my baby hates its father too?

He stops shouting eventually, having worn himself out, and goes up to bed with a resigned sigh. What a hero, coming home and playing with his son for three hours so I could do extravagant things like sleep and shower. I let out a dry little laugh at the idea of him ever having to beg me for a sliver of time to rest and wash, then him being expected to be thankful for it. Clever, kind, thoughtful, heroic Tony who would never be stupid enough to make any mistakes, like lose a phone or accidentally kill someone. What's he going to say when the police inevitably find my fingerprints in Dave's house, and on the slab of concrete I used to cave his head in, and they come and take me away? Tony will have bigger things to worry about then than contents insurance.

I swallow down the bile searing my throat and wipe my sweaty hands on my t-shirt.

'Call your mum back on my phone,' he shouts down the stairs before slamming the bedroom door.

I don't want to. I don't want to talk to anyone except Maggie. I start doing the maths. If Tony sleeps his usual seven hours, he won't wake up until five o'clock this afternoon. It's too long. I need to see Maggie now. She's the only person I don't hate right now, her and my babies.

Everyone else I want to kill.

TWENTY-SIX

I ring my mum in the end, because when you hate yourself, you may as well get others to join in. She picks up the phone on the second ring.

'Tony! Thank God you called me back. Is Lu OK? What about Riley?'

'It's me,' I say.

The line goes quiet.

'Where the hell have you been?'

I want to ask her the same question. Where have you been the last two years while I carried and birthed and raised your grandchild? Why didn't you worry about me? I'm *your* baby.

'Lost my phone,' I mutter.

She sighs. Everyone I know sighs so much.

'You sound terrible,' she says.

'Thanks.'

'Tony told me you haven't been yourself lately.'

'You spoke to him?'

Since when does my mum speak to Tony?

'Well, no, he texted me last night. Said he'd make sure you called me back. Said you'd had a few bad nights with Riley.'

A few. Yeah.

'Why did you tell Dan I was mean to you?' I ask.

My mother sighs again. 'Honestly, Louise. You've always been so sensitive. You're rude to me, you're rude to your brother. I try, you know. Surely now you're a mother yourself you understand how hard it is. No matter what I do, it's never enough.'

I can hear tears in her voice, and I wonder if it's me making her upset or if she's had another row with Dad. Their quarrels were the soundtrack to my childhood and why we moved around so much. Every time things got bad, Dad would get a new job or Mum would find a nicer house to rent and we'd start afresh. Their new starts meant new schools for me, new friends, new lack of friends. Dan never seemed to mind – he found all the change exciting, called me boring and ungrateful when I'd get upset and tell him I was lonely.

'You can always make new friends,' my parents would say. 'They might be better than the last lot.'

I think of Maggie. She's better than any friend I've ever had. Tony was a friend too, until he became something else. Something I had to carry along with our children.

'That's what adults do,' my brother would say when I'd tell him our parents' arguments scared me. He never seemed to care about it much. 'Arguments are normal in a marriage.'

I think about him and Kayla. She doesn't look the arguing type.

'There's no one more annoying than the one you've chosen to spend the rest of your life with,' Dad always says, and Mum laughs along. They think hating one another is funny. They think all that anger is passion. Maybe it is. Maybe you can only hate that which you once truly loved. I'm not sure. Isn't family meant to feel soft and safe?

'You there, Lu?' my mum shouts down the phone.

'Yeah, sorry. Long night. I was up five times with Riley.'

She makes a sympathetic sound and a hard ball forms in my

throat. She gets it. Dan and I were born just eighteen months apart. Of course she understands.

'You were the same,' she says. 'You hated sleeping.'

'It's so hard.' I'm on the verge of saying it, of telling her about the second baby, but she hasn't finished telling me what a terrible baby I was.

'You had me up all night, Lu. All bloody night, for years. But you have to suck it up and get on with it. That's the thing about your generation. You millennial lot. Everything is a disorder; everything's a problem. You have to get on with it. Millions before you got through it and millions after you will have to as well. What choice do you have? I've read about it in the papers, you know, how new mums today are going to the doctors in their droves and moaning about how having a baby is tougher than they thought – calling it postnatal this and psychosis that. What are you going to do? Get a prescription for motherhood?'

I think about my talk with the doctor and how little we spoke. He had pills for me. Mothers have always had pills, or gin, to get through it. Some poison their husbands... others murder their neighbours.

'Mums are strong,' she continues, warming up to her martyrdom. 'The more you suffer, the more you're loving them. Honestly, you have no backbone. None of you.'

She's right, I have no backbone; all my bones are made of jelly. My legs are soft, and my centre is weak, and I flop on to the sofa and close my eyes as she continues to tell me how everyone my age is useless. I hear Tony get up, his footsteps above my head; the water from the shower is white noise making my eyelids grow heavy.

Riley!

I jump up, making my head spin. Who has the baby? I'm out of the room before I hear a squeak and look behind me. He's still there, watching the TV I didn't realise was on.

'I better go,' I say to my mother, returning to the sofa.

'So how am I meant to call you now?' she asks. 'Honestly, Lu. Always losing things. Money doesn't grow on trees, you know.'

'Message me on Facebook,' I say. 'I'll check Tony's laptop now and then and send you pictures of Riley on there until I get a new phone.'

She doesn't pick up on my lie, that I can't take new photos of her grandson with no phone. Not that she cares. She's spoken to me and ticked that off her list and now she can go back out drinking with her friends, having fun and telling herself that she's a great mother and grandmother and how now it's her time to have fun after all the suffering I put her through.

I say goodbye, blink, and like magic Tony is standing before me in his towel. He has a strange look on his face, like he's been staring at me for a long time. His trips to the gym are paying off. He really is a good-looking man.

'I love you,' he says. 'You know that, right?'

Something small flips in my tummy. Not big, not like the fairground ride it used to be, but more like a tiny frog plopping into a shallow puddle.

'You too,' I say.

'Come here.'

He's pulling me up off the sofa, pressing me to him, his body damp and hairy, holding me too tight. Riley is pulling himself up by my leg and the children's TV presenters on the screen are singing out of tune and I'm hot and I can't move.

'Hey, what's the matter?' he says as I push him off.

Everything is always too tight, too heavy, too loud, too much. Someone is always on me. I can't breathe when everyone is always on me.

'Don't want you to be late for work,' I say.

I need Maggie. Tony has normally left by now and she's normally here by now, helping, listening, her voice soothing and her touch light.

'Nice chat with your mum? I can order you in a takeaway for later if you want,' he says, nodding encouragingly as he goes to get dressed. His voice is different, extra-jolly like the voice parents use on their teenagers when they're scared they're going to have their head bitten off.

Tony returns, dressed, and reminds me that I can email him at work if I need him and he'll order me a new phone once he's been paid. I don't even know what the date is today, but I think he gets paid on the first of each month. I can tell he's trying really hard to be patient, understanding, kind.

'I set up the Ring doorbell app on the laptop too, if you want to check it out,' he says. 'You know my password.'

Do I? I don't even know what doorbell he's talking about.

'Things are hard at the moment, but they will get better,' he says, looking like he means it. I wish I had his faith. 'You're strong, babe. You're one of the strongest women I know.'

'So then why do I feel so helpless?' I shout.

He wasn't expecting me to shout. Neither was I.

He tries to hug me again and I push him away.

'Lu, I'm worried—'

'Don't say it again,' I hiss. 'I'm fine. Go to work, Tony.'

He shakes his head slowly and pulls on his boots and coat as I scoop Riley up for his nap. We're behind schedule. He's normally down by two thirty and it's now close to five. Which means he'll be late to bed. Which means I'll have less time to sleep. How does Tony think he's helping me by messing with our routine?

By the time I put Riley down and get back downstairs Tony has left, and Maggie is waiting for me in the sitting room. She's smiling, her glossy lips twitching at the sight of me.

'Well, look at you,' she says as I descend the stairs. 'Have you done something new with your hair?'

'I washed it.'

I laugh and she smiles and inside my chest something hot

starts to glow. She leans forward, her nose grazing my neck as she inhales the scent of my hair. I shudder.

'Your face.'

I turn away but she places a soft hand on my cheek, and in an instant I'm looking into her cool blue eyes again.

'Who did this to you?'

'No one,' I say because I can't remember, and it hardly hurts anymore.

'Was it Tony?'

I don't think so. It was my son, or the wall I ran into. I'm not sure now. I remember Tony looking over me, standing there in his coat, me curled up in a ball on a bed rancid with old milk. Did he do this to me? Would I remember if he had?

'No,' I say, suddenly less certain. 'Just clumsy.'

She kisses my cheek so lightly I can hardly feel it. 'My poor love. And how's my baby?'

'Good.'

She places a hand on my stomach and the baby flips. This time it *is* like something from a roller coaster. My babies like her. I place my hand over hers and our fingers intertwine as she moves her hand round and round in small circles over my tiny bump.

I close my eyes, focusing on her touch. There's nothing heavy about Maggie; everything about her is light and calm and easy.

'Everything's going to be OK. I'm here,' she says, her hand remaining on my stomach as she steps behind me. I let my head fall back against her shoulder so her breath warms my neck as she speaks. 'I'm not going anywhere.'

TWENTY-SEVEN

It hasn't stopped raining. Tony comes and goes in a blur, and without my phone I don't know what day it is. Yesterday I went out and noticed the police tape had gone. There were some people outside Dave's but no one gawps at the house anymore when they walk past. Maybe everyone's forgetting about the murder. We all get bored of everything, eventually.

At the supermarket I found myself rooted to the spot, staring at the countless rows of cereal, unable to make a decision. I came back with six shopping bags hanging off the pushchair and more stuffed underneath but still managed to not buy anything that would constitute a meal, so I made omelette and chips for dinner.

I bumped into my neighbour Shona on the high street. She didn't notice me at first as I had my hood up, but she recognised Riley and made a big fuss of him.

'They still haven't found the killer,' she said to me. 'Must have been drugs related.'

'Must have been,' I said, gripping the pushchair handles harder to stop myself from shaking.

I don't want to leave the house again. Not for a while. I can no longer look in the faces of my kind neighbours who think I'm just a normal, nice mum. I can't risk the police driving past and seeing the guilt scrawled all over my face and realising the culprit was right there all along. Plus, I'm tired. Not just physically, not just because of the baby I'm growing, but bone-deep tired because my brain refuses to switch off I'm safer at home. Safer with Maggie. Maybe she can get my groceries for me. I'm sure she won't mind.

I'm in the kitchen and it's dark outside, a couple of sickly yellow puddles of light illuminating the street. I'm watching Tony run to his car along the wet pavement, head bent down against the wind, dirty water splashing up the back of his grey sweatpants. I'm quite certain now he didn't hurt me, he would never hurt me. As certain as I can be about anything right now. He keeps asking if I'll be OK. He keeps talking about work. Everything he says washes over me like rain.

I watch him get into his car and sit in it before starting the engine, rubbing his face with his hands, composing himself. The scene looks like a painting, the way the raindrops in the glass distort the light. Most things look pretend to me lately, like I'm walking through a work of art with the colour dripping off the canvas. Objects move, blurring around the edges; words flitter past me as I struggle to catch them. Nothing is sharp anymore; nothing but the stabs in my chest when I think of what I did or could easily do again.

Why isn't Tony starting the car?

Someone is walking towards him. It's not raining anymore; I can tell by how still the water on the paving slabs is. She has blonde hair and is wearing a bottle-green coat and smart shoes. Maggie.

She leans forward, the hazy shape of her a blotch of colour against the misty grey. He's talking to her. What's she saying? Is he touching her face? I blink. Is she reaching inside the car to him?

I turn away, as if I've interrupted an intimate moment, busying myself with Riley. Five minutes pass, maybe more, and then she's standing behind me, her flowery perfume filling the kitchen. Maggie is so quiet when she enters my house, like a cat. I think of Shadow. Where did he go?

'I've been talking to Tony,' she says, putting on the kettle, pouring hot water into a mug. I take Riley into the living room.

'I know. I saw you,' I shout out.

I sit on the floor with my son and build a tower of wooden blocks as he empties a box of toys over my feet. I've been doing that a lot lately, leaving whatever room Maggie is in as if I'm the one in her house getting in her way.

She enters the living room with a hot cup of tea for me and perches on the edge of the sofa. I take a sip and place it out of Riley's reach. I want to lean my back against the couch where she's sitting, feel her hand on my forehead the way a mother checks for a fever. Maggie doesn't have a drink, and she keeps her hands on her lap like the ideal wife. Or a doll. Something perfect.

'He's a good man, your Tony.'

I tense. She doesn't know him like I do. I take another sip of the tea even though it burns my mouth.

'He sounds very busy with work at the moment,' she says. 'You know what he's up to, right?'

'Yeah. All those extra hours he works are very convenient,' I say. 'That way he gets to take all the credit for looking after Riley and me without having to do any of the actual work.'

'You don't sound happy,' Maggie says.

I've never noticed how bright her eyes are. She keeps them trained on me, like a challenge.

'He makes me angry sometimes,' I say, drinking more tea even though it's beginning to taste bitter against my burned tongue. 'You wouldn't understand.'

Or would she? Would she understand if I told her the awful

things I see in my mind's eye? How he can be lying beside me during those rare moments when we're both sleeping side by side and I'll want to hold a pillow over his face even though I love him so much? It was always Tony; no matter how many boyfriends I had it was only ever Tony who mattered. Yet now, when I look at him, all I think about is how unfair life is. How we both have the same things yet I'm the only one suffering – although, unlike my mother, I see no virtue in it. I want Tony to suffer too, just a little bit, to make it fair. Enough so that being a father has also brought him a modicum of pain and discomfort like being a mother has me. We both get to be Riley's parents, yet he hasn't earned it enough – not physically or mentally. Not at all. And now I'm about to start the cycle all over again with another child. How am I meant to make peace with this?

'He's very handsome,' Maggie says. 'You could do a lot worse.'

'Too handsome for me?'

I don't know why this is making me tear up. Is it because I believe her, that Tony looks at me and wishes he had stayed with one of his beautiful blonde ex-girlfriends? Or is it because I want Maggie to think I'm pretty?

I finish my tea, putting the empty mug on the coffee table beside me.

Maggie is Tony's type. He loves a well-put-together blonde. Everyone he's ever dated is organised and successful and slim and neat. I'm never neat. I try, yet whatever I do I always look unkempt. Nothing hangs right on me. My make-up is always a little smudged. My nails always a little broken. All of me a tiny bit chipped at the edges like the cheap Ikea plates I've had for years that aren't bad enough to throw away but not good enough to put out for guests.

Maggie smiles. 'Tony doesn't know how lucky he is,' she says, leaning forward and playing with my hair. I shuffle back against her. 'I told him as much.'

She told him? She told Tony that he's lucky to have me?

Her knuckles stroke the back of my neck as she plaits my hair. I stay still, closing my eyes at the touch of her fingers on my skin, flinching but staying quiet as she tugs my hair so hard it hurts. But I like it. I like the sharpness of the pain cutting through my blurry world.

'What else did you say to him?' I ask, leaning further back against her lap until I'm looking up at her face. She smells of talcum powder and lavender and all things clean and calm.

'I told him I was envious of you.'

'Me?'

She stares at Riley as she strokes my head. 'You, your boy, the baby on its way.'

Did she tell him? Did she tell my Tony everything?

'W-what did you say about the new baby?' I stutter.

She smiles, that *Mona Lisa* smile of hers. 'Nothing. But you'll have to tell him eventually, you know.'

My eyes are growing heavy, and I feel myself falling. I'm so tired. Why am I always so tired when Maggie is doing all the hard work?

I must have fallen asleep because when I wake up I'm still on the sofa and Maggie is standing over me with a pair of kitchen scissors.

I gasp and scramble backwards. 'What are you doing?'

She's smiling. 'Riley is having a nap and I made you this.'

She puts the scissors down and hands me a ham sandwich.

'Thank you,' I say slowly, taking a bite, my eyes still on the scissors beside her.

Maggie never eats. I've noticed that. If she makes herself a drink it stays untouched, and when I go back into the kitchen in the mornings there is only ever one plate and one fork and one knife beside Riley's plastic plates.

'I have something fun planned for us,' she says, holding up a box beside the scissors. I squint at the label.

'Hair dye?'

She nods enthusiastically, raising one perfectly plucked eyebrow.

'And a cut,' she says. 'I used to be a hairdresser before I became a nurse. I thought you might fancy a change.'

I watch the way the light catches in her hair, how the blonde appears to be made up of so many different shades of gold.

'Something like yours?' I ask.

She shrugs, as if it hadn't occurred to her, even though the woman on the hair dye box looks exactly like her. My hair is a mousy brown, long, lank. The perfect canvas.

The baby is asleep, and the house is clean – there's no reason why I can't do something for myself. A frisson of excitement shimmers up my spine and Maggie grins at my apparent glee. I take three bites of my sandwich before she holds out her hand, leading me upstairs. The way her fingers thread through mine, our soft tread on the stairs as we head upstairs, the silence of the house thrumming around us... It feels illicit, like a dream, like I'm not really here and I'm watching what's happening between Lu and this perfect woman.

'Relax,' Maggie says as she unbuttons my pyjama top. I didn't realise I was still in my bedclothes. 'We don't want your top to get dirty.'

She turns me so we're both facing the mirror. The skin beneath my eyes is puffy and dark with sleep, and my breasts are straining in the bra I've been wearing to bed because my chest aches so much. I need a bigger bra. I need to look for my maternity underwear. I don't remember seeing any while unpacking the boxes. But then again there's a lot I can't remember. I really should tell Tony.

Maggie is raking her fingers through my hair, holding it up at various lengths, her eyes never leaving mine in the reflection.

She doesn't ask before she holds up a strand and snips four inches off, letting the cut hair fall to the ground.

'There,' she says, her breath like a cool breeze against the skin of my newly exposed neck. 'Doesn't that feel better?'

I nod. Everything is lighter already. She keeps cutting while I remain staring at my reflection, her face and mine starting to blend into one. She puts on the plastic gloves that are inside the box and paints the dye on. As she works, I'm listening out for Riley, but he stays silent. Such a good boy.

'Is this safe?' I ask Maggie. 'You know, with the new baby. I thought dyeing your hair while pregnant was dangerous.'

She keeps working as if I haven't spoken. Once my whole hair is covered, she looks up, meeting my gaze with hers. 'Would I ever do anything to hurt you, Lu?'

I shake my head. Of course not. Maggie would never hurt me.

TWENTY-EIGHT

I've forgotten all about my new hairstyle until I get up, woken by the sound of Tony's key in the lock. He visibly startles at the sight of me at the top of the stairs.

'Fuck, Lu. You scared me. I thought you were someone else.'

'Do you like it?' I ask, turning my head from side to side.

He takes off his coat and shoes, the entire time his face blank and pale. He's looking anywhere but at me as he climbs the stairs, where I'm waiting on the landing.

'It's very... Jesus, babe. What possessed you?'

He reaches the top of the stairs and I catch a glimpse of myself in the bathroom mirror, and it's Maggie staring back at me. The twitch of her lip as I smile at my reflection, the coolness of her stare as I imagine how it must feel to walk through life so effortlessly, with so much serenity and power.

Tony rubs my hair between his fingers, peering closer like it might be a wig. As if I'd be playing pranks at six o'clock in the morning. I look like Maggie. Does he wish I was Maggie, waiting for him to come home, standing at the top of the stairs in her underwear, beckoning him to bed? I bet her knickers always match her bra. I bet she's great in bed and knows how to tease a man until he's promising her the world.

'Well, I like it,' I say, putting my arms around Tony's neck. 'I fancied something different. Have you never fancied something different?'

He's looking over my shoulder at the bathroom and my old hair on the floor and the dirty plastic gloves in the sink. It's not like Maggie to not clear up after herself.

'What have you done?' he says, trying to take a closer look inside the bathroom.

I keep him still, holding his face in my hands, stroking the back of his head. Maggie wouldn't let her man worry about such trivialities as cleaning the bathroom. She would make him the centre of her universe, if only for an hour. Tony lets out a small moan as I kiss him like I imagine Maggie would, and he continues to respond as if I am her. As if I'm someone more interesting than me.

'Lu,' he says, more a rush of air than a word. His breaths are coming fast, and I realise I like this. Being this person. Because Tony is mine. This life, this world of ours, it's mine. And maybe I've only just realised how much I want it because Maggie said she envied it.

'What's going on?' he asks as I undo his trousers. He doesn't walk away or push me off; he likes this too. He likes me being someone else.

'I saw you speaking to Maggie,' I say, sliding my hand down his jeans. He makes a small sound but stays still, waiting, hoping for more.

'Who?'

I saw them together yesterday. I look like her now, which is why he's growing hard in my hand. I know what he likes, and I know Maggie was telling him how great I am. Because Maggie never lies to me; everything she says is not only true, but she says it to help me, to keep me safe, to protect me. But Tony doesn't think that way. He's always pushing, prying, trying to change me. Why is it everything he does is so suffocating?

I get on my knees, and I wonder what Tony is seeing when he looks down at me. Does my hair move the same way as Maggie's does? Does it swish from side to side like spun gold? Does he like it?

And while he leans back against the wall, his fingers in my hair, I imagine what it would be like to be her. How easy it would be to get what I wanted if I looked like her; so poised and serene. So beautiful. How would she kill a man?

Maggie would never allow herself to be dripping with blood like I was the first night she found me. She'd have dressed appropriately, and ensured she had adequate footwear on. She wouldn't even have broken a nail killing Dave, let alone injured herself, because she wouldn't have done it with a breeze block – she'd have chosen a thin, sharp dagger or poison. Something fast and clean and not at all messy. She would have entered and left his house like a shadow. Silent. Unseen. A ghost.

'Lu!' Tony cries out.

I stop and look up.

'Call me Maggie,' I say.

'What?'

'Say it.'

He says it and I continue. She might well be his type, but he won't want her anymore, not now he has me. I was always the one waiting in the wings but now I'm the main act.

Tony is saying something else but I'm not listening because it's not me here, it's her, and Maggie starts what she finishes. Maggie knows how to get what she wants. Maggie never takes no for an answer.

'I love you,' he says.

I get back on my feet and wipe my mouth with the tips of my fingers as she would do. Subtle, dainty, controlled.

'You know you're everything to me,' he says. 'You and Riley.

Please, tell me what I need to do to make your life easier. To make everything better.'

And all I can think of is... *Die.*

TWENTY-NINE

Tony has fallen asleep on the sofa, meaning an entire room is now out of bounds for me and Riley, so I use the opportunity to tidy up our bedroom. Most of the boxes have been unpacked now but we still have piles of clean laundry that haven't been put away.

I catch a glimpse of myself in the mirrored wardrobe and move my head from side to side. I look like Maggie. I feel like her too: capable, organised, like nothing can faze me. Tony felt the new me earlier too. I know he did. And he liked it.

I sit Riley in the corner with some toys and a plastic bowl, which are keeping him momentarily occupied. Deciding to sort out my bedroom feels like a momentous task, something I'm building my day around, even though I used to fit so much into one day before I was a mother.

I hold up a Babygro and peer at the label. It's from that expensive shop in town, Bebe Tu. The size says 12–18 months. It must have been a gift from someone. I wouldn't have bought him that; I've never set foot inside that store. I keep folding and sorting our laundry into piles – mine is mainly comfortable underwear and pyjamas because I don't go anywhere. Another new outfit for Riley, also from that fancy baby shop. Who's been buying him clothes? Tony would have said if he had but I doubt he's used his few precious hours before work to go baby clothes shopping. I hold up the fourth outfit. This one is tiny: it's for a newborn.

I place it over my stomach, a tiny bump I've been hiding well until now. Why is there an outfit for a newborn? I don't need that. We have a box of Riley's old clothes somewhere, although I don't know where they are anymore. Probably with my maternity bras. Tony kept encouraging me to throw things out, saying we needed the space. Maybe I gave them all away. No, I don't think I did. I can't remember. Although I do remember Tony kept all the things he hardly uses anymore, including his weights and five pairs of trainers he never wears.

I grab Riley's laundry and new clothes and lift him up, dropping him into the crib in his room while I put everything away.

He's nearly walking now, pulling himself up on the bars of his cot and sidestepping around the parameters like a squawking crab.

'I see you,' I sing-song, kissing his chubby cheeks and making him giggle. 'Clever boy.'

I open up his tiny wardrobe, marvelling at the rows of teeny outfits that used to make my tummy contract before I had Riley. Even when I didn't have a boyfriend, I'd still go to Baby Gap and put together outfits for a non-existent baby in my lunch hour, imagining different occasions and how I'd dress my child – weddings, summer parties, Christmas Day. All those fiddly outfits that are hard to wash and impossible to iron when it's so much easier to put the baby in tracksuit bottoms and a Babygro because everything gets stained with vomit and shit anyway.

As I add the new clothes to the others, something catches my eyes. There are boxes and bags stuffed at the bottom of the cupboard, from shops like The White Company and Bebe Tu and a few expensive boutiques I've only ever seen online. Inside the bags are cuddly toys, a train set and new shoes – the kind for children who can actually walk. The receipts are inside the bag. I recognise the last four digits of the card that was used to pay for them. That's our credit card – the one we only use for emergencies. I don't understand.

'I thought he'd like those little shoes,' Maggie's voice behind me says softly. 'They light up when they walk.'

Riley squeals with excitement and holds out his hands to Maggie, who places a kiss on the crown of his head. I hold my head up high, something she would do, and remind myself that I'm the one in charge here.

'What are you doing here?' I ask.

'I've come to help.'

'You're too early. Tony is asleep on the sofa,' I whisper.

'I know,' she replies. 'I saw.'

She let herself into our house, walked past Tony sleeping and found me upstairs like this is totally normal. None of this is normal. I tuck my bobbed hair behind my ear and stand taller.

'Did you buy these?' I say, holding up one of the little outfits on the hanger.

Maggie shuts Riley's bedroom door with a gentle click. It's not a large room. I'm hemmed in. I can't get to the door without squeezing past her.

'You're so pretty,' she says, untucking the hair from behind my ear. 'This new cut and colour really suits you.'

'I look like you,' I say quietly.

'I know.'

She takes something out of her bag and places it on the changing table. Two cards. One of them is my bank card, the other our credit card.

'You told me to buy Riley whatever he needed,' she says.

I rub my eyes. No, I didn't. Why would I tell her to do that?

'Sit,' she says, lowering me into the rocking chair beside the cot. 'You look tired. It should be you taking a nap, not Tony.'

She stands to one side and moves the chair back and forth, Riley's eyes following me as I swing forward and back, forward and back. My head feels so heavy.

'You took my bank cards,' I say.

She keeps rocking me, humming a tune I don't know.

'Do you have food in the fridge?' she asks.

'Yes.'

'And have you been to the shops lately?'

I haven't. It's been raining, so I've hardly left the house.

'I don't... I can't remember...'

What is she getting at?

'You asked me to do your errands, Lu. Said you didn't want the police tracking your movements. I went out, in the wind and rain, and I bought your food. And I also bought toys and clothes for your babies. And I did all of that because you asked me to.'

I'm dizzy from all the rocking, my head too full. Riley wants me but I can't reach him; it's like he's being pulled further and further away from me.

'Stop!' I shout.

The chair is going so fast now I feel sick. I hold my stomach, but she doesn't stop. I can't see her any longer, all I can feel is the force of the chair so that with each swing my head is flung around. I lurch forward and tumble on to my knees on the carpet, Riley laughing and clapping his hands.

'Do you think I spent any of your money on myself?' Maggie says from behind me. I can't see her, but I can sense her, her steady breaths and the flowery bouquet of her perfume.

'No. Of course not. Thank you for your help. You've been so kind,' I say, using the bars of the cot to pull myself up.

I have no way of knowing if she's bought things for herself, because the only way I can access our bank account is on the app on my phone. The phone she convinced me to throw away.

'You disappoint me, Lu,' she says.

It's getting dark outside, and the light of the room is

dimming. Maggie picks Riley up and he buries his head into her shoulder, his eyes growing heavy. It's his naptime. He's no longer reaching out for me, content in the arms of a woman I could never be. A woman angry with me. But what have I done wrong?

THIRTY

Maggie isn't there when Tony wakes up and I don't say anything to him. He doesn't need to know she was here.

'Is Riley still sleeping?' he says. He hasn't noticed that all the laundry has been put away. He cups my face in his hands and stares into my eyes.

I used to like it when he did that, the intimacy of it. Now I know it's all pretend. I'm a disappointment to Maggie and I know deep down Tony despises what I have become.

I turn my head, but he takes my hand before I can walk away.

'I liked what we did before,' he says,stroking my hair.

We didn't do anything; *I* did it all.

'I wasn't sure about the blonde look at first, but I could get used to it.'

See? It's not really me Tony wants. It's *her*. The woman I pretended to be for him while kneeling at his feet. I used to crave his adoration, his hunger, so much before – back when I would watch him with his girlfriends, wishing I was them. I craved Tony wanting me, the way he'd hunt me down in a crowded room, his eyes growing dark like a cat that's seen something moving in the grass, but never acting on it. Leaving that electricity there fizzing between us. But it's not me he wants now, it's a woman I'm not capable of being, no matter how much I try.

'I'm not in the mood,' I say.

He puts his arms around my waist, and I push him away. I can't let him feel my stomach and notice the hard bump. Not yet.

'Riley is awake,' I say, sidestepping Tony and climbing the stairs. I'm not sure if he is or not, I can't hear him anymore, but either way I'm going to take him for a walk to the shops. I need some fresh air. I can't stop thinking about Maggie and the baby clothes and all those receipts. If they were all put on our credit card, it won't take long for Tony to see them on our statement, and then how will I explain myself? What am I meant to say? *Oh, it wasn't me... I gave our bank cards to our neighbour so she could go on a shopping spree!*

I gather together the new items and put them in a bag. I'm taking them all back – I have a couple of hours before the shops shut. We can't afford such recklessness.

'Everything OK, Lu?' Tony shouts up at me.

Oh my God, can't he ever ask me anything else? And why is he always shouting? Everything he does is so loud, like the world was made for him. He sleeps where he wants, comes and goes when he wants, shouts and touches and demands like there's no one to stop him from marching forward. Because there isn't. I can't do that. I can't march forward because I'm carrying too much; the baby inside me and the baby that's always on me, everything dragging me back, stopping me from getting anywhere even though I don't even know where I want to go. Who I want to be. What the point of anything is anymore.

I want to scream at him, *Stop pretending we are a happy family. I am a liar and a killer and everything you claim to love is about to be taken away from you and you can't see it. You can't see that I'm breaking into pieces right before your eyes.*

Tony is staring up at me as I stand at the top of the stairs. He seems so far away, like I'm looking at him through the wrong end of a telescope. What does he want from me? Maggie was right, it shouldn't have been him sleeping on the sofa, it should have been me. When he woke up and saw Riley was napping, he should have suggested I go to bed instead of seeing it as an opportunity to have sex. Hasn't he taken enough from me?

Riley starts to cry, and I go to him. I have to leave the house, get away from Tony and his weaponised incompetence. I fleetingly think of the police, wonder if they are still outside watching and waiting, then brush it aside. I'd prefer to feel fear than the rage that will take over if I have to stay with Tony in this house one more second.

The high street is busier than normal because it's market day, which means it's a Sunday. I haven't seen one police officer or patrol car for at least an hour. I think they've stopped caring. I'm still twitchy though, still hiding behind my new hair and not making eye contact with anyone in case I'm spotted by one of the neighbours.

I took the clothes, shoes and toys back to the shops and had the money returned on the credit card. I was nervous, expecting the saleswoman in the fancy shop to be all snooty with me, but she was completely disinterested and didn't even make eye contact.

I'm at the fruit and veg stall, because they're packing up and selling off what's left in one-pound bags, when someone says Riley's name. The woman holding an armful of lettuces is saying hello. She has a little girl with her in a pushchair, wearing a big pink bow in her non-existent hair. Oh, shit. I can't pretend

I haven't seen her because I have. I know her, but what's her bloody name?

'Hi,' I say, plastering on a smile.

'Lu! I wasn't sure if it was you. Look at you!' She glances at my hair, her eyes sliding down my body and resting on my bump. I was feeling hot a few minutes ago and unbuttoned my thick winter coat. I have a jumper and leggings on underneath, but I didn't realise how much they accentuate my stomach. She doesn't say anything because everyone knows you shouldn't comment on a woman's body. What if I'm not pregnant but just fat? Or I *was* pregnant and then lost it? Or that's how my stomach stayed after giving birth the first time?

'You're looking well,' she says.

Liar. Wish I could remember her name. Tilly. No, that's the child's name. God, I forgot how much this woman can talk, and it's never about anything interesting. She's now telling me something about the playgroup and her husband and something funny her child did. I know the playgroup mum's name is that of a flower. Rose? No. Lily? No. I may not recall her name, but I do remember what she looked like dead. Bleached broken twigs and the snapped string of a marionette. Such a delicate cadaver. Fern. Iris. Daisy.

'Daisy!' I shout.

'Yes?'

'Daisy. Isn't it funny when you see someone away from the usual place and they look different somehow?' I say. 'Like when you were a kid, and you'd see your teacher in the fish and chip shop.'

Daisy lets out an uncertain giggle. She doesn't look the type who eats fish and chips. Sushi, maybe, but not fried fish. The wail of an ambulance in the distance makes me jump, but Daisy is inspecting some tangerines and doesn't notice. 'Well, you certainly look different.'

She's waiting for me to tell her I'm pregnant, but I'm not going to.

'I wasn't sure it was you when I saw you at the supermarket on Friday,' she adds.

I didn't go anywhere on Friday. I must be making a face because she keeps explaining.

'I recognised Riley, but he was with someone with blonde hair. I wasn't sure if she was a relative or maybe your au pair.'

Au pair? I try not to laugh.

'But it must have been you all along,' Daisy trills, pointing at some carrots and paying the stall holder.

It wasn't. I haven't left the house for ages. It was Maggie. Some of the receipts had Friday's date on them. She was at the shops, buying my food with my money. But how did she have my son? What is she doing taking my baby outside on her own without asking? Did she sneak him out while I was sleeping? My stomach churns and I have to grip the pushchair to steady myself. I really don't want to be sick all over Daisy's romaine lettuce. I close my eyes and breathe deeply until everything stops spinning.

'I'm not feeling too well,' I say, giving Daisy a shaky smile. 'Hopefully I'll see you at the playgroup again.'

She waves as I rush off, saying something about a playdate with the children and how we must try that new café down the road, but I can't hear her properly and I don't care. By the time I look around me, I'm already on my street and it's dark. I slow down as I pass number four. No police vans, no yellow tape, just boarded-up windows and some crumbs of glass on the concrete glittering like diamonds. Even the skip has gone. I wonder if he had family, if he had a funeral, if he died quickly or if he lay there for an hour choking on his own blood knowing how much he was hated.

With trembling hands, I let myself into the house, not having bought any food because I can't remember what Maggie bought or what's in the fridge. I thought Tony would have left for work already but he's still there, eating a slice of cheese on toast. The sound of his chewing turns my stomach.

'You look peaky,' he says.

I need to tell him everything. I need to tell him about the baby, and the credit cards, and that I killed a man three houses away from our own. That while he worked and our baby slept, I drove a brick into the face of someone I didn't know. He needs to know this because he needs to understand why I'm not the woman he needs me to be. I swallow down my tears, always one deep breath away from sobbing uncontrollably. Yet as soon as I feel the tears begin to gather in my eyes, that despair turns to something else – something sharp and bitter. Rage.

Tony doesn't move from the sofa and take my coat or lift Riley out of the pushchair or help fold it up. Look at him, sitting there munching through the last of the cheese. Look how thick the slices are. Cheese is expensive. I cut my slices thin so it still tastes the same, but it lasts longer. But not Tony. He simply takes what he wants then more automatically appears in the fridge the next day. He doesn't have to think about it, make a list, compare prices, go and get it, consider what we're all eating that week and how much we need or can afford or how long it will last. None of that matters to him because he goes to work and makes the money so whichever way he thinks about it, it's always him providing the cheese. That's why he can cut the slices as fucking thick as he fucking likes.

I want to ram that melted cheese down his throat. I want to watch him gag on the stringy strands and do nothing while his face turns pale then red then purple, and not help him as he grasps at his throat and stumbles around the kitchen unable to breathe. I see it all happen in the blink of an eye, then I hate myself because he's done nothing wrong. He's just got up, got ready for work, and is now eating cheese on toast before going out to make money for his family.

It's me. I'm the crazy one.

'Looks nice,' I say. 'I might make me and Riley some.'

Tony puts the plate by the sink and kisses his son on the head before putting on his boots and coat.

'No more cheese left, babe,' he shouts out, his heavy gym bag slung over one shoulder. 'Maybe you can go out and get some more later.'

I wish he was dead.

THIRTY-ONE

Tony spends ages hovering at the door talking about some client or other, but I'm too angry to listen to his boring work stuff.

'Email me if there are any problems,' he says. 'And I left my number on the side, just in case.'

Side? Side of what? His words wash over me as he gives me a long hug goodbye, his hold on me too hard, too rough. Sometimes his love feels like all the air has been sucked out of me.

'Remember I love you,' he says before closing the door.

Maybe I answer. I don't know. I'm still thinking about the cheese.

As soon as he leaves I feel like I can breathe again. Maggie must have been looking out of her window because the second Tony's car drives out of view, she's behind me in the kitchen.

'What happened?' she asks. I'm surprised she came back after last time, after I accused her of stealing from me and she called me a 'disappointment'.

'What happened when?' I say.

'You're upset. I can see you're upset.'

No, I'm not. Maybe I am, a bit. I'm confused. What does she want from me?

'It's that bastard,' she says. I balk. I didn't think Maggie used words like that.

'Who?'

'Your Tony.'

I'm glad she's called him 'mine', but I don't understand. A few days ago she was singing his praises, calling him handsome and telling me how lucky I was. It was me she had a problem with, not him. Has he done something I don't know about?

'I've been watching you lately, how you've changed,' she says. 'He's draining you, Lu. He doesn't appreciate you or everything you do for him. Does he know about me? Does he know about the woman who is saving the mother of his child?'

Saving? I stay quiet, which is all the confirmation she needs. She shakes her head at me. I'm such a disappointment, I can't please anyone.

'I'm going to the supermarket, you're low on pasta and cheese. You stay here – you don't want to risk the police seeing you coming and going.'

Coming and going where? Shopping isn't a crime. I'm in the kitchen and she's standing in the doorway, blocking my exit. Today she's wearing little diamond earrings and her top is light blue like her eyes; the same colour as the ice you find at the bottom of the ocean. The temperature of the room drops and my skin puckers.

'Why did you take Riley to the shops on Friday?' I ask her.

Maggie closes the distance between us, and although there's a part of me that wants to flinch from her touch, a larger part of me wants her to hold me and tell me I'm wrong. That I have nothing to worry about. She can sense this because she reaches out and takes my hand, stroking my fingers between hers.

'You asked me to,' she says. 'You said you were tired, so I left you to nap while I took the baby for a walk and bought some groceries. Just the basics.'

I asked her to? She keeps saying she's done all these things for me while I'm sleeping, but I don't understand. If I'm resting so much, then why am I so tired all the time? I rub my face as she takes a step closer. For a moment she doesn't move, her eyes boring into mine, then she pulls me to her. My head falls heavy on her shoulder, and I breathe her in –flowers and washing detergent and the scent of her hair. Everything clean and feminine. It smells like safety. The sound of a siren grows in intensity outside then fades away, making me tense. She holds me closer.

'Oh, my love,' she purrs in my ear. 'You poor, poor thing. Why am I the only one who sees how hard life is for you right now?'

I sniff, fighting back tears.

'You can cry,' she says, holding me tighter. 'Let it go. Everything is OK now. I'm here.'

So I do. I let the tears come until they erupt into a heaving sob that has me weak at the knees. I'm on the kitchen floor, in a ball, in her arms, and she's holding me tight. I'm a failure. I hurt people. I can't even be a good partner, mother, daughter, friend. Why does she still care about me? I'm dangerous.

'It shouldn't be like this,' she's saying. 'He shouldn't make you feel this way.'

I look up at her. Maybe she's right – it's not me, it's him. This is all Tony's fault. It should be *him* on the floor, holding me, rocking me. But all he does is leave.

Every time I think of him, I fill with red-hot anger, a sour indignation that eats away at me. It's never about anything big, it's all the tiny things, each new selfish thing he does becoming yet another scurrying ant burrowing its way into every crevice of my mind. With every wet towel on the floor and cupboard door left open and ingredient for dinner eaten at night in the dark of the kitchen by the light of the open fridge, the resentment builds and bubbles like a corrosive burning acid, gnawing at my guts and making my gums sting. Yet right now, in

Maggie's arms, I'm weak. What is it about her that turns my rage into something liquid and warm? Everything seems so difficult, so insurmountable, until she's with me. Then it's all so simple.

Maggie goes out and comes back with food. She makes dinner for me and Riley, helps me put him to bed, cleans up and eventually tells me I'm so tired I need to go to bed myself. She's right. I'm so exhausted I can hardly walk.

I expect her to leave at that point, but she doesn't. She waits until I'm in bed then sits on the edge of the mattress stroking my hair until my eyes feel heavy and the world slips away.

'It doesn't always have to be like this,' she says, her hand lying gently on the duvet covering my bump. 'And it won't be. You know what you need to do, Lu. You know.'

I nod and mumble something. The last thing I remember as I fall asleep is the feathery touch of her lips on my cheek.

THIRTY-TWO

I don't even wait for Tony to take off his shoes and coat before I hit him over the head. I don't know where I got the hammer from, but I hear it, the way it meets his skull and the soft thud as he hits the floor. Blood pools around his head, not red but black, and all I can think about is whether it will stain. I don't know how I move him, but I know I do because I'm marvelling at the patterns his hair is making in the tracks of blood on the floor, thankful I don't have carpet downstairs. I'm also glad I have wooden flooring because it makes sliding a body along the ground easier. I feel the cold slap of air on my face as I step outside, the rough texture of the patio tiles beneath my bare feet, Tony's shoelaces snapping as I drag him by his boots into the garden.

I smell the bleach as I scrub the floor and feel the pain in my knees from kneeling, much like I knelt for Tony a few days ago. I think back to how he tangled his fingers in my new blonde hair. How he said my name, *her* name, his head thrown up to the ceiling, eyes closed. Oblivious. Now his eyes will be closed forever.

I wake with a start, panting, face wet, pyjama top drenched.

I switch on the bedside lamp, relieved it's sweat and tears and not blood on my face or soaking through my nightclothes. Again. I check – my hands don't smell of bleach. My knees don't hurt.

Yet it was real. So real.

I look at the time. It's gone seven in the morning and Riley is whimpering. How long has he been crying for?

I rush to him, holding my stomach because the weight of it is beginning to pull, my other hand over my heavy breasts, everything dragging and slowing me down. I'm in Riley's room, then I'm changing him, then he's in my arms, everything happening staccato, like a song with only the chorus. I blink, and he's in a new Babygro. I blink and he's in my arms. Maybe I'm still sleeping. Or maybe I'm still in the hallway scrubbing Tony's blood off the cheap wooden floor.

It's still dark outside but I keep the bedroom light off, watching as shapes glow silver out of the window. I can see our shitty little garden from here, with its bare tree and patchy grass and plants that used to be bushes but no longer have leaves. We haven't even been out in it since we moved here. Tony had been excited about the idea of a garden. Describing his grand plans for a barbeque area and pretty flower beds and inviting friends we don't have over for parties. From Riley's bedroom window I can see the patio, the overgrown shrubs and the broken fence that leads to derelict fields that lead to a railway track that leads to somewhere better.

There's movement out there. The wind in the bare trees, spindly branches scraping at the windowpane like fingers, a full moon as heavy as the life curled up inside of me. But there's something else staring up at me in the gloom of the early-morning light. Someone else.

Her hair shines white in the fading moonlight, her face tilted up to the framed scene of mother and child silhouetted in the window. She's smiling at us. Maggie, in my garden, before the sun has risen.

I blink and she's gone, and I wonder if perhaps I'm still sleeping, and Riley's still sleeping, and it's still the middle of the night. But then my baby kicks from the inside and Riley wriggles in my arms on the outside and I'm awake. At least, as awake as I can be. And I know I had a nightmare – that all the violence and blood is all in my mind – and yet I can't stop shaking.

I keep busy. I make us both breakfast, then I clean up and get ready for the day. It's not until nine o'clock in the morning that I realise... Tony hasn't come home yet. Where's Tony?

THIRTY-THREE

I'm not sure why Tony is late home, but I carry on as normal because what else am I meant to do? Without my phone I can't call him, and he can't call me.

I try not to think of the visions I saw in the night. Not memories, only nightmares. But they're beginning to mingle with the flashes of Dave and the blood and the bodies and the crack over the head... and I don't know what's real anymore.

By eleven o'clock I'm getting worried. Where is he? I need to get in touch with Tony, but even if I use someone else's phone, I don't know his number off by heart.

Wait. I wrack my brain, he said something about a number. It was a long time ago, when I told him I'd lost my phone. He said he left his number on the side. The side of what? I run into the kitchen, looking for a scrap of paper or Post-it note. I search though the fruit bowl, an apple so brown my finger pokes through it. I run back into the living room, look at shelves and the windowsill and... what side?!

Maybe I could ask one of the neighbours to use their internet, look up where he works and call him there. But Maggie said I had to keep a low profile, that the police are monitoring what everyone on the street does. It's why she's gone to the shops for me so much. It would look suspicious if I told anyone that my partner is missing when a man three doors down was murdered a few weeks ago – it drags me straight back into their line of enquiry. Every time I hear a siren, I imagine the police throwing me against the wall, cuffs on, ripping my baby from my arms.

We know you wanted him dead!

I did, but I don't now. I'm sure he's fine. I'll wait a little longer and ask Maggie what I should do. I can use her phone.

Oh, God, what if Tony has had an accident at work? I feel awful that I hope that's the case, because it's still better than what I did to him in my nightmares. It makes no difference whether I close my eyes or if I keep them open: stills of Tony in a pool of black ink play like a movie on loop before me. I can't make them stop.

My stomach starts to spasm. At first I think it's the baby, pulling and pushing against my skin, dancing on my bladder, but it's not. I grab Riley and rush upstairs to the bathroom, sitting on the toilet just in time. No one tells you this about motherhood, how you can't even have diarrhoea without either making your baby watch or putting them in their crib to scream for ten minutes, twenty, half an hour, while you suffer. Whatever you're going through as a mother, your baby is always right there beside you.

He's crawling on the bathroom floor, pulling himself up on the bath, making me imagine all the ways he could hit his head and knock out his only teeth while I sit powerless on the toilet, spilling my guilt and fears out into the pan. Maybe Tony has left me? Maybe I hurt him? No. What I saw and experienced last night was just a nightmare. Just? There was nothing small about any of it. But if he's left me, if he's gone of his own volition, why was Maggie in our garden this morning staring up at Riley and me?

I need a shower, and I can't wait until it's Riley's naptime, so

I put him in the bath with me and wash myself while he shows me his rubber ducks and wobbles precariously close to the metal taps. My stomach is growing hard and round. I won't be able to hide this new baby for much longer. Light blue veins climb from my pubis to my belly button, the stretchmarks from last time still red and raw and gaining in length like claw marks on the outside from the creature on the inside.

'It's going to be OK,' I say to the baby, rubbing my belly. I feel a flutter beneath my palm and tears spring to my eyes. It's real. All of this is all too real. I sit down in the bath so I don't slip and fall. Then in a flash I'm seeing what that would look like: me falling and hitting my head on the tap, blood everywhere, my unborn baby dying as I die, Riley left alone, no one coming to our rescue. No family. No friends. Would Maggie turn up? Would she help me, or would she take Riley as if he were her own and never look back?

I shake my head, push the thoughts away and hold my wriggling, wet boy close to me.

'It's going to be OK,' I say to him too. 'Mummy is going to make all of this better.'

But it doesn't matter how many times I say the words out loud, I know it's not true. Nothing is OK. And I don't know what to do about it.

I wish I hadn't thrown my phone away. I wish I could remember what Tony said to me as he was leaving for work. I wish I could call him without bringing attention to myself. Tony mentioned me emailing him, but I don't remember the password for his laptop. The last few times I've used it, he's left it open for me. And anyway, what am I meant to say to him? *Where are you?* I'm sure he's busy at work or something has come up, something normal.

I can't have hurt Tony. There would be evidence. A body.

Yet I remember hitting him and dragging him and digging in cold mud. I look at my nails. They're clean. Maggie was in the garden. Is he out there, in the scrubland behind my house near the train tracks? Did she help me?

I rub at my eyes with the heels of my hands, pushing the tears back in because I'm too tired to cry. I haven't got the time to crumble. I love him. I love Tony and I would never do that to him. I don't understand what's happening.

I look around and I'm in the living room. I've made Riley his lunch; he looks happy in his highchair with his scrambled egg and peas and pieces of ham cut into minuscule squares. I remember seeing a slab of cheap chocolate in the fridge. I go back and take it out and break off some squares, hoping the sugar will wake me up. It doesn't; it makes me feel sicker.

I'm on the sofa and *Teletubbies* is on the TV. My hair is still wet. I forgot to dry it after my shower.

'You need to eat more than that,' Maggie says, appearing in the living room.

I don't have the energy to look up. She hands me a bowl of pasta. It's red and hot, and there's cheese melted on top. When did I buy more cheese? Maybe she bought it.

'Do you have a phone I could use?' I ask her.

She shakes her head.

'Not even Jim?' I say. 'Could we ask him?'

She sits down on the sofa beside me, so light and dainty the sofa doesn't even sag.

'Eat up,' she says, nodding at my pasta. 'You can't think straight if you don't eat.'

She looks pretty today. Her lipstick is freshly applied. Her hair perfect as always.

'Were you in my garden early this morning?' I ask.

She motions for me to eat, and I do while she clears Riley's lunch mess and helps him down. He's on the rug pointing at the TV, pulling himself to standing without using the furniture. At this point he normally falls back down on his bottom, but this time he stays standing. He's swaying on the spot, contemplating lifting a leg, and I stop chewing and hold my breath, the solid macaroni sitting like a slug on my tongue.

'You're not making any sense,' Maggie says.

'What?'

I continue to chew slowly, my eyes trained on Riley as he tentatively lifts his right leg. I'm silently willing him to do it, to take that first step, but then he drops down and crawls over to his toy car.

'You're not well,' Maggie says, holding the back of her hand against my forehead.

I move my face away. 'I'm fine.'

'You feel hot.'

'I'll turn the heating down.'

'You look tired.'

'I'm always tired,' I say, shoving another mouthful of pasta in my mouth. It's helping. I feel less shaky, less floaty. But it's making me sleepy.

'I don't know where Tony is,' I mumble.

Maggie smiles. 'Of course you do.'

I go to ask her what she means but Riley is standing again, and this time he's not falling.

'Did you see that? Riley nearly took his first step,' I say with a grin that soon disappears as I think of Tony. He should be sitting next to me right now, not Maggie, as we marvel at how clever our son is and he tells me how excited he is about the new baby. I'll tell Tony everything when he gets back. And if Riley walks before then, I'll pretend he didn't so he gets to see the first time too.

'Riley is already walking,' Maggie says.

I swallow down my final mouthful of pasta as she takes the bowl off me, disappearing into the kitchen with it.

'No, he's not,' I say.

'He was walking yesterday, remember? Or maybe you were napping,' she calls out.

I look at my boy, who's waving at the purple Teletubby on the screen. She's lying. Why would she say that? I'd remember if he was walking.

'Watch,' Maggie says, entering the living room and sitting beside me.

'Riley,' she calls out. His face lights up at the sight of her. 'Come to Mummy,' she coos. She's right next to me. She's talking about me.

Riley slowly rises, his little bottom sticking out as he goes from a crouch to a wobbly stand, his pudgy arms lifting to balance himself, his gaze fixed on Maggie. He grins and he takes a step, then another, until three steps later he launches himself into her arms and she catches him, laughing and holding him close as she rocks from side to side.

'See?' she says. 'He's been walking for a couple of days now.'

'I didn't realise,' I mumble. 'I must have forgotten.'

'Silly Mummy,' she says in a high voice, rising and kissing my forehead. 'Always forgetting something. I'll take him for a nap and then we can have a nice cup of tea.'

I go to stand, to join them, to wash up or do something important, but a wave of exhaustion washes over me and my head falls back on the sofa. I don't feel well – maybe I'm coming down with something. Maybe my upset stomach wasn't stress but some kind of viral infection.

'Rest,' Maggie says, leaving the room with my boy.

I can't keep my eyes open. I need to sleep.

When I open them again it's dark outside and Riley is in his crib crying, and Maggie has gone. And there's still no sign of Tony.

THIRTY-FOUR

It's only me and Maggie now. There's no line between day and night, when she's here and when she's not. I'm not entirely sure if she's sleeping at my house – or even if she sleeps at all.

I open my eyes and she's there, looming over me, a thermometer in her hand.

'You have a fever of thirty-eight-point-five,' she says.

I try to stand but she pushes me back. Tony. I need to find Tony.

'Where is he?' I mutter.

'Riley is fine.'

'Tony. I need to find Tony,' I say

'Not right now. You need to rest.'

Rest? But all I do is sit and sleep and watch her do all the things I'm meant to be doing. When I'm not sleeping, I'm worrying, and when I'm not worrying, I'm reliving all the visions I've had of Dave and Tony and everyone else I've wanted to bring harm to. I need to find Tony. What if he's been hurt? What if his work has been trying to get hold of me? Surely they'd send someone to the door if something has happened to him. Unless it's me who has done something to him.

'Hush, you're mumbling,' Maggie says, plumping my cushions and putting a bowl of soup beside me. It's pea and ham. My favourite. I want to taste it but I'm too weak to lean over and take a sip.

'I need to use someone's phone,' I say. 'To report Tony missing.'

'No. You need to keep your strength up,' she says. 'I have it all under control.'

I'm too weak to move, to think, to understand what she's saying. I don't know how long I stay in bed for. Maybe it's a few days or maybe a few hours, but at one point she wakes me up and says I have a hospital appointment and my fever has gone. I sit up and stretch and she's right, I feel better. Not rested, I never feel rested, but I feel less dizzy.

'Is that today's date?' I ask, pointing at the TV. She's putting Riley's shoes on and ensuring there are enough nappies in the bag.

'Yes,' she replies.

Seventh of December? That can't be right. It's nearly Christmas. When did I last see Tony? I don't know how many days have passed because I don't know when he left. I run back into the kitchen and peek between the slats in the blinds. I haven't seen any police for a while but our car is outside. Tony must have come home the day I saw him leave for work. But then what happened?

'You need to stop looking out of the window,' Maggie says, appearing beside me with Riley on her hip.

'I need to file a missing person's report,' I say.

'So that the police can suspect you even further? You're not out of the woods yet, Lu. Remember what you did to Dave. You want them to think you did that to Tony too?'

I shake my head. 'But... but I don't know where he is.'

She smiles. 'Yes, you do, Lu.'

'I don't. I'm going to call his work.'

Her face clouds over and she thrusts Riley into my arms, her face inching so close to mine the tips of our noses are nearly touching.

'Don't you dare do anything stupid. Not now we've come this far.'

I do what Maggie says and do nothing.

'Thanks for reminding me about the appointment,' I say to Maggie an hour later as I drive us to the hospital. 'And for looking after me so well.'

The appointment is for the twenty-week baby scan, although I'm further gone than that now.

'It's in my interest that you stay healthy as much as it is in yours,' Maggie says as I pull into the car park. I want to ask her what she means but she still seems angry with me, so I stay quiet.

She remains stony silent as I check in at the hospital reception and take a seat with all the other pregnant mothers. No one looks at Maggie; they're too busy smiling at Riley in the pushchair, who's waving at all the women.

'Will you come in with me?' I whisper to Maggie, who has remained standing.

She shakes her head. 'Leave Riley with me,' she says.

No. I don't want to. What if she takes him for a walk and I can't find her? My name is called, and I pretend I didn't hear Maggie as I manoeuvre the pushchair into the hospital room, where a nurse is waiting with a large machine. Memories of my twenty-week scan with Riley flood my mind and I bat away tears at the guilt that I'm here alone, without Tony. The nurse tells me what the procedure is, but I know the drill.

'Twenty-three weeks,' she says to me a few moments later as she pushes the scanner over my jelly-smeared stomach. I'd forgotten how they make you drink so much you're desperate for a wee but aren't allowed to go, and then how hard they press against your bladder as they look inside your womb. I imagine the baby inside getting angry at all the prodding.

I try to focus on the grainy black-and-white image on the screen but all I can think about is what all of this would be like in prison. Would I be made to give birth while handcuffed to a bed? Would they let me hold my baby before they ripped it away from me? I can't think that way. Tony is probably fine, but where the hell is he?

He should be here, watching Riley walk and seeing our new baby. I miss him. I keep trying to remember why I was angry with him, what he did that made me so furious. I have to stop telling Maggie about my fears because every time I say anything, she tells me I'm overreacting and that after Dave I should stop talking about it, forget it all. But how do you forget something you can't even remember?

'My friend is in the waiting room. She came with me,' I say to the nurse or doctor or whoever she is. She's been too professional to ask why I'm alone, but I can feel it like an unsaid heavy weight between us. Or maybe she doesn't care and it's all in my head.

Riley is in his pushchair, fidgeting, straining at the straps. I should have left him out there with Maggie, but I wouldn't have been able to focus on this moment if I'd been worried about him.

The woman smiles benignly and asks if I've been feeling OK.

'Bit tired,' I say.

She glances at Riley. 'That's normal with two babies so close together. Have you been getting enough help and support?'

I think of Maggie and nod, although my eyes are filling with tears.

She hands me a printout, which has a date on it. The fifth of April. Is that the new baby's birth date? That's Tony's birthday.

I'm confused and the tears are making it harder to see and think. Every time I want to cry, I swallow it down and it turns into something sour, something hard and angry. I only have two emotions now: tired or angry.

'There's nothing to worry about,' the nurse says. 'Everything looks good here. You have a happy, healthy baby. Would you like to know the sex?'

I don't know. I haven't thought about it. She prints out a photo of the baby and I tell her to write it down on the back of the scan so I can decide to look later if I want. She smiles and says that's a good idea, pops it in an envelope for me, and passes me some tissues to wipe my belly with.

'Get some rest,' she says, as if tired people choose to be tired. As if it has never occurred to any of us walking dead to have a lie-down or a lie-in. Getting enough sleep isn't about making the decision to; it's about having the opportunity and ability to. Two things many of us can't control.

I thank her, wheel Riley out and head back to the waiting room. Maggie is there, shining like a bright beacon in a sea of black winter coats and tired, worried faces. She smiles but stays silent until we're in the car, where she grasps my hand.

'We're having an early April baby,' she says. 'How lovely.'

We?

'I didn't tell you the date.'

She tuts and rolls her eyes at me. 'The doctor told you that you were around twenty weeks over the phone, so I did the maths.'

Maths. Always with the maths. I pull my hand away and focus on the traffic. I want to be alone when I get home, but I don't know how to tell her. Beside me Maggie continues to smile while staring at nothing, and behind me Riley has fallen asleep in his car seat. I keep checking the time, thinking how I need to get back because Tony needs the car for work, then remembering he doesn't, then trying to still my heart as I picture it clawing its way out of my mouth and exploding over the windscreen like a dead bird.

'I need to know what happened,' I say quietly while staring straight ahead.

Maggie doesn't react but I know she's listening. 'I told you when we first met that everything is going to be OK. I've looked after you until now, haven't I?'

I swallow. She has.

'You're safe, aren't you?' she says, her voice rising a little. 'No one playing music at night and keeping you awake. No man telling you what you can and can't do. No more questions from the police. You get to rest while you grow a life and someone else is helping to care for your baby, shopping for you both, feeding you. What more do you want, Lu?' She turns to face me, but I keep my gaze locked on the traffic. 'Why are you never happy?' she shouts.

'I am,' I say quietly. 'I'm really thankful for all you do for me. For us.'

'I love you both like my own,' she says.

'I know.'

'You said you needed somebody.'

'I know. I do. We do.'

She places her hand on mine. 'I promise everything is going to be OK, my love. You'll see.'

'What do you want?' I ask, eyes fixed ahead.

'I want you to be happy.'

I blink back the same tears I've been holding in all day, my eyes itchy and aching. It takes a lot of effort to focus on the road. I shouldn't be driving. This doesn't feel safe.

'But why are you doing this for me? For us? Why?'

My voice is no longer quiet. I don't want to wake up Riley, but I don't understand. Where is this going? Does she think she's going to be part of our life now? Is she going to move in with her brother and see me indefinitely, every day until the new baby arrives and beyond? Maggie's hand is still on mine on the steering wheel. Her grip tightens, her nails digging into my skin.

'Let me do this for you, Lu,' she says. 'It's the only way. And don't forget I know everything.'

She knows everything. She knows me as well as I know myself and none of it is pretty. She can choose to make our lives better, and just as easily rip our lives apart. She owns me, which means she owns Riley. My choices have all gone. All I can do is say yes to her.

'Thank you,' I say, and she pats my hand and smiles into the distance again.

I wish my tears could turn to anger around Maggie, but they never do; instead they fall silently, plopping on to my lap as I drive. I don't say another word but inside my mind is screaming.

I want Tony back. I want to go back to when it was just us and I'd never met Maggie. I don't know what to do. She's never going to leave.

THIRTY-FIVE

It's raining. It's been raining for two days, maybe longer. I don't know. I can no longer tell the difference between tears and raindrops. I wake up and, once again, Tony isn't here. Sometimes Maggie is, sometimes she isn't. Every time I try to talk to her about Tony, she tells me to hush, that it's OK, I've not done anything wrong. But I'm not sure. This morning I found some coins under the sofa cushions and considered ringing his work from the payphone at the end of the road, but I'm not sure it even works anymore, and I don't know the telephone number without looking it up online, and I have no access to the internet. The same thoughts swirl around in my mind, round and round and round, like water down a plug hole. I'm cut off. Alone. Maggie is my only connection to the real world – and she controls what we do.

Riley has light temperature, maybe the same virus I just recovered from. He's grumpy and not sleeping and my stomach is growing and everything about me feels so big. There's always food in the fridge and I eat and drink everything Maggie gives me, but I don't know if today is still today or if we're already in tomorrow. Either way it's always so dark and most of the time

I'm either sleeping or crying or watching Maggie do everything I should be doing.

'Stay home,' she says. 'It's safer that way. You don't need to do anything outside, not in this weather, not if you're tired.'

Every minute of the day is monotony tinged with fear. The ever-growing threat that I know something bad has happened... and there's nothing I can do about it. My life is on a loop: a constant cycle of feeding and changing and TV and sleeping and screaming and crying and worrying and hiding from everything and everyone. Even myself. I no longer live inside my own body. Sometimes I watch myself, shuffling around the house in my slippers, wearing the same clothes because I don't need to wash them. I don't move enough to sweat, and I don't do anything interesting enough to make them get stained or dirty.

I'm like a character in a computer game, the one in the background that looks the same every day and their only job is to walk up and down for no discernible reason. No one knows anything about them, and the game would continue as well without them. I'm a backdrop, filler, wallpaper. Nobody notices me. I'm simply here to fill the gaps while others take the stage. And in the meantime, one man is dead, and another is missing, and nobody knows what happened to them. Just me. But I don't want to remember.

Maggie is tidying Riley's toys up and the patter of rain at the dark window is making me sleepy. I don't know if it's the afternoon and Riley is having his nap, or if it's already night-time and I should be going to bed. I don't know if I even go to bed anymore. I often sleep on the sofa. Sometimes I start off in bed and wake up in Riley's bedroom, my face pressed up against his cot, red lines on my face like a barcode. What would it say if someone scanned me?

I remembered about Tony's laptop today. His voice popped into my head as I was dozing on the sofa, and I remembered he'd said something about emailing him. Something about work and emails and what if his work has emailed me? What if people have been trying to call me and they can't get through, so they've emailed? Do people post letters anymore? I've not seen any post for a long time. Maggie sometimes opens it, says I have nothing to worry about. Our bills are paid by direct debit. She says I need to rest.

Sometimes I watch her like she's a character on TV, the perfect housewife in an old sitcom, hating that the sight of her soothes me. I like the way she moves, how gently she manoeuvres herself around the house, her hips swaying and her face always so serene. She catches me staring and smiles, and I hate that something in my chest swells, making me immediately crave her touch. When she looks at me like that, I yearn for her to sit next to me and pull me on to her lap. I want to curl up against her chest as small as a cat as she rocks me, hushing inconsequential words into my ear, stroking my hair, telling me it's safe to disappear for a small time. I want all of that... but I also want her to leave me alone.

'What are you doing?' she asks.

I'm sitting cross-legged on the sofa, Tony's laptop on my lap.

'I remembered the password,' I say.

She looks alarmed, like I'm a toddler with their fingers jammed in the electrical socket.

'Should you be doing that?'

'Doing what?' I ask. 'I'm allowed to access my partner's laptop.'

She crosses the room and kneels at my feet. 'Show me.'

'Show you what?'

'The emails from Tony.'

There are no emails from Tony because I can't remember the password for my Gmail account so I'm seeing what else is open.

'I'm on Facebook,' I say.

'Tony hardly ever posts on his Facebook account.'

He doesn't, but how does she know that? I turn the screen to show her what I'm looking at. It's photos of my mum and dad at a dinner table with friends – the discarded shells of pink prawns and two empty bottles of wine, palm trees in the background, and eyes glossy with midday drinking.

'They look happy,' I mutter.

'They do. Because they're not thinking about you.'

I keep scrolling. More pictures of them. One on a boat. Another one on the beach. All with a glass in their hand.

There's a message for me. I wonder if it's my mum. Have they booked their flight for Christmas yet or Riley's birthday? But it's not from them, it's from my brother, Dan.

Been trying to call you all week, Lu. What's going on?

The message is dated the ninth of December. When was that? I look at the date on the laptop. He sent it today. Which means Tony has been gone a few days. A week, maybe? I don't know. It feels longer than that. I send Dan a message back:

I lost my phone.

He replies instantly:

I need to talk to you.

I can't talk to him. He'll know something is the matter as soon as I open my mouth. I'm thinking about what to type when the laptop starts to ring. He's calling me on Facebook. I don't even know whether I can answer him via the computer.

I glance at Maggie. She's on all fours under the table, picking up toy cars. She's staring at me, her eyes flashing cold blue, shaking her head slowly from side to side. I half expect her to prowl over to me, head bent, low on her haunches, teeth bared.

I stare at the screen, the call icon flashing, the ringing isn't stopping. Maggie is still staring at me. Waiting.

I answer.

'Hello?'

'Lulu.'

The familiar timbre of my brother's voice makes something inside of me fall a little, making whatever I keep swallowing down rise up. I need my brother. I do. I need my family – even if they're all selfish and useless.

'Hi,' I say.

'What the fuck is going on?'

I can't cry. If I cry, he'll worry, and if he worries, he'll come and see me, and then if he sees me, he'll know I did something bad. Maybe more than one bad thing.

'Nothing's going on. What's the matter?'

'I've been trying to call and WhatsApping you and messaging on here.'

'I just told you, I don't have a phone anymore,' I say. 'I told Mum. I lost it.'

He lets out a rush of air. 'You OK?'

'Yes.'

He goes quiet. Where is he that it's so quiet? He has a busy job and two children. How is he existing in such silence?

I close my eyes, forcing myself to open them again when he starts to speak. I'm no longer looking at Maggie, but I can feel her. She was always the lightness in my day but she's growing heavy now too.

'I can't get hold of Tony,' Dan says. 'His phone keeps going straight to answerphone. I have tickets for that Man U game in January and I need to know if he wants them, or my mate says he'll have them.'

Tony's not picking up his phone? All this time I've been

telling myself that maybe it's nothing, maybe Tony has been away, that he isn't hurt. That I... that we... haven't hurt him. But if he's not answering the phone to my brother, his best friend, then it must be serious. It's been nearly a week. What the fuck have I been doing sitting here, hoping it will all work itself out, when Tony has disappeared? My mouth is opening and closing, no words coming out, my hands sweaty and lips trembling.

I look over at Maggie, who has remained still as a statue. She's sitting on her heels, listening to every word we are saying, her head bent to one side. She's waiting for me to answer, seeing what I will say.

'I'll tell Tony you called,' I say to Dan. 'Got to go, baby's crying.'

My brother is saying something about Kayla having been abroad on business and how she's in London for a short time soon but I'm not listening. I click on the red button and hang up. There's a buzzing in my ears. I can't see and I can't hear anything. I'm underwater and I can't breathe. I'm on my feet, searching the room for a glass of water. Maggie is always bringing me drinks. Why is there nothing to drink?

She's next to me now, passing me a glass of orange juice. I used to like that she can read my mind, now I'm not so sure.

'You did well,' she says.

I look at her as if she's speaking another language.

'Well? I did well with what?'

'You were vague. Didn't give anything away about Tony.'

'Because I don't know anything about Tony,' I say. 'I don't know where he is.'

I don't want to think about my nightmare. The hammer. The red streaks on the wooden floor as I pushed a sheet under him and used it to drag him to the garden. My stomach was heavy and my chest was heavy but he wasn't. It was almost as if it was meant to be. Is he buried somewhere wrapped up in the same sodden sheet?

Maggie gives me that faint smile of hers again.

'Kayla is beautiful,' she says, stepping closer to me. She's never even seen a photo of her, has she? Has Maggie been looking at my Facebook account? Has she been looking at photos of people I follow and piecing together all the broken shards of my life?

'Too pretty for your brother.'

A flicker in my chest starts to expand into something solid and sharp. What does she know about my brother?

'Don't you think it's strange that Kayla has been away on business the whole time Tony has been missing?'

I rub my eyes. Didn't Tony and Kayla used to date? No, I met him at their wedding – it was her best friend he was going out with. I think. I don't know. What has that got to do with anything? Kayla *is* incredibly beautiful though. Very put together. Tony likes a woman put together. I see him, his head surrounded by that black inky halo on the hallway floor. Human heads aren't that strong. I thought a skull would be harder to crack, like a stone, except they're more like brittle plastic. I look through Maggie, behind her, where his body lay. Did she help me get rid of his body? Or is he in the arms of another woman? He wouldn't be answering the phone to Dan if he was sleeping with his best friend's wife.

'You're better off without him,' Maggie says, snapping me back into place.

'I'm not.'

She takes a step forward, making me edge back until the backs of my knees are on the edge of the sofa. She's a little taller than me, slender and refined but strong. Stronger in so many ways.

'I'm here for you. I'm the only one who is, Lu. Not your parents, your brother, the father of your child. Me. Yet you keep pushing me away.'

'I d-don't,' I stutter.

I close my eyes at the touch of her soft hand on my cheek, her thumb brushing away the tears.

'It's just us,' she says. 'Us and our babies.'

Our babies?

'What do you want?' I ask her again because I don't understand why she's here. I can't think clearly anymore, I can't remember why she's making me uncomfortable. Why is nothing sharp enough, or in the right order anymore? Reality has no edges and keeps dissolving and changing into other things.

'I told you. I'm saving you,' she says, her breath warming my lips.

'From what?'

'Yourself.'

I'm up against the sofa, teetering, about to fall back, but I don't want to fall. I nudge her away so I can regain my balance.

'No,' I say. 'What did you do with Tony?'

Maggie smiles. Unfazed. She thinks this is amusing.

'You are so ungrateful, Lu. Dave kept you awake all night. Now he's gone. Tony was driving you mad. Now he's gone. Be happy, Lu. Everything is good now.'

'No!' I shout, pushing her back.

She doesn't react, so I do it again until it's her with her back against the wall.

'You can't do this!' I shout. 'You can't convince me that any of this is OK.'

'You wanted it,' she says quietly. 'You made this happen. I'm only here because of what you want. What you need.'

I can't see her properly through the blur of my tears, but I know the expression on her face is soft. And I know she's right. I need her. I can't manage without her. But I don't want her here.

'Leave,' I say. 'I need to be alone.'

'No. I'm not going anywhere,' she snarls. 'You have the perfect life now, and if you won't make the most of it, then I will. Riley loves me, and the new baby will too. You're not indispensable, you know.'

She's heading for the hallway. My son is sleeping upstairs. This is it, this is why she's here. She wants my babies.

'Leave us alone!' I shout, standing between her and the stairs.

And for the first time I see Maggie like I've seen all the others. Dead. Hurt. Suffering. I see her crumpled form on my living room floor, a knife in my hand, her clothes turned burgundy, her blonde hair pink, her painted lips a dribbling crimson maw. She doesn't even put up a fight. Sliding the blade inside of her is like slicing fresh mozzarella. Too easy.

Maggie is holding the tops of my arms, her fingers pushing into my flesh, holding me back or maybe pulling me forward. She thinks she knows me better than I know myself, but she's controlling me. She's been slowly pushing me out of my own life, and I've been letting her.

I shove her off me, but she digs her thumbs into me deeper, getting closer, so close it's like she's trying to climb inside of me. I push her back again, this time far enough away that I can hit her. Her face is harder than I thought it would be, like hitting a wall.

'Leave us alone!' I scream.

She lets go of me but doesn't move.

'Go!' I shout in her face, pointing at the front door behind her. Her nostrils flare and her lips twitch, but she stays silent. I open the front door and she steps outside, disappearing into the darkness.

I'm breathing so heavily it's hurting my chest. She's gone, but for how long? If I lock the door, can she still get in? If I ignore her, will she still insist on being part of my life?

All this time I've been thinking everything would be better if I could be more like Maggie, but what if she wants to be me?

What if she wants all that I have? And there's nothing I can do about it because she knows too much to ever let me go.

THIRTY-SIX

Maggie didn't come back last night, and I eventually fell into a fitful sleep full of angry dreams and strangled breaths. It's morning and I keep blinking until my eyes adjust. I moved Riley's cot into my room last night and jammed it against the door so it couldn't be opened. I can taste blood in my mouth and my fingers ache. I switch on the light and pull back the covers to find my nails and pyjamas black with dirt. What have I done?

I jump to my feet, my toes also brown and muddy, and run to Riley's room. He's asleep, his cot in its usual place. I must have moved it back in the night. My heart thunders as I imagine where I went last night, or who could have got into the house, but I check, and every room upstairs is empty. I squint as I walk down the stairs, checking the key is still in the door. It is. The rooms downstairs are also empty. OK. It's OK. Maggie is not in my house. With a sigh of relief, I open the back door and take a deep, clearing breath. The cold December air fills my head and lungs, painting everything clearer for a moment, even though all is still and black outside. I don't put on shoes or slippers, feeling the rough hew of the patio beneath the soles of my feet. Grounding me. It finally stopped raining yesterday – the tiles should be dry, yet my foot is standing in something wet. I inspect it, staring at the dark marks on my dirty toes.

Blood? Mud? Maybe I was in the garden last night.

When we moved here Tony said there was no point doing any gardening at the start of winter. The grass has remained long, the hole in the fence large, what lies beneath nothing but derelict land churned up and boggy in places. There are marks in the grass, like someone has been walking through it. Or something has been dragged.

Was I out here last night? Was I looking for someone or hiding someone?

I go back inside the house and look at my feet again in the light. Then I turn off the lights and take a long hot shower. The water runs dark, my feet clean once again, but I keep having to turn the water off to check if the noises I can hear are real, if it's Riley crying or birds singing or a woman screaming. But it's nothing, just things trapped inside my head. So much of my life is no longer happening in the real world. It makes me wonder how much of anyone's life is shared, or are we all sleepwalking through our own alternate realities? Maybe I'm not here. Maybe I never have been.

Without Maggie I lack direction, like a phantom in my own home. I wander from room to room, moving objects from one place to another, watching the minutes tick by like they're hours. I feed Riley, I bathe him, I change him and we play, but I'm not here. Not really. I'm hovering above my body, my corporeal form and my soul slightly unaligned like I'm no longer solid enough to be encased in skin. I follow my son around the house as he toddles from new surface to new surface, his entire world looking different from his new height now he can walk. My world is looking different now too.

I try not to think about Maggie and what she said about

Tony and Kayla, but the more I consider it, the more it makes sense. All my sister-in-law's trips to London, and all the times Tony left for work earlier than he had to. And who works seven days a week anyway? What if some of those nights he wasn't working but fucking? Is that where he is now? Having sex with my brother's wife? Part of me hopes he is, so that he's alive and well.

But Tony wouldn't do that to me and Riley. He wouldn't do that to his best friend. And if Dan suspected Kayla, he'd have told me. But what if I knew something before and I've forgotten, and that's why I hurt Tony? I look at my hands, now clean, and the cut from a month ago now healed. Are these the hands of a killer?

I consider going for a walk, but the rain has started up again, pelting at the windows so hard I can't even see outside. I haven't seen police on our street in ages. I don't know what that means, but it must be good. What happens if they don't find Dave's killer? At what point does a case grow cold? If only I knew, I could stop worrying about being caught.

I stumble upstairs with Riley and put him in his cot for a nap then collapse on to my own bed. I have to lie on my side as my bump has grown bigger and harder in the last few days and my breasts are too sore to put pressure on. I sleep deeply yet alert, like a soldier on patrol. Do soldiers have my ability to start running seconds before they open their eyes?

I pull the duvet over myself, but it's still too cold and I remember I turned the thermostat down the other day. Can I afford to turn it back up again? How much more will one degree cost? The money in the bank won't last forever if Tony is dead. I shouldn't have listened to Maggie; I should have reported him missing. But it's too late. It looks far too suspicious now. How long has he been gone? A week? It feels like a year.

I'll say we had an argument and he walked out on us. That's what I'll do if anyone asks.

As I sleep I dream, even though my eyes are not yet fully closed. Arms snaking around my middle, a murmur at the back of my neck. Tony. Maggie. Which one is in my bed?

Riley wakes me from my nap and I no longer care that it's now pouring with rain, I have to leave the house.

It's six o'clock in the evening and there's still no sign of Maggie. I think I hit her yesterday. I shouldn't have hurt her. An image of her broken body fills my mind, her clothes red, golden hair matted pink, reality and dreams and my imagination melting into one. What if there is no difference between the three? How do any of us know what is truly real?

I bundle Riley into his pushchair, but he's refusing to put his arms and legs into his new snowsuit. It's like trying to stuff a wriggling octopus into a plastic bag. He thinks it's a game and laughs as he keeps his arms and legs rigid. I don't even know where the snowsuit came from.

I don't have time to get wet outside because I'm only going next door. Jim answers the door with a smile, as if expecting me to be someone else.

'Oh, Lu!' He peers down at my son and waves. 'And little Riley. To what do we owe this pleasure?'

'Is Maggie home?' I ask, feeling like a ten-year-old knocking for her friend to come out and play.

His brow creases. 'My sister?'

Has she said something to him? Did she tell him I hit her? I should never have hit her. What else has she told him?

'She's not here,' he says.

Shit! A police car has entered our street and I grip the handle of the pushchair tighter, keeping my face turned to Jim so the officers in the car can't see me. Maggie knows everything. She knows who I've hurt, the things I've seen, what I'm capable of. She knows where Tony is and insists I do too, even though I don't remember. She's not here but the police are. What has she done?

'Could you tell her I need to speak to her, please?' I plead, my voice shaking at the edges and my eyes filling with tears. I can't let him see me cry. They take babies away from crazy, violent mothers.

'Can I help?' Jim asks me.

I notice he no longer has a cast on his leg. He can't be needing a lot of Maggie's help anymore if he can walk now, yet his sister has stayed. For me? What does she want with my family?

I shake my head at Jim's question. 'Please tell her...' To keep quiet? That I'm sorry? Not to take my babies away from me?

'Would you like her telephone number?' he says. But that's no use to me, not without a phone of my own. I tell him I have it and that I'll text her. He looks like he wants to say more, perhaps even invite us in, but I've already embarrassed myself enough and the police car is still circling.

I get home, shut the door behind me and slump on to the floor. Maggie's not gone back to her brother's, but she hasn't left. Jim would have said if his sister had returned home. She's stayed. Has she stayed to help me... or hurt me?

The sharp ring of the doorbell makes me jump. Hardly anyone has knocked on our door since we moved in, and I'm reminded of Tony saying something about us having a Ring doorbell and how he linked it to his laptop – not that I have any idea how to access either. What a waste of money that was.

I scramble to my feet, wondering if it's Maggie. Wondering if she isn't using the key because I locked her out last night. But it's not Maggie – it's the police. Two of them. A man and a woman, again.

She's done it. She's told them everything. Or maybe it's about Tony. My heart is beating so loudly I can't speak.

'Oh, were you on your way out?' the female officer asks me,

glancing at Riley sweating in his snowsuit. How long has he been sitting in his pushchair while I was on the floor?

'No, no, just got back,' I say, unfastening him and letting him toddle off to his toys. 'What's happened? Is everything OK?'

I can't let them in. If I let them in, they'll see I haven't washed up and they'll know everything Maggie told them was right. I'm a bad mum. I don't deserve to have my babies.

'Only a formality,' the male police officer says. 'Some new evidence has come to light about the murder at number four and we're giving neighbours the opportunity to come to the station and answer a few questions.'

'Evidence?'

I can't remember what story I told them last time. Did I say I was asleep? Do they know I was locked out that night?

'A woman was seen running down the street at the time we believe the murder took place.'

'A woman?' I say.

Maybe if I keep repeating everything they say back to them, they'll eventually go away. The policewoman looks at her tiny writing in her tiny book. 'You told us you put the bins out at around eleven o'clock. Is that right?'

I shrug. 'I think so. Maybe a bit later. I could hear Dave's music.'

She hums, as if that's very interesting. 'And did you see anyone in the street?'

I shake my head. 'I wasn't really looking. There might have been. I was in my nightclothes, so I was trying to be quick. I didn't want anyone to see me.'

The lies slip out so easily, like I want this story to be true so much I'm making it real simply by saying it aloud.

'But then you got locked out?'

'Yes. But not for long. Jim has a spare key and his sister, Maggie, helped me.'

The police officer is writing something down. What more can she fit in that stupid little book? What is she writing in there?

'Thank you, that all tallies. We already have your original statement but should anything else come to mind and you wish to add anything further, we are giving everyone the opportunity to speak to us.'

'I don't know anything,' I stammer. Why does she keep on pushing? Perhaps she can tell I'm hiding something. Can she see my hands shaking? Riley starts to cry, and I widen my eyes like an apology.

The female officer smiles kindly. 'Don't let us keep you,' she says, although I'm already at the doorway of the living room with images of Riley hurt and bleeding filling my mind. He's fine. He's struggling to fit a ball into a box.

'I'll get in touch if I remember anything further,' I say, the door already closing on them. 'Thank you,' I add.

Thank you for being so terrible at your job, I don't say, secretly thanking Maggie in my mind. She's clearly kept quiet... so far.

THIRTY-SEVEN

I wake up on the sofa to the smell of burning. I'm on my feet before I've had a chance to realise I'm not alone. Maggie is standing before me, Riley in her arms, a cup of tea and some burned toast on the coffee table beside me.

'Good morning,' she says.

She's changed Riley, and all his toys have been tidied away.

'You came back,' I say.

'You wanted me back.'

I hate that she's right. She could have told the police and her brother everything, but she didn't. I should have trusted her. Why do we fear the things we need? Is it because we're scared that they'll change us?

'I'm sorry,' I say quietly. 'For overreacting. I know you mean well.'

'Yes, Lu. I'm not the bad guy.'

A thin haze of pale grey smoke settles towards the ceiling. I open the window, even though it's drizzling outside, and the air cuts sharp as a knife. Maggie places Riley in his playpen and hands him a cuddly lion. Is that new too?

'I burned the toast,' she says.

I take a bite. Dry charcoal. I wash it down with the weak tea. 'Thank you.'

She smiles benignly at me, straightening her dress. This one is floral and looks too summery for the dark days of wind and rain we've been having.

'I like your nail polish,' I say. 'Baby blue.'

She looks at her fingers, as if it's a surprise. I've never known her to paint her nails before.

'I need to get some nappies and formula,' I say. 'Would you like to come with me?'

Neither of us has mentioned me hitting her. Perhaps it didn't even happen. Perhaps I only wished it so. Yet, I wished Dave would die and he did. And I wished Tony would disappear and he has. Is anyone safe from me?

'Let me go,' Maggie says. 'I'll take Riley to the shops, and we can feed the ducks on the way home. You're probably not feeling up to it.'

As soon as she says that I start to feel weak and lower myself to the sofa. Maybe she's right. Riley could do with some fresh air, and we do need groceries. It's not like she's not gone to the shops for me before and taken my son. I owe her some respect after the way I've treated her.

'Food,' I say, handing her my bank card. 'Nothing else. No toys or clothes this time.'

She takes the card silently and I close my eyes, falling into a deep sleep.

Three hours have passed, and Maggie is still not back with Riley. I'm pacing the living room, unsure whether to go out and look for them or stay put. Why haven't I bought myself a phone yet? Why did I think I could function in today's world without one?

My head is thumping, something hard pressing over my left

eye. I rub the back of my neck, pinching and massaging it, but it makes no difference. The pain is like a vice and all I can think about is my baby.

What if she's kidnapped him? Was this her plan all along – to steal Riley?

I peer out of the window, then through the back door and into the garden. What am I looking for? I should call the police. No. I can't call the police. You can't say your friend went to buy you milk and bread with the baby and has been gone a couple of hours. That's not a crime. Killing your neighbour and potentially your partner is a crime, but I don't have proof of either of those incidents either. All I can offer the police is my paranoia.

I hear a scraping of keys in the lock and pull the front door open. On the doorstep is a giant pink teddy bear. And behind it are Maggie and Riley.

'We're back!'

'What took you so long?' I cry.

'Sorry, but Riley saw this teddy in a shop window, and I couldn't say no. Look how happy he is. Don't be such a sourpuss, Lu. It's not good for the baby.'

I pull the stupid bear into the hallway and help her with the pushchair that has three bags of shopping hanging off it.

Maggie is smiling and Riley is asking to be let out of his constraints. I unclip him and he wanders off to the living room, where I've left the TV on.

'I bought milk, eggs, bread and those nappies that don't leak like the others do.'

'What's with the bear?' I ask.

She laughs. 'He likes it. It's not like Tony can complain about it anymore.'

She's right. Tony would have hated a giant teddy bear cluttering up the house.

'What did we do?' I say quietly. 'Please. Tell me. Where's Tony?'

Maggie cups my face in her hands, and I close my eyes at the touch of her cool skin on mine. Her mouth is so close to mine I can smell the scent of her lipstick. I think she's going to tell me, or embrace me, but she does neither.

'I'll put the shopping away,' she says.

She leaves me in the living room with Riley and all I can do is stare at the wall, willing my mind to tell me something. Anything. What did Tony say as he left for work? Did he come home the next morning?

My head is ringing, and it takes me a while to realise it's the doorbell. I pick Riley up and balance him on my hip. Please, God, don't let it be the police again. Can a woman be arrested if she's pregnant and holding a baby?

I turn to look at Maggie as I head for the door, but she keeps her back to me. She's not going to help me with this one. But it's not the police, it's my neighbours Shona and Beth. A hard ball of relief plummets to the pit of my stomach. Shona is holding a bunch of carnations that look like they've been coloured in with felt-tip pen and Beth has a plate in her hand that's covered in tin foil. I take a moment to think about today's date and check it's not my birthday. It's December – my birthday is in June. What do they want?

'Victoria sponge,' Beth says with a timid smile, nodding at the plate clasped in her two hands.

I'm still holding the door open, but not all the way, just a fraction. I glance to my right to the kitchen doorway, where out of the corner of my eye I can see Maggie staring at us.

Are my neighbours expecting me to invite them in? Am I meant to say something? There are a few beats of silence and then Shona jumps in.

'We wanted to check you're OK,' she says.

Me? Why? 'I'm fine,' I reply.

Riley is getting restless and whining, burying his head into the crook of my neck. He must have not slept in the pushchair earlier when Maggie took him out. Shona and Beth look like they want to give me my gifts, flowers and a cake, but my hands aren't free. I try to place Riley on the ground, but he starts to wail so I hold him to me.

'He's tired,' I say.

'And how are *you*?' Shona asks in a gentler voice than I've heard her use before. I'm wearing a baggy tracksuit top so I know they can't see the bump.

'I'm fine,' I say again. I use that word a lot lately.

'Do you need any help?' Beth says, still holding the cake. 'You know, with settling in and the baby and all that.'

'I'm getting some help,' I say. They look relieved. 'Maggie.'

They glance quickly at one another. What does that look mean? They've seen me out and about with her before, I'm sure they have. There's no reason for them to look surprised or concerned.

'Jim's sister,' I add. 'Jim at number eight.'

'You're friends with Maggie?'

'Yes, she's been really kind.'

I can still see her, watching us, her eyes shining in the darkness of the kitchen. Why isn't she coming forward to say hello? Why doesn't she take the cake and flowers? Shona and Beth are still waiting for me to invite them in, but I can't. My house is a mess and it's clear Maggie doesn't like them, or she'd have said hello.

'I didn't have Maggie as the nurturing kind,' Shona says to Beth with a raise of her eyebrow.

'Jim said she was pretty reluctant to come and help him, to be honest,' Beth replies. 'She always was a livewire. Remember all that drama she caused a few years back with that guy she got involved with?'

'Oh my God, yes. But, you know, I'm glad she's been kind to you, Lu.'

'Get rid of them,' I hear Maggie say softly from the kitchen.

I must have turned my head a little because Beth and Shona peer over my shoulder.

'That's a big teddy,' Beth says. I forgot the huge cuddly toy was still in my hallway. 'Saw you earlier with it.'

They saw Maggie, but hidden behind the huge toy of course they'd think it was me.

'I dyed my hair,' I say.

'Yes,' Beth says. 'We noticed. Nice nails.'

I glance at my hands. My fingernails are the same shade of blue as Maggie's. When did she paint them? While I was sleeping?

The three of us stay standing, smiling awkwardly at one another, until they eventually hold out the gifts, which I take with one hand.

'Riley's getting tired,' I say, and they take the hint and step back from the door.

'Look after yourself,' Shona says, her hand resting on my arm. 'If you need any help at all, we're only down the road.'

I nod and thank them for their kindness, and keep nodding and smiling until they turn around and I can shut the door with a sigh. What the hell was all that about?

'They hate me,' Maggie whispers. 'Old busybody bitches.'

I don't have the energy to ask what drama they were talking about. I place the gifts in the kitchen with all the shopping, put Riley down for his nap and return to ask Maggie why they hate her.

But when I come back downstairs, all the shopping is still in the bags and she's gone.

THIRTY-EIGHT

'Stay away from them,' Maggie says.

I didn't notice she was back. I must have dozed off on the sofa after putting Riley down. She's in the kitchen, all the food has been put away and the house is tidy once again.

'Who?' I ask, joining her at the sink. She washes, I dry.

'Beth and Shona. They've lived on this street since they were kids. Always sticking their noses in everyone's business. I wouldn't eat that cake of hers if I were you.'

I notice the flowers are already in a vase, and the cake is on a plate I don't recognise.

'Why? What's wrong with the cake?'

She makes a face and throws it in the bin, plate and all. I don't stop her. Maggie has been right so far, so I'm not going to question her about this.

'After what you've done, you're safer not talking to anyone,' she says. 'Keep yourself to yourself.'

'Tony's been gone a week,' I say. I think I'm right. I can't hold anything down anymore. A week! Where the hell is he? A week is not a long time to be gone if someone has left his wife...

but it is a long time if that man is missing, and his wife hasn't reported it.

'He's away on business,' Maggie says. 'That's what you tell them. He's away on business.'

I want to ask Maggie if he's dead. She was in my garden the morning after I remember hurting him. Was it also that morning that I woke up muddy, with dirt under my nails? Or was it the following day? I need to know what we did! Why won't she tell me?

'Except he's not away on business,' she adds. 'He's having an affair with Kayla.'

I swing around to face her.

'Tony wouldn't do that,' I say, although that would explain why he's not here and not answering the phone to Dan. 'Kayla isn't even in the country right now.'

'Really? That's her car,' Maggie replies, pointing out of the kitchen window.

I join her. She's right. My sister-in-law's car is pulling up outside the house. How does Maggie know what car Kayla drives? And why is she outside my house?

'You're getting a lot of visitors today,' Maggie says. There's a steel to her voice. It's practically accusatory.

'Yeah. Weird,' I mumble.

'What have you told them?'

'Nothing. I promise! You answer the door,' I say to her.

She shakes her head.

'Please,' I beg. Kayla can't see me like this, she'll know something is wrong. She'll know I've done something bad. My sister-in-law isn't a woman who is easily fooled. The easy one to fool is obviously me. 'Tell her I'm not in.'

'That will only make them more suspicious,' Maggie says. 'I told you to keep everyone away.'

'Stay with me,' I say quietly as Maggie backs into the kitchen.

'I'm here.'

I close my eyes and take a deep breath, waiting for the doorbell to ring before opening the door.

'Hi, Kayla. What a surprise!' I don't know if my voice sounds as fake as I think it does, but unlike my neighbours Kayla doesn't wait to be invited in. She pushes past me into the hallway, her head swivelling left and right.

'Where's Riley?' she asks.

'Sleeping.'

She bounds upstairs but I stay by the door. What's going on? Maggie is still in the kitchen, her eyes narrow, her face stony. It's clear she doesn't like Kayla and I can see why. Perfect Kayla pulling up in her BMW, barging in on a cloud of expensive perfume, her Burberry mac flapping behind her. Kayla who is too good for my brother. But is she too good for my man?

She comes back downstairs slowly, her brow furrowed with concern as she places her car keys into her bright red handbag.

See? I want to say. *My baby is fine. Now fuck off.*

'What's going on?' I ask, opening the door wider, but she's already taking off her jacket.

'Let's have some tea,' she says.

I shut the door, take her coat and handbag, and signal for her to go into the living room.

'I'll make it,' I insist, suggesting she sit down and take a load off her ridiculously high heels. Where is she going dressed like that anyway?

Maggie is still in the kitchen, shaking her head at me slowly. I shrug. What can I do? Kayla is on the sofa waiting for tea. She's talking fast but I'm across the hallway so can't hear her properly. The kettle is loud, my head is full of noise, and Maggie is whispering to me.

'She's with Tony,' Maggie is saying. 'She's seeing how much you know.'

'She's not sleeping with him,' I hiss back.

'Then she's here to check up on you so she can tell your brother you're failing as a mother. Look at her. Women like Kayla love to drag other women down.'

Kayla is talking about her work and Dan and Spain. Her words are like bubbles floating through water, muffled until they reach the surface and pop. Only a few are pointed enough to cut through the fog of my mind. I catch the odd word...

'Tony.'

'Your parents.'

'Mobile phone.'

'I know it's tough.'

I make the tea, and while throwing the sodden teabags away I notice that the carnations Shona bought me are in the bin too.

'Rotten,' Maggie whispers.

I bring the two mugs into the living room, where Kayla is balancing on the edge of the sofa as if she's worried the fabric is going to stain her tight grey dress. Isn't she cold? It's winter. I'm sure it's December already.

Kayla's nails are long, pillar-box red, not like my stumpy, flaky nails painted in a shade of baby blue. I think of Maggie in the kitchen telling me to get rid of her. She's right. If my sister-in-law works out that Tony is missing, she'll start to ask questions. Questions that I don't have the answers to.

'Dan is worried about you,' Kayla says, sipping her tea. She makes a face and puts it down. I forgot she doesn't take sugar. 'We're all worried about you, Lu.'

'Why?'

She crosses her legs – her impossibly long legs clad in sheer tights that shimmer in the weak winter light. I can't remember the last time I wasn't wearing tracksuit bottoms or leggings. I'm glad I have my baggy jumper on today because I don't look pregnant; I just look fat. Kayla won't care about that. She can add my lack of self-care to the list of things she already judges me for.

'You don't have a phone, you don't answer your Facebook messages, we can't get hold of you. I have enough on my plate, but I came here anyway so I can see with my own two eyes that you and Riley are OK.'

'Are you not here on business?'

'Yes, but... that's not the point. Is Tony still at work?'

Maybe Maggie is right after all. All these trips abroad Kayla takes and her visits to London. How do I know it's not my man she's really interested in?

'Don't you normally take the train into central London?' I ask.

She looks harried, like I'm wasting her time. She must really resent having to see her dull, annoying sister-in-law twice in as many weeks. Or months. I can't remember how long ago our dinner together was.

'Are you OK?' she asks me again, this time placing a hand on my arm. Like Shona did earlier. I look behind me, to the kitchen, where I know Maggie is waiting for me. I can imagine what she's saying about Kayla, how stuck-up she is, what she must be thinking of me. Kayla, the perfect woman with her perfectly flat stomach and nice clothes and big house and beautiful children with their stupid names.

'You look exhausted,' she says, frowning at my outfit. She means fat. She thinks my baggy jumper is hiding big hips and a flabby tummy. 'Maybe Dan and I should take Riley for a few days.'

'No!' I shout. I'm not letting them take my baby.

She raises her hands up as if in surrender. 'Or you can come to ours with him. Change of scenery?'

Why is she here? Is it Tony she wants or is she checking up on me? Judging me? Maggie looms behind her, watching me. I know what she's silently saying to me. Kayla is a threat. She's going to take everything away from us.

Kayla looks up as Maggie raises her hand. She's holding

something. It's silver and long, the light from the living room windows bouncing off it as she drives it into Kayla's neck. I watch but I don't move as Kayla falls to the ground. I blink. And there's blood on the floor, dark crimson puddles. I blink. And Kayla is reaching out for me, her grey dress now black and her eyes pleading. I blink again and it's all gone. Kayla has gone and the floor is clean and I'm on the couch and Maggie is telling me not to worry. That everything is OK. That she's looking after me.

Where's Kayla? Did she leave? Is she dead? What did Maggie do?

'I've made everything better for you,' Maggie says.

I feel safe. I feel scared. I feel so confused.

THIRTY-NINE

I wake up but it's as if my eyes are still glued shut. My head is pounding. I'm in my bed but I'm not alone. There's someone beside me. My heart leaps. He's back. I reach out, expecting to feel Tony's hard shoulders, his hairy chest, but the person beside me is smooth and soft, with curves. I run my hand from their shoulder along the dip of their waist and hip. They turn, their arm drapes over me, and I drift back off to sleep.

Riley's cries wake me up and this time I'm already on my feet, my eyes springing open. Light is fighting through the cracks of the blinds at my window, which means it must be late morning or I fell asleep during his naptime. I don't know what's night or day. I don't think it even matters anymore.

I pick him up and cradle him, tell him how much I love him, change him and tidy his room. Everything is so clean now that Maggie is helping me. We're so lucky to have her. No. Wait. Something flashes in my mind.

Kayla. My sister-in-law was here yesterday.

I go to the landing and look out of the small window at the front of the house. She was here but I don't remember her leaving. What I remember can't be right. Maggie with a knife.

Maggie in my bed. Maggie telling me she's made everything better. I squint against the milky light of morning and there it is, Kayla's car, still parked outside my house.

She didn't leave.

My arms are shaking, and my chest is tight, and I have to put Riley back down in his cot because I'm scared I'm going to drop him. Kayla didn't leave. It was real. The blood and the knife and her hand reaching out to me. The hand I never took. I was scared – she wanted to take my baby, so I took her life. Maggie took her life. But she did it for me, so it's my fault. Dave, Tony, Kayla... it's all my fault.

I leave Riley safe in his cot and run downstairs, gripping the banister so I don't fall.

Maggie isn't here, not in the living room or the kitchen where she normally is. Everything is in order, all the washing up put away and the floor mopped. The only thing in the sink is a knife. It's clean, I can't see any blood, but the mop and bucket are out. I don't remember cleaning.

I lower myself down on a chair by the small kitchen table and hold my head in my hands. The pounding returns, a sharp pain above my left eye. Riley is crying, shouting, 'Ma, ma, ma,' but I'm rooted to the spot. When I look up, Maggie has him in her arms and he looks happy enough.

'I didn't hear you come in,' I say.

'I've been here the whole time.'

She has?

'Kayla was here,' I say. 'My sister-in-law.'

'She knew too much,' she says. 'She was looking for Tony and talking about taking Riley.'

She was. I remember now.

'You did the right thing,' Maggie says.

What did I do? Nothing. Maybe Tony has left me for Kayla. Maybe that's what she was doing here – to tell me and take my baby.

'I wouldn't hurt her,' I say quietly, looking up at Maggie's cold blue eyes.

'No, you wouldn't,' Maggie says.

But she would. I can see it. I can see what she's thinking behind the ice of her gaze and the twitch of her lips. She wants me to herself. Me and the babies. She wouldn't let the neighbours come in, she threw away Beth's cake and Shona's flowers, and she killed Kayla. Didn't she?

'I need a bit of space,' I say to her. 'I might go out for a walk.'

'In this weather?' Maggie says.

It's bright outside. I know it is – I looked out of the window earlier. I look now and it's dark and raining.

'I might take Riley to the playgroup,' I say, thinking of Daisy and her daughter. Maybe I can talk to her about how I'm feeling. No, I tried that. Daisy thinks every second of motherhood is a blessing. Daisy's idea of a difficult day is not finding the matching pillowcases to her duvet.

'I'll come with you,' Maggie says.

No. 'Let's stick the TV on,' I say.

I don't know what Maggie does to busy herself, but she's gone and it's just me and Riley and a cartoon. I've given him some baby biscuits, which he's happily sucking on while pointing at an animated dog and his friends.

I need a phone. That's what I need. I'm clearly not a suspect anymore or the police would have said something. I'm safe. I'll buy a cheap phone online and a pay-as-you-go card from the supermarket. Then I can ask Dan for Tony's number and I'll call him and he'll answer and say... I don't know what he'll say. I'm terrified of what he will say. I reach for Tony's laptop and open it. I don't know my email password, but my Facebook is still open and there's a message from my mum.

How are you both?

I reply.

> We're all good. Hope you're having lovely sunny weather. Won't stop raining here.

That's OK. Talking about the weather is OK. Play it nice and safe.

The next messages are from my brother, Dan, spanning the last two days.

> What the fuck is going on, Lu?
>
> Why won't you answer your messages on here?
>
> Did you pass my message on to Tony?
>
> Have you seen Kayla?
>
> Kayla told me she was coming to see you.
>
> Lu, where's Kayla? She's not answering her phone! Is she still with you?

Shit. Kayla hasn't gone home, and her car is here. She never left my house. I didn't imagine it. I didn't imagine any of this. Oh God, what did I do? What did Maggie do?

I shut the laptop, hide it beneath the cushion on the sofa and go back to watching Duggee the dog with Riley. The cartoon changes to a woman in dungarees counting numbers, then *Thomas the Tank Engine*, then a cooking show and I realise it's lunchtime.

I peer around the doorway. It's quiet in the kitchen. Maggie is normally good at knowing when it's time to eat, when I'm thirsty, when Riley needs something. I stifle a yawn and pull myself up from the sofa, my belly like a bowling ball pinning me down.

'Maggie?' I call out.

Silence.

I glance out of the back door. It's stopped raining but it's still grey and damp outside, the kind of day where the air is full of water and the cold seeps into your bones. I think I can see someone at the end of the garden, through the bushes. Is she out there? What is she looking at?

'Let's go,' I say to Riley. 'Let's get something to eat in town.'

We've not done this before. We never go for a walk around town like other mothers and babies, wandering around the shops for fun, grabbing a sandwich along the way. It's too wet for the park but maybe if the sun comes out and we don't finish our lunch, we can feed it to the ducks.

'Duck?' I say, and Riley staggers to his feet and claps his hands.

I change him and bundle him into his snowsuit, making sure I've packed bottles and snacks and nappies. I do this in a haze, on autopilot, not quite here but not completely gone. I can't see the back garden from the hallway but I'm moving fast. I don't want Maggie to join us. I need to clear my head. Alone.

I shut the front door silently behind us and I'm halfway up the road when a familiar face stops us.

'Lu!' Jim exclaims. 'And little Riley. How are you both?'

Why does everyone keep asking me that? Do I look crazy? Am I unkempt? I'm not as made-up as Kayla and Maggie, but I look OK. Don't I? We're standing beside Kayla's car, but I refuse to look at it. Maybe I'm wrong. Maybe it's not hers.

'We're fine,' I say, glancing over Jim's shoulder. Fine. The magic word. 'Just heading to the shops.'

'I've not seen your husband come and go the last week or so,' he says. 'Is he unwell?'

I can't be bothered to correct him about being unmarried.

Why do we have to do this, anyway? Why is it expected of near strangers to stop and exchange such mindless, useless pleasantries?

'Tony's away,' I reply. 'Work.'

That's what Maggie told me to say, and Jim buys it.

'Your sister has been a great help,' I add.

He makes a face. 'You're still in touch with Maggie?'

Why does he find this so hard to understand? Where does he think she is every day and night? Don't they speak?

'She's very kind. Very caring.'

He laughs. I didn't expect him to laugh.

'Maggie? Caring?'

Something inside me burns hot. This isn't funny. Why is he laughing at me?

'Well, she *is* a nurse,' I say.

Jim's face falls and his laughter stops like the turning of a tap.

'Maggie, a nurse? With *her* temper?' he says with a snort. 'Whatever gave you that idea? Even her own daughter complains about her bedside manner.'

I mumble something and say I'm in a rush and he says goodbye and I'm at the end of the road before I turn back. I can see my house from here, and my kitchen window, and someone looking out of it.

Maggie was watching me talk to her brother. Maggie who isn't a nurse. Who has a child and a temper. Who has lied to me about everything.

FORTY

I don't want to go home.

I'm standing in the high street, staring at the window of a discount card shop, wondering how to get Maggie to leave. She told me she was a nurse with no children. I'm sure that's what she said. She also said she used to be a hairdresser, but she probably made that up too. I don't understand why she would lie about that. And how old is her child if she's been at my house for so many weeks? Did she leave her with the father or is she older? Maybe there isn't even a man in her life. Maybe she did something to him too. All this time I've been worried about what I'm capable of when it's Maggie I should have been focused on.

Riley has fallen asleep in his pushchair, so I make my way to a bench on the high street and sit down. I bought myself a coffee and some chocolate, but it does nothing to wake me up. I didn't know it was possible to feel this tired while having so much adrenaline surging through me. I want to vomit. I want to scream. I want everything to stop.

I close my eyes and try to straighten out my thoughts. If my visions aren't nightmares but memories, then it's Maggie who's dangerous. The woman in my house, the woman who has made it her job to care for me and my baby, might be a killer. And I might be next.

I go to take another square of chocolate, but I've eaten the entire bar. I sit and twist the tin foil casing into intricate shapes. A swan, a butterfly, a worm. I don't want to go home, but I have to. I don't know what Maggie is playing at, but I need to get my keys back off her and she needs to leave my family alone, or I'll... I don't know what I'll do.

Maggie is waiting for me when I get home. The house is exactly as I left it, so I don't know what she's been doing while I've been gone or what she's been planning. But I no longer trust her.

'Did you buy food? We're out of formula,' she says like I'm a feckless husband and she's the harried wife stuck at home all day.

I completely forgot to buy anything. I've become so used to her managing everything, I can't do the simplest things anymore.

She helps me with the pushchair, taking my keys out of the lock and placing them in her pocket. The second I cross the threshold Riley wakes up screaming and reaches up for Maggie to hold him. Not me, her. Why does he like her so much? Is she a better mother than I am?

I shrug my coat off but before I have a chance to take off my shoes, Maggie has unbuckled the baby and scooped him up in her arms, cooing things in his ear to make him giggle.

'So...' I start, then tail off. I've been thinking about how I'm going to word this all the way home, how I'm going to be gentle but firm. Yet now I'm in front of her the words get stuck in my throat.

'You must be wanting to go home soon,' I say.

She turns to face me, her head tipped to one side, her lips pulled into a pout of confusion.

'What do you mean? I *am* home.'

My heart is hammering in my chest. I breathe deeply so it will slow down, so I can think straight.

'I mean back to Devon. Didn't you say you lived in Devon? With your... daughter?'

Is it my imagination or is she holding Riley tighter. I want to snatch him out of her arms, to hit her head repeatedly against the wall, to drag her out of my home by her perfectly coiffed hair. But I've seen what Maggie is capable of. I've seen that dead look behind her eyes.

'My family no longer needs me,' she says. 'There's no rush to go back.'

No mention of her child.

'What about work?' I ask. 'Doesn't the hospital need you back?'

'Hospital?' she says.

'You told me you're a nurse.'

She gives a light titter. 'Whatever gave you that idea? Me, a nurse?' She laughs louder. 'No, I'm self-employed. I'm an artist. I paint pictures of the sea. There's no rush for me to go back.'

'What about your husband?' I stammer.

I don't know this woman. I've let her into my home, my life, my *family*, and I don't know her. Everything she has told me is a lie. I force myself to keep breathing, even though my throat has closed over and my head feels like it's going to fall off my shoulders. She wheels around, my son still clamped firmly against her chest. 'You're asking a lot of questions, Lu. Why all the questions?'

I want to rip my boy out of her arms, but I have to play it carefully. I can't anger her. I've seen what she does when she's angry. And I've seen how she comes back after she's been told to leave.

'I thought maybe your husband might be missing you,' I say.

She rolls her eyes. 'Ex-husband. He disappeared.'

Disappeared?

She tilts her head at me, like a little curious dog. 'Oh, don't look at me like that, Lu. Men disappear all the time. They can't hack being parents or partners or responsible members of society. Look at your Tony. He doesn't care about you or your son. He's simply vanished into thin air, like the selfish bastard he is.'

People don't vanish. They leave or they die, but they don't 'disappear'. Whether Tony has left me or something terrible has happened to him, either way I'm alone. I bite my lips together to stop the tears from falling. I need him. I need him right now more than ever.

'I can't do this anymore,' I say, my voice thin and shaky, my chin trembling. 'I think it's best if you leave.'

Maggie gives me a long and steady look. 'Leave?'

I nod and she laughs.

'I don't think so. You're tired, my love. You're not speaking any sense.'

She's wrong. This is the clearest I've been able to think for a long time.

'Please,' I say, holding my hands out for Riley. She steps back, twisting her body so I can't reach him.

'Why don't you rest?' she says. 'All this stress isn't good for the baby. Would you like a cup of tea?'

Tea, tea, tea. She's always making tea. I don't want any of her fucking tea. Then everything starts to slow down, every tiny piece of the puzzle going from a blur to something solid like snow settling on a rooftop. Is that why I'm so tired all the time? Has Maggie been drugging me? Sandwiches, pasta, so much tea! A surge of electricity shoots through me and I make a lunge for Riley, pulling him into my arms. I do it so quickly Maggie doesn't have time to react.

I hold him to me tightly, breathe him in, ground myself as

my legs threaten to crumble beneath me. My baby. Both my babies are safe now, and I have to keep it that way. Riley laughs, thinking it's all a game.

'Get out of my house,' I say calmly, not wanting to shout and scare the baby.

Maggie shakes her head, her perfect blonde hair moving as one. Slowly, her face as blank as a mask, she leans past me and locks the front door with her key then places it in the pocket of her trousers along with mine. I forgot she'd taken my keys until I hear the two of them clink together.

'I think it's best if we all stay at home today,' she says. 'Too many busybody neighbours sticking their noses into our business.'

I back away from her until I find myself in the living room.

'What do you want?' I say, a sob escaping my throat. I hold Riley to me tighter. He's stilled, sensing my fear.

'I'm just looking after you both,' Maggie says. 'Somebody has to. Your community doesn't care, the father of your child doesn't care, even your family judges you. But not me. I'm the only one who's been beside you during everything.'

'No,' I say, although no sound escapes my lips. 'They *do* care. Tony loves me. My brother and my parents love me.'

She's still shaking her head slowly as she cups my face with her cold hands, holding me in place. Her fingers are strong, her grasp tight. Hands that could kill.

'You're safe now,' she says, pressing her soft lips against my cheek. 'Safe and sound.'

FORTY-ONE

I need to call the police, but even if I could I'm not sure what I'd say to them. Everything would sound ridiculous or get me into further trouble. What would I tell them?

My helpful neighbour is becoming obsessed with me?

My new friend won't tell me what happened to my partner or my sister-in-law?

I might have killed a man.

There's nothing I can say that makes sense. Nothing I can tell them which won't get me in even more trouble than it will Maggie. I place my hand on my belly. I can't go to the police.

'I'm going to put Riley down for his nap,' Maggie says, lifting him out of his playpen, and I nod in agreement because all my words have left me.

She leaves the room and I turn the TV off so I can think. I know she wouldn't hurt him. Would she? I want to chase after her, stay where I can see my boy at all times, but I need her out of the room so I can do something to get us out of here. I find Tony's laptop under the sofa cushion and open it, listening out constantly for the slightest sound upstairs. I place the cursor over the Google search bar, but I don't know what to type. What do I need? What's the next step? I'm frozen, staring at an empty screen, when I hear Maggie re-enter the living room. I'm not fast enough.

'What are you doing?' she asks.

I snap the laptop shut. 'Nothing.'

'People are going to start getting suspicious about us.'

'What people?'

She sits beside me, squeezing me between herself and the armrest of the sofa.

'Your family. The neighbours. When they realise Tony has left you and I'm here, they're going to start asking questions. Even Jim has been asking what I do here, with you, all day.'

She's lying. Jim has always acted surprised that I know Maggie. She doesn't tell her brother anything.

'We've done nothing wrong,' I mumble.

She takes my hand in both of hers, transferring it on to her lap, stroking my fingers as she speaks.

'I know. You and I, all we've done is be good mothers. We've cleaned and cooked and cared for the babies and one another. This is how it was always meant to be, you know. The men out there, making the money, and us... a tribe of women... caring for one another. It takes a village,' she says. 'Or, in this case, one very helpful friend.'

That's not true! My dream isn't to be stuck at home all day and I never wanted Tony for his money, I wanted him because I loved him. *Love* him. Her hands are warm and dry even though my own is growing clammy in hers. I try to move but her grip tightens. My heart is beating so fast and my mouth is so dry. And she can feel it, my fear; she knows I want to run and it's making her angry. Whatever I do I can't make her angry.

'We need to go,' she says.

Go? I turn to face her. She keeps her left hand in mine while using the other to tuck a stray strand of hair behind my ear.

'I have your car keys,' she says, stroking the side of my face. 'We should get out of here. Just you and me, and the babies. I have a cottage in Mousehole. Right by the sea. No one will find us there.'

What's she talking about? Wait, I've heard of that place. I watched a cookery show set there a few days ago. A man was making seafood dishes outside a little cottage by the sea on the Cornish coast. I remember saying to Maggie how cute the name was and how idyllic it all looked. She's lying. She lives in Devon – why would she have a second home nearby?

I'm trembling, my veins running with ice. Can she see I'm shaking? I grit my teeth and try to steady myself. I need to get my car keys off her. I don't know why it didn't occur to me sooner. I can drive to my brother's house in Liverpool. I know where he lives, vaguely. Even without my phone or GPS I can get there. It's six hours away. My brother always boasts he can do it in five if he leaves the house early enough. I could sneak out tonight. As soon as Maggie leaves, I'll pack a bag and leave quietly, and when I get there, I'll tell my brother that I need his help. He'll ask about Kayla, and I'll tell him the truth. I'll tell him Maggie hurt her because I'm sure she did. She must have. Because I know it wasn't me. I wouldn't do that. I wouldn't.

Another trickle of cold washes over me from the crown of my head, over my shoulders, right down to my feet. I suppress a shudder as Maggie keeps chattering on excitedly.

'This is going to be glorious,' she says, booping me on the nose with one finger. 'We can plan our trip now while Riley's sleeping, then this evening I'll make us all a special dinner and we'll pack. Probably best that we leave before dawn, so no one sees us. I'm sure that won't be a problem for you, Lulu. It's not as if you sleep much anyway.'

Lulu. That's what my brother calls me. Not Maggie. Maggie isn't allowed to call me that. I stand up, snatching my hand out of her firm grasp.

'I'm not going anywhere with you,' I growl.

I don't recognise this voice; it's not one I've used before. But she doesn't react. As usual Maggie stays poised, graceful, elegant, a picture of the perfect woman.

'Come, now. No need to overreact. You'll be fine. I'll look after you.'

I'm so cold. Is the heating on? Maybe she turned it off. I rub my arm through my jumper, my skin prickling like the flesh of a plucked chicken.

'I don't want you looking after me,' I say.

'You're struggling, Lulu,' she says, trying to take my hand again.

'No, I'm not!' I shout. 'I can do this. I can look after myself and my babies. I don't need you!'

Maggie stands up and I flinch. I always forget she's taller than me.

'Let me make you a cup of tea.'

'I don't want another one of your fucking cups of fucking tea!' I scream, pushing her off me. 'I want you to leave us alone.'

She stumbles but stays on her feet.

'You're tired,' she says, smoothing down her hair. 'You don't know what you're saying.'

'You're a liar. You lie about everything, and I think you've been hurting me.'

Her eyes widen and she reaches out to touch me, but I slap her hand away.

'I would never—'

'You have! Every time you're here, and I eat or drink something you've made me, I'm suddenly exhausted. And then I fall asleep and when I wake up you've done everything around the house, you've turned my own child against me, you've taken over my life, and now you want my other baby. I know you do. You're going to kill me like you did all the others. You won't even tell me where Tony and Kayla are. I don't know what's happening. I don't understand anything, and nothing makes sense, and...'

I'm crying huge, wracking sobs, my throat tight, a silent wail erupting out of my open mouth as I double over grasping my stomach. It hurts. All of this hurts so much, and I'm not entirely sure that I'm even here. Inside my body. Pinned down. For a moment I can see myself and Maggie, as if my back is flat against the ceiling. I see myself crouched into a ball of crumpled clothes and greasy hair and Maggie looming over me – beautiful, pristine Maggie, who has been so kind and gentle and supportive.

I don't know what to believe anymore. Perhaps *I'm* the evil one. Perhaps it's me my children should be scared of, and it's Maggie who is keeping us all safe. And I can't run from this nightmare because I can't escape myself.

She's holding me now, rocking me as I wail into her shoulder. I want it all to stop. I want Tony back, and I want my mum and dad and brother, and I want someone to tell me everything is going to be OK.

'It's going to be OK,' she says, her words smooth in my ear. 'I love you, but I will destroy you if you defy me, Lulu.' She smells so clean and light. I let her hold me to her, rocking me, making soothing noises into my lank hair. 'You're dangerous,' she says to me. 'You're an unfit mother, but I can keep you safe. I can stop you doing anything bad. Do as I say, or you will never get to hold your babies again. Do you understand?'

I nod and shake my head, and she holds me tight, my chest so raw from the pain of crying I can practically hear my ribs cracking. Maggie is all I have. Maggie is keeping me from harm. Maggie is the cage in which my monster must live.

FORTY-TWO

The milky winter light turns to a purple haze and all I've done is sit on the sofa and stare at the TV on mute. The shadows on the wall shift and play as day turns to night but I don't move. If this was a movie, I'd be a still character in the foreground as everything whizzes by me. A solitary figure, a statue, rooted in one place as my baby toddles up and down, playing, crying, sitting, running. Maggie tending to him and cooking and cleaning and wiping, life in perpetual motion like a spinning wheel with me as the stationary hub.

'I found this suitcase,' Maggie is saying, her voice blending with the howl of the wind outside and the whir of Riley's toys and the roar of the kettle.

She comes and goes, showing me clothes and telling me she'll pack the nappies and bottles in the baby bag and take a pack of nappies separately because they take up too much space in the suitcase. I don't even nod. I can't. Maybe if I stay still and silent enough, time will start to slow and maybe it will go backwards and backwards until it's only me and Tony and Riley, and I can admit I'm struggling. Tell him that I can't do it all by myself. That I need help.

Maggie is grinning, her blood-red lipstick-slick lips like a wound that refuses to heal. Riley is picking up on her energy, clapping his hands and screeching, aware that something exciting is happening. He only has eyes for her as she dashes up and down the stairs, rifling through my belongings as if they were her own, deciding what to take and what to leave behind the way she decides who stays in my life and who doesn't.

Move, Lu! I'm screaming inside my head. *Get out!*

But I'm not listening. I'm numb. I'm no longer here.

'I'll need to go back to Jim's to get my belongings,' Maggie says.

I look up.

'What did you say to him?' I ask. My tongue sits like a wet fish in my mouth, too big, too heavy. The words sound slurred and thick.

'I told him it was time for me to go home. He's better now. You're both better.'

'I'm not better. Everything you have done has made me worse.'

She doesn't answer me, scooping and rising as she clears the toys from the floor and folds up the highchair. Riley has had his dinner. Is it that late already? Have I eaten? I don't think so. My mouth is dry. I need to stand up. If I stand up, I can walk to the kitchen and get water. And if I can manage that, then maybe I can do more.

Maggie is upstairs so I get up slowly, my head too heavy for my shoulders, my fingers numb. I stagger to the kitchen, holding my stomach. My poor babies, having a mother like me. They deserve better.

I glance behind me as I turn on the tap, waiting for Maggie to appear. To shout at me. To knock the mug from my hand. Nothing.

As the cold liquid settles in my stomach, my head starts to clear. I glance out of the kitchen window at the street outside, pools of amber spotlights dotting the damp pavement. They've fixed the streetlamps. All is quiet outside.

Kayla's car is still parked a few doors down. Of course it is, because Kayla is no longer here to drive it. I don't know where she is. If I harmed her, then where is the body? Is there a body in my garden or in the wasteland beyond? Are there two?

My heart starts to race again, and I don't realise why until I'm searching through my kitchen drawers and looking inside old carrier bags. Maggie has my car keys but what about Kayla's? She put them in her handbag. I remember her handbag. It was red. I took her coat and her bag into the kitchen. Does Maggie know that? Is Kayla's bag buried with her body?

Escaping in Kayla's car isn't ideal, it has no car seat, but Riley is big enough to sit up. When Maggie goes next door to get her things, I will use the suitcase like a booster seat in the front and put a seatbelt on Riley. It's not legal and maybe not safe but if the police stop me, I will tell them we're running for our lives. Surely that's OK? Surely a pregnant woman being imprisoned by a crazy woman won't get in trouble for not having a car seat for her toddler. I don't know. All I do know is that I need to get as much distance as possible between us and Maggie.

At least I have a plan now. That's a good plan.

'Everything OK?' Maggie asks, appearing behind me. She slips her arms around my waist, her hands resting on my bump, her words hot on the back of my neck. 'You're getting bigger.'

I don't move. I don't even breathe.

'Don't you have to go?' I ask.

'It's Riley's bedtime,' she says, her hands moving in slow circles over my stomach. The baby likes it. I don't want the baby to like it.

'I'll put my son to bed,' I say.

She hums in my ear, and I close my eyes. I need to stay focused. I need to stay present.

'Get your clothes from your brother's,' I say, placing my

hand over hers. 'The sooner you say goodbye to Jim, the sooner we can leave.'

'We're really doing this?' she says.

She can't see me close my eyes and hold my breath. She doesn't know I'm counting the seconds until she lets me go.

'Yes,' I say. 'First thing in the morning we'll leave.'

Her hold on me tightens. 'Everything will be so much easier when we get to my little cottage,' she says. 'You'll see.'

I stay in the kitchen, facing the window, as she lets me go and silently leaves the house. I don't hear the door open, but I do see her pass the window as she heads next door to her brother's house. The door is unlocked. I'm finally alone. The adrenaline hits and I burst into action.

FORTY-THREE

I run into the living room and scoop Riley up.

'I know you're tired, sweetheart,' I say, holding him close and breathing him in. 'But we need to get out of here.'

His pushchair is folded up in the hallway. With one hand I set it up and place him in it. He arches his back, making his body straight as a board, screaming in protest. Of course he doesn't want to get in the pushchair, it's his bedtime. He wants to watch *In the Night Garden* and have his bottle of milk and go to sleep.

'Not now,' I whisper. 'Please, just get in. For Mummy. Please.'

I manage to buckle him in then I race upstairs, grabbing what I can in the darkness. Two blankets, his coat, a change of clothes, his nappy bag. There are already three empty bottles inside the bag and two cartons of baby milk. I bring it all downstairs, where Riley is still straining at the straps of his pushchair.

I find a dummy in the bag and pop it into his mouth. It calms him enough for me to get his coat and shoes on, pushing the blanket around his legs. I have a woollen hat for us both, but I know he won't keep his on. This is taking too long!

I push my trainers on and grab my coat, putting my purse into my pocket. Maggie has had to use my keys to unlock the door and she's left them in there. My heart skips a beat and I grab them too, putting them in my pocket along with my purse. I haven't got time to look for Kayla's car keys now. If her handbag was still in my house, I'd have seen it by now. I can't take her car, which means I can't drive to my brother's... My only choice is to run.

Do I have everything? I can't think. I have food and snacks for the baby, and clothes and nappies. But what about me? What do I need? I glance at the clock. This has taken ten minutes already. Maggie isn't going to take long to get her things together. I haven't got the luxury of time right now. As long as Riley has everything he needs I'll be OK.

I open the door quietly and slowly, peering around the corner. The wind outside is icy, the street grey and empty. People's houses are decorated with lights, trees shining in the windows. How many days until Christmas? My coat isn't warm enough, but I don't have time to think about that either. I need to get some distance between me and Maggie and *then* I can think. Quietly I shut the front door behind me, and I run. Then I stop. Where am I going?

All the houses in the street have their lights on. A row of burning squares, some stripy with blinds and others framed by curtains, all of them warm and inviting. One window has the silhouette of a woman cut out of the light. She disappears and the door opens. It's Shona.

'You all right, hun?' she calls out as I cross the road.

I glance behind me. Riley is crying, his dummy lost to the dark. He's pulling at the straps of the pushchair, bucking against his constraints. He's tired. He wants his milk.

'I need to get out of here,' I say.

My cheeks are numb with cold, my tears leaving scalding tracks as they fall. I didn't mean to cry. I thought I was managing well, all that adrenaline bursting through me long enough to get everything and get out. But now the biting wind and the reality of what I'm doing are pushing me back, clearing my head, reminding me that I made a mistake. I'm not safe out here, in the open, with other people. Maggie's right. I'm useless and dangerous. No one really cares about me, no one understands, only her. Maybe I should go back.

I glance over my shoulder again, batting at my eyes with the back of my bare hand that's dry and raw from the sting of the wind. I should have grabbed my gloves. I didn't even pack any spare clothes for myself. It's too late now.

Shona is looking back at my house, the only unlit one in the street. The only house not decorated for the festive season. Can she see something I can't?

'Is it your other half?' she asks quietly. 'Are you in danger?'

Yes. I'm in danger.

'She's going to hurt me,' I say. 'She wants my babies.'

'Who, hun? Who wants your babies?'

Shona's door is open, and three teenagers and a man are peering out at us. She's somehow already got me and Riley into her front garden, inching me up the path.

'Get inside,' she's saying. 'It's too cold out here.'

A girl, maybe fourteen, maybe eighteen, has opened the door wider and Shona is manoeuvring Riley's pushchair inside. The heat of her home hits me while I'm still standing on her path, a moth before a flame, the warmth seeping into me like a hot bath. Their tree is decorated in reds and golds, little tartan ribbons tied to the boughs. I don't have a tree. Why didn't I think to buy a tree? Her house smells of comfort food. Roast chicken and something sweet. Is it Sunday today? I don't want to interrupt their dinner.

'Come in,' the man is saying. He's smiling at me, that hesitant smile you give to a stranger who's acting strange.

I hear the door click behind me and I'm inside, although I

don't remember walking through her door. Shona is talking to me but I'm still looking over my shoulder even though there's no window behind me, just a wall. Maggie will find us here. We're not safe until we get far from this street, or London, or the country.

'Do you need me to call anyone?' Shona is saying.

I shake my head.

'Do you want a drink? Tea or something stronger? I have some... oh.'

She's seen my stomach. I should have put a jumper on, but I was rushing. I'm wearing leggings and a tight t-shirt that never used to be tight, but it is now. It's really hot in her house. I could take my coat off but then I'll have to sit down, and if I sit down, I won't be able to keep running.

'We can't stay,' I say. 'She's going to get us.'

'She?' Shona is saying. 'Who's after you, Lu?'

They must know. Her and Beth. They're always in their front gardens chatting, they must have seen Maggie going in and out of my house. Shona must know.

'Maggie,' I say.

She gives me a strange look.

'The neighbour,' I add. 'She's going to hurt me.'

'Jim's sister?'

Shona's husband is by her side now. I don't think he's worried about what I'm saying, I think he's there to make sure his wife is safe. He knows. He can tell by looking at me that I'm not a good person. It's not *my* safety that concerns them, it's *theirs*.

Shona's kids are making Riley laugh and he's babbling back at them like he has so much to say. What would he tell them about his mama if he could talk? Would he admit that I'm a killer?

He's drinking his milk now – they must have found it in the bag – and I'm holding a mug. It has a picture of a snowman on it. I don't remember accepting a cup of tea. Their house is laid out differently to mine, but I can see a table in the living room with plates on it. The plates still have food on them. I've interrupted their dinner.

'I better go,' I say, reaching behind me, my hand finding the door handle.

Shona is saying something, but her voice is far away, and I can't make out the words. All I can hear is the buzzing in my head. If I open this door Maggie might be waiting on the other side, ready to tell Shona and her lovely family everything about me, about how dangerous I am and how I hurt innocent people. They'll tell the police I turned up out of the blue acting strange, desperate, totally mental.

Take her babies, Shona will tell them.

She doesn't deserve to be a mother, Maggie will agree.

Because I'm nothing like Shona and her lovely family and their wholesome roast dinner together in the warm rosy light of a winter's evening. Safe. Happy. Together. I bet Shona has never wanted to hurt her husband. She knows she's blessed.

'I have to go,' I say again, pulling open the door, grabbing the pushchair and scrambling out into the bitter cold.

Shona tries to say something but it's too late, I'm already running. I run through her open gate and down the street and on to the main road, the pushchair clattering along the cracked paving slabs. I turn right, along the thick hedges that hide me from view, and the broken lamp posts, and the cars that never move because they have wheels missing. I don't feel my feet hit the hard ground and I don't hear anything but the soft thud of my heart as I run and run, my tits heavy and full, my stomach hard and aching, and my throat dry and sore.

The shops in the high street are all shut. There are bars and restaurants, breathing out short puffs of warmth as their doors open and close, laughter trickling out, couples hand in hand getting into the festive spirit. But no one stops the mum rushing down the high street with nowhere to go, her pushchair whooshing along the wet pavement as she runs, glancing behind her with every stride.

I don't stop until I find myself outside the park where I take Riley to feed the ducks. He's quiet now, probably from the bumpy ride and the cold night air.

'Ducks are all sleeping now,' I say into the wind as I enter the park. Maggie won't find me here, it's too large and too dark. I hide behind the hedge and get my breath back, thinking about what to do next.

Maybe Maggie will leave for her cottage without us. Maybe if I go back in a few hours my house will be empty and I can change the locks and we'll be safe again. Then I can think about Tony and Kayla and I'll remember what really happened.

As my heart rate and breathing slow back to normal, a shooting pain hits my side, making me double over. I grasp the handles of the pushchair for support, nearly tipping the baby backwards. It's only a stitch, I tell myself. I'm not fit like Tony; I'm not used to running such distances.

'Mummy needs to sit down,' I say, yawning and staggering in the direction of the large pond. My phone is in that water, somewhere beneath the duckweed and mud. I wonder how many missed calls I have. How many angry messages from those who supposedly love me.

I find a bench and sit down, wincing at the stabbing pains in my abdomen. If I stay here and rest for a few minutes, I'll be OK. I take the second blanket from under the pushchair and place it over me. It's a baby blanket, it's not big enough to cover me, but it's soft against my face as I hold it up to my cheek and breathe in the scent of talcum powder and washing detergent.

I yawn again and rub my eyes. I was awake so early this morning. I haven't done my sleep maths in a long time, but it doesn't matter anymore. I've not been sleeping – I've been drugged. Riley is quiet. Finally asleep. I lay my head against the grainy wood of the bench and rub the wool of the blanket against my face. I'm just resting my eyes. Just for a little bit. I'm going to need my energy tonight if I'm going to somehow get away from all of this and keep us safe.

As I drift between consciousness and the insistent pull of sleep, a million different scenarios flicker though my mind like a kaleidoscope. I don't have a car but maybe I can catch the Tube to King's Cross and get to my brother's house from there. I'm certain that's where I caught the train from once. I can't call him, but surely the trains run until midnight. I'll head that way in a minute. I'll calm down and have a little rest and then we'll go.

I close my eyes and think about trains and timetables and how many days are left until Christmas and my mother and my brother and Tony and Kayla and all the things I've done that maybe I didn't do until eventually everything grows heavy. Dark. Quiet.

FORTY-FOUR

I wake up with a start, my vision struggling to adjust to the pitch black of night. I'm not in my bed or on the sofa.

My cheeks are pinched tight with cold, and my hair is snagging on a hard surface. Damp splintered wood. There's the soft lap of water nearby, something rustling, the honk of a duck. I'm outside. What am I doing outside?

It takes a moment for me to remember Maggie and the suitcase and Shona and running. I fell asleep. I'm still holding on to Riley's pushchair and I rock it back and forth instinctively as I sit up and move my neck side to side. I need to find out what the time is and head to the station. It doesn't matter that I can't call Dan – I have my bank card so I can just go, even if I have to wait in the station until the first train tomorrow. At least Maggie won't find us there.

Riley's blanket is on the ground, glowing white, its snowy-soft corner in a puddle. I pick it up and shake it out. He needs it. He's probably cold with only one blanket. We have to get going.

I turn the pushchair around to face me. It feels lighter than normal. I place the blanket over my baby but there are no legs dangling beneath it. Nothing solid to cover. I stare at an empty space.

Riley?

The pushchair is empty.

Riley isn't there.

At first, I do nothing. I can't process what I'm looking at. The pushchair is empty, and my baby is gone. He can't have got out of it by himself, I know that. I cognitively know that a nearly-one-year-old can't unclip buggy straps. They are specifically made to stop babies from doing that. Yet I'm still on my feet crying out his name. I'm running behind bushes, ripping at the foliage, falling to my knees, my leggings soaking up the same mud that's now caked beneath my fingernails.

'Riley?' I'm screaming. 'Riley!'

I look at the pond. Did he go in it? How long was I sleeping for? He could have got out hours ago. Anything can happen to a baby in that time, all sorts of dreadful accidents: wild animals, falling into a ditch, getting run over, drowning.

If he's in the water, I need to wade in. I don't care that it's cold, that the edges are white with thin crystals of ice. I'll throw myself in. I'll die before he ever does.

Then I notice the nappy bag has gone. My baby didn't get out on his own, he was taken… and I know who has him.

FORTY-FIVE

I'm running again. I'm running so hard I don't think about the pushchair or the blanket or my hat. I left them all behind in the park. All I can think about is my son.

The twigs of the hedges lining the street catch on my coat, scratching my hands and face as I scramble on to the main road and keep running. I don't know what time it is; it could be eight o'clock in the evening, it could be three in the morning. It's not until I near the high street that I see the restaurants and pubs are still open so it can't be that late. I slow down, resting my hands on my knees, my stomach pressing against my thighs. Lungs burning, hands cold with sweat, I push my hair away from my face and take a large gulp of freezing air that makes me choke.

Maggie. Maggie has my baby. She's the only one I can think of who would follow me and take him. Has she left for Cornwall already? Has she kidnapped him? So many questions run through my mind, like why did she take the nappy bag but not the whole pushchair? Was it so as not to wake me up?

A door opens beside me, and the light bathes me in orange. I look up. I'm outside the church, the same community centre where I first took Riley before Maggie became a permanent fixture in my home. There's a sign on the door – 'Eating Disorder Support Group. Tonight, 8.30pm.'

Banging and scraping sounds are coming from the hall and I peer inside. There are no rubber mats on the ground this time, no toys and plastic slides scattered around. This time there's a table pushed along one wall with leaflets and orange juice, and a pile of chairs that are being unfolded and arranged into a circle.

'Lu?'

A woman is walking towards me. Everything is hazy, my breaths are still coming in rasps. I squint as she nears me. It's Daisy. Skinny, perfect Daisy with the cute daughter and the helpful husband. Boring, tedious Daisy with her spindly pale arms and neck that could snap like a twig. Perhaps life isn't so easy for her after all. We all crack and splinter in our own special ways. Her delicate porcelain hand is on my arm and she's looking at me with wide eyes.

'Are you OK?'

I look at my own hands. They're caked in mud and bleeding, but only a little. Light scratches like claw marks criss-cross my skin where brambles grasped at me as I hunted for my son through bushes I couldn't see inside. My face stings but I don't know if that's from more scratches or from rubbing at my teary face.

I shake my head. 'I'm not OK.'

Daisy goes to hug me, but I step back. 'I'm looking for my son.' I sound like a robot. Like I'm drunk. Like I'm losing my mind.

'Riley?'

She thinks I'm crazy. Why would I be looking for a baby at a church hall at night? I scan the hall but it's just her and a man I don't know and nowhere for anyone to hide. Did Maggie run past the church with my son? No one would think that was strange, a woman holding a sleepy baby in her arms at eight thirty at night.

'My friend Maggie was taking him home and I've lost them,' I say with a laugh. It's a pathetic laugh that's fooling no one. 'It's late and past his bedtime. Ha ha.' I actually say the words 'ha ha'. 'You know Maggie. She's the one you saw in the supermarket the other day.'

Daisy shakes her head. She has no idea who I'm talking about.

'Are you OK?' she says again. Maybe it's her who's the robot, but I'm no longer looking at her. I'm peering over my shoulder at the exit. I have to find my boy. 'Only, the last time I saw you here you didn't say hello.'

What's Daisy talking about? I haven't been back to this playgroup since she told me she never gets angry. I can't think straight. I don't know. 'My friend and I look the same,' I babble. 'Same hair. Sorry. I have to find her.'

Daisy is still talking when I run out of the hall and back into the freezing black air. I attempt to run, although my stomach is aching so it's more of a stagger. My chest is full of spiky things and my teeth are aching from the cold air and exertion, but my road is just up ahead. I turn into it and my stomach somersaults when the first thing I see is my parked car then Kayla's. Oh, thank God. Maggie and Riley are still here.

As I approach Shona's house, I turn my head and cross the road. She already thinks I've lost my mind – I can't let her see me returning without the pushchair. Without my son! What would she do if she knew I'd taken my baby to the park at night and he's now missing? She'd call the police. She'd have me sectioned.

I speed up as I near my house, my trainers silent against the wet pavement, my hips aching from running. All the lights are out but that doesn't mean Maggie isn't inside.

My fingers are so cold it takes forever to get my key out of my pocket and into the lock.

'Maggie!' I'm screaming before the door is fully open.

She's not in the kitchen or the living room. Everything looks the same: the suitcase open on the sofa with my clothes spilling out of it, Riley's extra pack of nappies and my passport and paperwork in a neat pile beside them. Nothing of Maggie's is here. Now I think of it, I've never seen any of her belongings in my house. I look upstairs. All the doors are shut, and the curtains drawn. Nothing. No Maggie... and no Riley.

I race downstairs, grasping the banisters, my muddy shoes leaving marks on the carpet runners. The front door is still ajar, and I look outside. Jim's house is all lit up. That's where she is!

I bang on his door, not bothering with the doorbell. I'm already shouting her name before he has a chance to open the door fully.

'Where's Maggie?'

He stares at me with incomprehension, his eyes screwed up as if the sun is shining. He strokes his beard. It looks freshly trimmed.

'Are you OK, Lu?' he asks, looking behind me and around me. He's searching for my pushchair, my main accessory, because I never go anywhere without it. Shit, the pushchair. I bet someone has stolen it already.

'No, I'm not OK, Jim!' I shout. 'I'm far from fucking OK. Where's your sister?'

He's blocking my entrance, his door only partially open. Maybe he knows what's going on. Maybe he's in on it all.

'Where's Maggie!' I scream again, pushing his door open and running past him. He's too stunned to stop me and I'm in his house before he has a chance to say anything. The layout of his home is the same as mine, which makes it easier for me to run from room to room. But they are all empty. I've never been here before and it's not what I expected. I thought Jim would have one of those bland brown bachelor houses, where everything is made of wood with maybe a dartboard on the wall or a display of novelty beer tankards on a shelf. But it's not like that. It's very white, the surfaces all clear, and there are pink roses in a vase on the table. Maggie must have bought them. I wonder if Jim ever had a wife. Or a family.

'What the hell is going on?' he roars, bursting into the living room, where I've finally ground to a halt.

The hallway was dark, but here in the living room all the lights are shining and he even has a small tree in the corner draped with fairy lights. At the sight of my face, Jim gasps and recoils.

'What happened to you?'

Must be the mud and the wet leggings and the scratches. I touch my cheek. It stings. My fingers come away red with blood.

'She has my son!' I shout. 'Your sister has taken my baby.'

Jim is shaking his head like I'm talking in a foreign language. Why isn't he moving? Why isn't he saying anything?

'Jim! Tell me what's going on!'

He furrows his brow, his mouth hanging half open as if there's so much he wants to say but no words are coming out.

'Maggie isn't here,' he says eventually. He looks scared. What's he hiding?

'I know she's not here, Jim. I can see that!' My voice is too loud and I'm too dishevelled to be standing in this spotless living room, getting mud and grass on his clean floors, my shrill voice reverberating off the white walls. 'Where is your sister? Where has she taken my son? Don't make me call the police.'

My throat is tightening up and I have to squeeze the last sentence out. I don't want to call the police. I don't even know where I'd start.

'Lu. Believe me. Maggie doesn't have your baby. We need to get you help.'

'Yes! I need help... *looking for my son!*'

Thick, hot tears are running down my face, making my skin sting even more. I run my hand through my hair, my fingers picking out small leaves and a wiry twig. Why is Jim not doing anything? Why is he not taking me seriously? He's holding a mug out at me.

'I put some brandy in there. Warm you up.'

Coffee? Why does everyone keep making me hot fucking drinks? I want to throw it in his face, watch the boiling water turn his skin bright red, smash the ceramic mug and slash his face with it.

Jim puts the mug on the table when it's clear I'm not going to take it off him.

'Maggie is in Lanzarote,' he says.

It's such a strange statement that all the terrible thoughts racing through my mind grind to a sudden stop and I'm dragged to the present. Am I hearing him properly? I left my house an hour ago. My car is still here. Riley has no passport. There's no way she's gone abroad with him.

Jim keeps talking. 'Look at me, Lu. Look at me. My sister, Maggie, left my house exactly one month ago.'

'No.' I'm shaking my head in tiny motions. 'That's not true. I was with her today.'

He takes his phone out of his jean pocket and taps at it. He shows me a Facebook page with Maggie's face all lit up. She's in a swimming costume on a beach with a bald man on one side and a young woman on the other. Maggie's hair is brown in this photo.

'See?' Jim says.

'Why are you showing me an old holiday snap?' I spit. 'I don't have time for this. This is serious!'

'Look at the date, love. It was taken two days ago. She left here the morning after she helped you when you got locked out. Remember? The twelfth of November. Today is the twelfth of December. She's not been back since. But I figured you knew that seeing as you said the two of you had got close and been chatting.'

I can't stop staring at the photo and the date above it. In the photo Maggie has brown hair. And she's abroad. I don't think Jim is lying, but I don't understand. The photo is real, but that doesn't make sense. If Maggie hasn't been here, then who has been in my house every day? And who the hell has my child?

FORTY-SIX

'Maggie left the day Dave was discovered dead?' I hear myself ask.

I'm holding Jim's phone and scrolling through his sister's Facebook photos. Maggie with brown hair at a beach bar, a bright orange drink in her hand. Maggie sitting on the edge of a pool with the bald man, his nose red from the sun. Maggie in a flowing red dress wearing chunky wooden jewellery and no make-up. That's not how Maggie dresses. Maggie would never wear anything bright and baggy and hippy.

'That's right. She left that morning, when all the commotion was happening. You don't remember? I do because she had to pick her way around all the police vans and yellow tape, and they asked for her phone number so they could take a statement. That's why I remember the date because the police kept mentioning 'the night of the eleventh'. She had to get back to Devon, back to Andy and Hannah because they had their Lanzarote holiday booked the following week. They always like to have a long sunny break before Christmas.'

His words are washing over me but none of them are sinking in.

'Her hair.'

'Oh, yeah. I know. She dyed it before her holiday. She reckons it makes her look younger and more sophisticated,' Jim replies. He hesitates for a moment. 'I can call her if you like, you can talk to her yourself.'

I nod dumbly and he takes his phone gently out of my hand, pressing the screen before handing it back to me.

'Hiya, Jim!' Maggie exclaims before I've said a word. 'You'll never guess what Andy's doing right now. Karaoke. Bloody fool.'

It's her voice, but it's not Maggie. Not the Maggie I know.

I cut her off. 'It's not Jim. I'm using his phone. It's Lu.'

Silence.

'His neighbour,' I add.

'Oh my God, is he all right? Is my brother hurt?'

'He's fine. I was just...' What am I meant to say? This isn't Maggie. Not the real Maggie. 'Have you been helping me look after Riley?'

More silence.

'Sorry, sweetheart. I don't understand. Who's Riley?'

'My baby.' The room is undulating, like I'm inside a jellyfish.

'Oh, Lu! I remember you. Sleepwalking Lu. How are you? I heard about that business with the neighbour. Shocking. Been telling Jim to get out of London for years.'

'Sorry. I shouldn't have called,' I say. 'Enjoy your holiday.'

I hang up and stare straight ahead of me at the white wall.

'Lu!' Jim is saying, shaking my shoulders. 'Where is the baby? You're making me worried. I'm calling the police.'

'No! I'm... It's... I don't understand,' I stammer.

'Sit down. Please. You're trembling.'

He's staring at my belly as he takes his phone back. He's asking me if I want water – I guess no more brandy is on offer. He's asking if he should call Tony or a friend. He's talking about the police again. He's right, I'm shaking. My voice has gone. I no longer know what to say. Nothing makes sense.

Maybe I *should* call the police. They won't ask about the neighbour's death, or where my partner is. They'll only care about my baby, but... what do I say? I fell asleep on a park bench and woke up to find my baby missing. I don't know who's been looking after him for the last month. I've had a woman in my house obsessed with my family, but I don't know who she is or what she wants or where she's gone. Is that what I'm meant to say to them?

'And I know the Patels at number twelve said they were getting a Ring doorbell, not sure if they got one in the end though, and then Pete at number two said he might get one in the Boxing Day sales,' Jim is saying. Why are we talking about doorbells?

Jim is shimmering, his outline blurry. I rub my gritty eyes, but it only makes them hurt more.

The adrenaline has started to drain from my body, making my head heavy and my guts churn. Every inch of me is growing limp and weak. I'm going to vomit, or faint. My teeth are chattering together, and I can't think straight. I don't understand what's happening. I don't know what to do.

'We have a Ring doorbell,' I manage to mumble.

'That's a good place to start,' Jim says, like this is a game. Like my missing baby is an escape room challenge. 'If you're looking for someone, you should check the app. Let me call the police and—'

I grasp his wrist.

'No. It's fine. I'm just tired and confused. My memory isn't great right now,' I say, pointing at my bump as if it's my unborn baby's fault that I'm such a terrible, neglectful, awful mother. 'I'll call Tony. I remember now... his sister said she'd babysit.'

Jim doesn't believe me, but I don't care. We have a Ring doorbell, which means I have video footage of Maggie, or whoever the hell this woman is, and even if that doesn't tell me where Riley is, I can show it to the police. Tony said he installed the app on his laptop. That's what I need to do. I need to check his laptop and collect evidence.

I stumble out of Jim's house and let myself into mine, my hands shaking so much I drop my keys three times. I can feel Jim watching me.

I get in, slam the door shut and lean against it. It's too quiet in here. Too dark. Too empty.

Tony's laptop is still on the sofa where I last left it. I sit down, not caring about my muddy clothes, and log in. I stare at the screen, but I don't know what I'm looking for. Some tabs are open: Google Maps, Facebook and Gmail. I don't remember looking at my emails. I don't even remember the password. It must be Tony's account.

I scan the desktop and there it is: a blue square with 'ring' in the middle. I click on it and a small screen appears entitled 'Front Door'. It's the view of our street. A live view. Everything is dark, a few twinkling windows in the distance. There's no movement except for an empty box from the fried chicken place blowing in the wind.

I search the menu on the left: 'History'. It's listed as 'Live View', 'Motion' and 'Accepted Ring'. It goes all the way back to when Tony installed the doorbell after the murder. Thank goodness we didn't have this the night I went sleepwalking or there would be footage of me dripping with blood on my doorstep.

I click through various dates. Tony going to work and coming home. Tony, who did nothing but work hard and love us. An Amazon delivery. A takeaway I don't remember ordering. Me leaving the house with Riley and coming back with shopping. The sight of my baby makes my breath catch but I need to keep going... I need to find footage of this woman. Whoever she is, she has my baby!

I can't remember what days are which. What I've been

doing and when. I click on 'Accepted Ring' and there's Kayla. Oh God. So she was really here, I'm not imagining it. That's definitely her car outside because she's on the video leaving it and walking up to my door. I keep clicking. The next footage is of Kayla leaving my house and walking past her car.

I rewind it and watch it again. And again. I zoom in. She's alive? My hands are sweating as I watch Kayla leave my house and make her way to the end of the street. She's not hurt. She doesn't even look angry. If Maggie didn't kill her, then maybe Tony's OK too. Relief floods through me as I click on the image again, peering closer at the screen. Where was she going and why wasn't she driving?

She's saying something. Does the Ring doorbell pick up sound? I rewind it again and turn up the volume.

'... event is a whole week. Makes no sense to drive into central London and pay for parking and the congestion charge so I'll leave it here and take a train in.'

I'm saying something but I can't hear my voice as clearly as hers. So Kayla left her car here on purpose? She left my house, with her red handbag and high heels, and she walked to the station? My ears are ringing. I feel like I've been struck by a wave, but I have to keep going. I have to clamber to the surface and keep watching this. I need to get everything straight in my head: Where did Tony go? Who is this woman? Did I leave the house with my baby, and did she come back with him? I need to know then I'll go next door and call the police. I don't care if they take me away. I don't care anymore. I just want my son back.

I keep clicking further back. There's Tony leaving the house with a bag and walking past his car, heading the same direction Kayla did. And there's no footage of him coming home. I look at the date – Sunday the third of December. Today is Tuesday the twelfth. Tony has been missing for nearly ten days, but where is he? If he didn't come home, then that means I can't have hurt him. That awful nightmare, hitting him and dragging him into my garden, none of that happened.

I burst into tears, my breaths coming in painful pulls. I may not be a killer, but my man has still left me. I want to curl up on the sofa and sob and sob until I'm wrung out, but I can't. My son is missing and whoever the hell was pretending to be Maggie has him. I need to find her!

With shaky fingers I keep sifting through the footage. Where the fuck is my Maggie in these videos? I click and click and click but still no sign of her. Why can't I see her coming and going? She was here every single day for a month. I go to the most recent day. She took Riley to the shops yesterday. I think it was yesterday, or the day before. It was the day they came back late, and I was worried. There she is! I see her. I see her blonde hair peeking out behind the huge teddy bear. I turn the volume up.

'We're back,' she's saying. 'Sorry, but Riley saw this teddy in a shop window, and I couldn't say no. Look how happy he is. Don't be such a sourpuss, Lu. It's not good for the baby.'

Except it's not her behind the bear and it's not her voice, because Maggie doesn't have blonde hair anymore. I do. I remember pulling the pushchair into the hallway and Maggie telling me all the things she'd bought, except in this video it's me pushing Riley into the house, and it's me manoeuvring the giant bear through the door, and it's me talking to no one because I'm talking to myself.

I look around me, the house silent, the giant bear in the corner glaring at me with its beady eyes. I rub my face then hold my hand over my mouth as I let out a strangled wail. That's not Maggie on the doorstep holding that teddy bear, it's me. I click and I click and it's all me in every single one of these shopping trips. It's me coming home with the baby and the bags from

Bebe Tu and other clothes shops. It's me talking to an invisible person beside me as I leave for the park. It's me standing on my doorstep, shouting at no one, then storming back inside.

All of it. Every single moment with Maggie, it was me. I have been alone all this time.

FORTY-SEVEN

I'm struggling to breathe. My mouth is open, but no air is coming in. I'm going to die. This is how I'm going to die. I clasp at the sofa, drag some air in, but it doesn't fully fill my lungs. I'm panting. Is this small amount of oxygen, lying in a thin layer above my lungs, enough to sustain me? What about my baby? Am I drowning my baby?

My hand is shaking as I re-watch every single video in the Ring app, trying to make sense of what I'm seeing. I spoke to Maggie on the phone just now and she had no idea who I was. Jim showed me photos of her looking nothing like the Maggie who has been keeping me company for the last month – the Maggie I loved and the one I'm scared of. And now I can't find evidence of her on the Ring footage, only images of a woman who looks how I remember her. Me. I wasn't resting while Maggie helped me, I was doing it all then passing out when I couldn't push myself any further. No. No, no, no. This can't be happening. I run my hands through my blonde hair and pull at it, flinching at the sharp bite of pain as I pluck out one strand then another. I need to wake up. This isn't real. It is. I'm here. This is happening. My son is missing!

I go on Facebook but all I see are more messages from my brother asking if I'm OK. He says he's been talking to Kayla. Kayla, who left her car on my street to attend a work event in town. Kayla, who isn't dead because nobody hurt her. She must have come over because she's been worried about me. And to park on my street. That's all.

I scan the rest of Facebook. I haven't posted anything, but Tony has. Tony hardly ever uses social media, but he has been this week. There are pictures of beer and sausages, and lorries, and a street covered in graffiti with pretty tables adorned with flowers outside. There are comments below the photos. Comments from me!

The photos were posted yesterday, and I replied with, 'We miss you. Glad it's all going well.'

I close my eyes and try to pull another deep breath into my lungs, but they only fill halfway. The screen is beginning to go fuzzy, doubling up, the words becoming a blur of dark stains on the screen. I look at the other tabs. Gmail. Whose Gmail have I been using?

I look at it and it's mine. I didn't know I remembered the password. There are three emails unanswered at the top. One from Dan with the subject line 'ANSWER MY FB MESSAGE AND GET A NEW PHONE FFS!' There's an email from the doctors, one from Bebe Tu announcing their pre-Christmas sale and a couple from Tony.

I click on one.

> Hey babe! I can't wait to see you both tomorrow. It's been great to meet the team in Berlin but it's been exhausting. Last day of training went well but I can't wait to get back to normal and have our first Christmas as a family. How are you feeling today? xx

I scroll up. We've been talking. For over a week Tony and I

have been talking. I close my eyes and try to remember. Hazy threads of dreams and memories float before my eyes but I can't catch them. I remember waking up wishing I could remember my password so I could email him and see if he was OK. I also remember the taste of his blood on my lips as it splattered over my face when I killed him, the crunch of his skull beneath the hammer, the marks on the floor that took so long to scrub off. I remember telling him that Riley was walking. But I also remember the look on Maggie's face as she stood on my patio, right at the back of the garden, looking up at the bedroom window. The way the light of the moon caught her face, highlighting the gap in the fence at the back that leads to wasteland and the perfect place to bury a dead body.

My emails to Tony are upbeat and positive.

> It won't stop raining but Riley and I are making the most of it. Lots of cuddles and cartoons and plenty of snacks. You should see the cute outfits I've bought him. He's growing so fast, even in the week you've been gone!

> I've made friends with the neighbours. Two of them even brought me some flowers and cake. Everyone on the street is friendly. We're counting down the days until we see you!

Who is this person? For a moment I imagine Maggie sitting on my sofa while I sleep, replying to Tony, telling him everything is going well while she plots the kidnapping of my child. Then I remember that the Maggie I know doesn't exist, I made her up. She helped me once, only once, and after that it was me. It was all me. His latest email simply reads:

> Can't wait to see you tomorrow.

I check the date on the screen again, and the time. Then I

check the email. It was sent this morning. It's now nearly ten o'clock at night. Tony is home tomorrow, and I don't know where his son is!

I stand up so fast the room starts spinning and my legs wobble and nearly give way. I hold on to the arm of the sofa and try to gather enough energy to stumble to the door. Who has my baby? How have I lost my baby?

The police. That's who I need. I can't call them without a phone, but Jim can help me. Maybe he has already called them. The police can't suspect me of anything because everyone is safe. I've done nothing wrong, and I couldn't have had anything to do with Dave's death, because I'm not evil. I know that now. I just don't know where my baby is. Oh my God, how do I tell them that without them locking me up for being crazy and neglectful?

I blink twice and I'm already at my front door. My baby. Someone has my baby.

'Please!' I'm screaming into the night, grasping the door handle to steady myself.

A pain shoots through my belly and has me doubled over. I'm trying to shout but nothing is coming out.

'Someone,' I gasp. 'Help me. Please.'

All is still and quiet outside. I see a cat in the distance, black against black, and I think of Shadow, the cat I've been feeding for weeks that no one else knows about. Does Shadow exist? If Maggie doesn't, then maybe the cat doesn't either. Or maybe they both exist, and I don't. Maybe I'm sleeping right now, or I'm dead. Maybe it's me who died and I'm watching all the different ways my life could have panned out.

There's movement in the night. It might be trees or someone leaving their house. I hear voices. I hear sirens. No, not sirens, that's me. I'm screaming. I don't know this sound I'm making but it's not human. It's the cries of an animal moments before death, of grieving women, of something feral and dark and primal.

Blue lights melt into black. I can hear hushed urgent voices. And people running. I can't let them get me. They will take my unborn baby. They already have Riley, and now they're coming for the other one. Someone is after me, they're going to get me. I don't know who or why or how but...

Everything is shifting and melting. I turn back into my house, grasping the doorframe, my voice sore and hoarse, the ground rising up to meet me. Then I'm gone.

FORTY-EIGHT

I dream of blood.

Maggie is beside me, her blonde hair matted red, her lipstick smeared across her face. She's smiling over me, her teeth sharp, her eyes colourless.

'I got what I came for,' she's saying, two bundles in her arms. Riley is balanced on her hip with his arms around her neck, and in the other arm is a baby wrapped in a yellow blanket. My arms are empty, and my bump has gone.

'My babies,' I mumble.

Maggie smiles

Riley smiles.

The baby in her arms smiles.

'Goodbye,' she says, turning on her heels and shutting the front door behind her. There's a bang and a flash of light and I sit up with a start.

'Riley?'

My son's name is always the first word at my lips.

I'm in my bed. The sheets smell clean and fresh, cool against my hot cheeks, the single bulb bright as a sun searing my eyes. We really need to buy a lampshade.

'Riley is here, darling.'

I touch my stomach. It's whole and solid and the baby gives a tiny kick that has me letting out a lungful of air. I look up, searching all the faces staring down at me, searching for Maggie. She's not here. The woman I imagined doesn't exist. She's not real. No one is taking my children from me.

'He's safe,' says the voice again.

I focus and it's my father. Beside him is my mother. In her arms is my son.

I reach out for Riley, and he clings to me, burying his head in my chest. The woman he's been calling 'Ma' was me, not Maggie. Always, and only, me.

This is a dream too, but I like this one better. The faces of my parents swim in and out and they're saying something to someone. My brother. Kayla. They are all talking over my head. So many hushed whispers.

This is what it must be like to be dead, I think.

Is this heaven or is this my last goodbye before I descend to my dark fate, a hellish world full of darkness and blood?

When I open my eyes again Riley has gone, and a cup of tea is being placed beside me. I flinch as I imagine Maggie forcing me to drink it, but the arm is hairy with a gold ring on one finger.

I blink until the image comes into focus.

'Dan?' I croak.

My brother sits beside me, making the bed sag to the side.

'You scared the shit out of us, Lulu.'

I take the tea off him and take a sip. It's not too hot and he's put extra sugar in it. He grins because he knows he's made it exactly how I like it.

'Is Riley...?'

'He's in the sitting room with Mum and Dad.' I must make a

face because he grins again. 'Oh yeah, we're all here. Do you not remember anything?'

I shake my head and take another sip of the tea. I can't tell him what I do remember because I can no longer separate dreams from illusions from reality. It wasn't that long ago that I 'remembered' killing his wife, but I can hear her voice and Mum's too, so I know Kayla's not buried beneath my patio. A wave of scarlet shame floods my cheek and I keep sipping the tea, wondering at what point all these pieces will start to slot together and make sense.

A milky light is bathing my bedroom in light shadows. It could be early morning or early evening. But what day, I don't know.

'How long have I been asleep?' I ask.

'Fifteen hours.'

I sit up straighter, trying to do the maths.

'It's three in the afternoon. We found you last night on your hallway floor, at eleven o'clock at night. You'd passed out and were delirious. You seriously don't remember?'

It's like unpicking a pile of necklaces that have got knotted. As I pull one shiny strand another tangles. I know the last time I saw Dan was when we had that stupidly expensive dinner together, and I'm quite certain Maggie helped me the night our neighbour was killed, and Tony has been away with work for some time. Anything else is a jumble of *Sliding Doors* moments, any version of which I could easily believe.

'You've not been right for a while,' Dan says in hushed tones, glancing at the door, clearly trying not to alert our parents that I'm awake. 'I said to Kayla when we met for dinner that I was going to have a word with Tony about it. I promised her, then I forgot, and she went off on me, talking about postnatal depression and stuff like that.'

'That's what the doctor said I have,' I say. 'But I don't think it's as simple as that. I'm not sad, Dan. I'm just... I *was* just really fucking tired.'

He takes my hand and squeezes it, making tears spring to my eyes.

'I know. Extreme sleep deprivation is dangerous and none of us took it seriously. I'm sorry. We're all sorry. How do you feel now?'

I look into the distance and think. Yes, I can think. It's a start.

'Better,' I say. 'But also...'

He looks down at where I'm looking, at the bump beneath the duvet, and he makes a face that would normally make me laugh.

'Mum changed you into your pyjamas and said she thought so but couldn't be sure. Does Tony know?'

I shake my head. 'Not yet. I think it sent me a bit over the edge. You know, the stress of moving and Riley keeping me awake all night and finding out I'm pregnant. Then Tony went away, and I started to think things. Bad things.'

Dan's still holding my hand, his grip growing damp.

'How bad? Did you want to, like...'

'No! I never wanted to kill myself or harm Riley or anything like that.' I can't say it. I can't say out loud all the things I've seen and imagined doing to people. People who have been kind to me and tried to help. 'You know my neighbour was murdered?'

He nods. 'Yeah, Jim said.'

Jim? Has my brother been talking to people on the street?

'It was all a bit dramatic last night,' he says. 'Kayla told Mum and Dad yesterday that you were in a bad way. She's been in London for this event, and she told Mum and Dad to fly over. Wouldn't take no for an answer. I came down on the train, kids are with her mum, and we all got here about the same time. And just in time too. The ambulance was here, you know.'

My heart is racing again, and I take three deep breaths to

calm down. I can remember some of last night now. The lights and faces and someone taking my blood pressure.

'Jim, next door, said you'd been acting proper mental, and then your neighbours Shona and Beth, they came running over with Riley saying how you'd dumped him at Shona's and run off with the buggy saying someone was after you. She'd called the police and they'd found you passed out. We got here the same time as the ambulance. You were filthy and cut up and there was an open suitcase in the living room. Lu, we all thought...' Dan takes a deep breath and bats at his eyes with the back of his hand. 'Anyway, they said you'd passed out and were exhausted but all you needed was rest. They gave you a sedative. You've been out cold all day.'

I can't process all of this. It's a lot.

'The pushchair,' I say. 'I left it in the park. And my hat.'

'Fuck the pushchair, I'll buy you another one,' Dan says with a laugh, wrapping his arms around me and holding me tight. His voice is cracking as he keeps talking quietly in my ear. 'I thought... When we turned up and saw you on the floor and the ambulance and... Don't scare us like that again, OK?' He sniffs and laughs again. 'You have to ask for help. I promise we'll listen this time. All of us.'

The bedroom door opens, and my parents come running in, both of them talking at once, telling me how much they love me while Kayla stands at the back, Riley on her hip, a smile dancing on her lips. I nod at her, and she nods, and I burst out crying.

And that's how Tony finds us ten minutes later, all of us on the bed, sobbing.

'What the hell is going on?' he cries.

'Shit,' Dan says. 'I forgot to call Tony.'

FORTY-NINE

It's dark and Riley's asleep and everyone has left, insisting that they want to stay a few more days and the hotel up the road will be fine. It won't be, it's a dump, but I appreciate the sentiment.

I'm struggling to keep my eyes open as Tony hands me a bowl of soup and buttered toast.

'It's a lot to take in,' he says. 'I can't believe I had no idea, Lu. I'm such an arsehole. I'm the worst husband in the world.'

I take a mouthful of toast and answer, 'We're not married.'

'Well, maybe that should change too.'

I raise my eyebrows and swallow. 'Is that how you're going to propose to me?'

'No!' He waves his hands in the air. 'Forget I said it. I'll do it properly. A proper surprise in the new year or something. Shit. Sorry.'

I pull him to me and kiss him on the lips. I never thought I'd get to do that again. I nearly start crying but take a mouthful of soup instead and swallow it down. I can't use up any more energy on these tears.

'Where did you get the soup?' I ask.

'Your mum made it.'

'Bloody hell,' I mumble.

'This is all our fault,' he says. 'Honestly, Lu. We let you down. The lot of us. And you stayed so strong for Riley. Thank you for keeping him safe while you were struggling.'

I did, didn't I? All those times I thought Maggie was cooking and cleaning and caring for my boy, it was me. I never did have long naps on the sofa – I was at the shops and playing with the baby and splitting myself in two in order to be who I thought my son needed me to be.

'I've been talking to your parents, and they want to pay for Riley to go to nursery, so you can have some days to yourself. And I'm going to talk to our doctor and get you some help. Proper help. I mean, you may need the pills he prescribed – that's OK if you do and want to take them, or if you don't – either way you should get therapy too. Plus I've spoken to my boss and taken some time off until the new year.'

I raise my eyebrows. 'You've been busy. I'm impressed.'

'You shouldn't be, Lu. Jesus, it's all too little too late.'

'It's not,' I say with a yawn. 'It's perfect timing.'

I take his hand and slip it under the covers. He gives me a quizzical look which turns to surprise when I rest his hand on my stomach.

'What the…?' he mouths. 'Fuck.'

'Are you angry?'

His eyes are brimming with tears and he's biting his lips together. 'What? *Angry*? Is that what you thought? Is that why you kept this from me?'

I nod and this time it's me who's crying. Maybe all these tears need to come out after all. He kisses them away, telling me how much he loves me and our babies and that everything is going to be OK.

'I went for a scan,' I say.

All this time I've been emailing him, pretending, lying,

keeping the important stuff to myself. I point at the bedside table drawer, and he opens it.

'See that envelope. There's a picture of the baby in there. It's due on your birthday.'

Tony no longer holds back the tears, letting them fall down his bewildered face. He opens the envelope and stares at the grainy black-and-white picture, shaking his head slowly from side to side.

'Are you worried?' I whisper.

He keeps shaking his head. 'I'll look after you,' he replies. 'I promise. I've been a selfish bastard; I know I have. Your parents will help too, and Dan and Kayla, and work is going well. It will be OK. And our neighbours care, you know. They've already been round with flowers asking if you're feeling better. Shona, Beth, Jim, some woman called Daisy.'

I think about Maggie and how I'll never see her again – because she was never my friend to begin with. The woman I thought was my only friend never even existed. Pieces start to slot together: how I drove to the hospital with her, but she waited in the waiting room, and how she never spoke when we were around other people, and how she would stroke my stomach and call our baby hers. It was me. Alone. Being my own mother and my own best friend.

'Turn the scan over,' I say, remembering something else. 'What does it say?'

He squints at the writing through the gloom. 'Girl. Wait. We're having a girl?'

I nod but I'm crying so hard now I can hardly speak. A girl. A sister for Riley.

'What day is it?' I ask.

'Thirteenth of December. Christmas soon. I'll do it all, Lu. You have nothing to worry about. Your parents are staying all month and we'll celebrate Riley's first Christmas with them and his birthday and then we'll plan for this little lady.' He rubs my tummy and I smile. 'And all you have to do is sleep and rest and take it easy, OK? And we'll get you professional help and you'll feel better soon, I promise. You're not alone, Lu. Not anymore.'

He holds me and I hug him back and he kisses my forehead, and over his shoulder I see her. Maggie. She's standing in the corner of our room, not quite solid, not quite there, and she's smiling.

FIFTY

Christmas was fun. I never thought I'd say that, but it was a success.

We decided our house was too small for everyone, and Dan and Kayla were too far away for us to get there, so we had Mum and Dad at ours for Christmas Eve and then my brother and his family came down and we all had a family lunch at a nice pub on Boxing Day. But Christmas Day was just the three of us – me, Tony and Riley. Four of us, including the bump. Tony bought a tree and decorations, and he cooked while Riley played with all his new toys. Then we sat on the sofa watching *The Snowman* and any bad thoughts that flittered into my mind soon melted away. I'm not taking any notice of them anymore; I'm not giving them any power. My new doctor says I shouldn't get complacent, that sleep-deprivation mixed with anxiety and pregnancy hormones are a tough combination. She says I'll be assessed before and after the baby comes too, to be safe. But knowing I have so many people looking out for me is already making me feel solid, like I'm really here and I can manage stuff. I think I'll be OK. I really do.

'What do you want to do for New Year's Eve?' Tony asks me.

He has his arm around my shoulder as we walk back from the shops. It's Riley's birthday tomorrow and the day after that is the last day of the year.

'Nothing,' I say. 'Mum and Dad are coming around for Riley's special tea party then all I want to do is eat and watch TV.'

'Sounds perfect,' he says, planting a kiss on the crown of my head, and I smile beneath my scarf. Light flakes of snow are falling but nothing has settled yet. Riley is bundled up asleep in the new pushchair his uncle bought him, the handles laden with carrier bags full of even more gifts for him. He's going to hate having his birthday so close to Christmas when he grows up, but we'll deal with that later. Not everything has to be perfect right now.

'Do you think he'll like nursery?' I ask Tony.

My parents are paying, and Tony has sorted it all out. The idea of having three full days a week to myself is both wonderful and terrifying. I don't want to be apart from Riley, but equally I can't risk getting overwhelmed again.

'He's going to love it,' he replies. 'And it will be good for you too, Lu. You need to have some time to yourself before the baby comes.'

Riley is no longer referred to as 'the baby'. He only started walking a few weeks ago but he's already our 'big boy'.

'And he's going to love having a little sister,' I say as we turn into our street.

'Yeah,' Tony replies. 'God, I'm so happy, Lu. You both make me so happy. I promise I'll never take it for granted again.' He slows down and I stop to look at what he's pointing at.

'Is that a black cat on our doorstep?' he mutters. 'Is that good luck or bad?'

Shadow. So I didn't imagine him.

'Definitely good luck,' I say. 'I think he's a stray. I fed him a few times.'

Tony looks at me and I make a face and shrug. He hugs me to him.

'Looks like we have a cat, then,' he says, kissing me again. 'Just make sure it shits outside.'

I laugh and make a mental note to ask the landlord if we can install a cat flap. We cross the road and Tony slows down again.

'Wait up. That's Jim. We should go and wish him a happy new year.'

The snow is falling harder now and it's difficult to see who my neighbour is talking to. A woman is standing on his front doorstep, a suitcase in her hand, a man and older teenager by her side. My stomach flips and I grip the handles of the pushchair tighter.

Jim has already seen us.

'Hey there, you two!' he calls out. 'How was your Christmas?'

Tony answers for us and I'm thankful because all my words are lodged at the back of my throat. It's Maggie, with her family. Maggie with her brown hair tucked beneath a woollen hat. Her daughter is blonde – she looks like a younger version of the Maggie I remember, but shy and awkward. Maggie turns to us and catches my eye as the two men talk of turkeys and Boxing Day football.

'How are you?' she asks carefully.

I have to take a deep breath to clear my head. The cold winter air hurts my lungs but in a good way. I've worked so hard banishing the Maggie I know from my mind and now here she is, a darker-haired version, asking me how I am as if she really cares. I have to remind myself that this woman hardly knows me.

'I'm fine,' I say. 'A lot better.'

Jim says he'll help Andy with the cases – they must have

been staying with him over Christmas – and Tony says he'll take Riley inside because it's properly snowing now, so Maggie and I are left outside staring at one another.

'Jim told me,' she says. 'You know, about your funny turn. I'm sorry, I know how hard being on your own with a baby can be. It all must have been very scary for you, moving here and the murder and all that.'

I'm so embarrassed. Did Jim tell her everything? Does she know I hallucinated about her helping me and my son? I can't imagine how she must have felt hearing that. If I were her, I'd have crossed the street to avoid me. I watch her mouth as she speaks, lips exactly the same as I remember, and I think back to the touch of those same lips as they kissed my cheek. My face itches with heat and I clear my throat.

'Hormones,' I say with a fake laugh. 'They send us all a bit bonkers, eh?'

She glances down at my belly, now protruding through my old winter coat that doesn't quite do up anymore. Tony wants to buy me a new one in the sales next week. He's trying really hard to the point where it's beginning to grate, but it's better than being ignored.

'Oh. Wow!' Maggie exclaims, patting my belly. 'Congrats. How far along are you?'

'Nearly six months.'

'Do you know the sex?'

'A girl.'

She grins. 'Oh, baby girls are brilliant. I remember when Hannah was tiny, she was such a little doll. Got any names in mind yet? You should call her Maggie,' she says, keeping her hand on my stomach.

I wait for the laugh or the 'I'm only joking' addition, but it doesn't come. Instead, we stay like that, frozen in time. Her pale eyes stare into mine, her hot hand on my swollen stomach, and it feels so much like it used to. I want to place my hand over hers, feel her touch against my skin, hear her whisper that she'll be there for me. But I'm being silly. That Maggie isn't real. It was just my imagination being dangerous.

'I never did properly thank you for looking after me that night,' I say. 'You know, when I was sleepwalking. I should have realised back then how much I was struggling.'

Maggie doesn't take her hand off my stomach; instead she steps closer until I can smell her scent. It's the same floral perfume as before – I must have remembered it that night and kept it with me. My stomach tightens and I wonder if she can feel it.

'It's me who should be thanking *you*,' she whispers, bending her head forward so her lips brush my earlobes.

'Me? What have I done?'

She straightens up and waves at her husband and daughter, who are standing by the car waiting for her. Then, in a flurry, she pretends to hug me. I remember now, how her breath smelled of mint and how it tickled my hair as she spoke.

'You kept quiet,' she says.

'About what?' I reply, but she's holding me so close, so tight, that I can't move.

'You kept quiet about the whole Dave thing. That night when you saw me at his house. When you tried to save him but couldn't. And all this time you haven't said anything to the police. Thank you.'

'It was you?' I say, so quietly I'm not sure she's heard me over the howl of the wind.

'I didn't mean it to happen. It all got out of hand. It wasn't meant to go that far,' she replies. 'We'd both had a few drinks, and a kiss and a cuddle. Andy, my husband, and I were going through a rough patch and... Well, then of course that bastard Dave wanted more and wouldn't take no for an answer. I couldn't get him off me, Lu. I ran and he chased me outside, and

I had no choice. It was the only way I could make him stop. You know that. I told you.'

She told me? What did she tell me? I can see something forming in my mind's eye, hazy at first then in sharp relief as if I've stepped into a photograph. I can see Dave on the floor and the brick in Maggie's hand. Not my hand. Hers. Dave had chased me in my nightmares when in reality he'd been chasing her. Maggie. His victim... and his killer.

'I feel terrible for leaving the way I did,' she mumbles into the crook of my neck as she holds me tightly to her. 'I dyed my hair and went on my holiday, hoping all the fuss would die down and it did. I'm so sorry, Lu. I had no choice but to protect myself. But it all worked out in the end, eh? We got away with it.'

'We?'

She lets me go and I stay frozen, arms by my side, my limbs filling with concrete. I'm a statue once again encased in stone that refuses to release me. I remember now. I remember everything.

Riley had woken up in the night and I'd just settled him, going downstairs to the kitchen for some water. That's when I saw her. Maggie, in Dave's arms, drunk and stumbling. He was leading her back to his house and she was laughing, until she wasn't. They went out of sight, and then the music started thumping. I was heading back upstairs when I heard a scream cut through the techno, so I ran outside. It was instinctive, the way I run when Riley screams for me. Running before thinking.

But I was too late. I saw Dave bolt out of his house, grabbing out at something, someone, and then he was on the ground. As I neared his house Maggie stood up straight, dropped what she was holding, and ran. I attempted to help him, his blood soaking through my pyjamas as I knelt beside his body and tried to stem the flow from his head. When I looked over my shoulder Maggie was already closing the door to her brother's house.

That's what happened. I know it. The truth is Maggie left me alone with the man she killed then acted like my saviour. She let me think it was me who killed him.

The snow is falling so thick that as soon as Maggie steps away from me, she's lost in the blizzard. To my right I can see the outline of Tony waiting for me in the doorway of our home, Jim waving from his, and across the road is Maggie's family waiting for her by the car. She turns her back on me once again and walks away without another word, leaving me standing in the snow staring after her.

The world has turned as white, thick and fluffy as Maggie's dressing gown the first night I met her. All around me, so much white. Yet all I see is red. My blood boils hot in my veins, sharp thorns piercing beneath my skin. I bite down on the inside of my cheek until I taste iron. I nearly lost everything because of her. She won't get away with this.

A LETTER FROM NATALI

Dear reader,

Thank you so much for choosing to read *While My Baby Sleeps*. It's thanks to readers like you that I get to keep writing books which I hope are entertaining, insightful and thrilling. If you enjoyed *While My Baby Sleeps* and want to keep up to date with all my latest releases, please sign up at the following link. Your email address will never be shared and you can unsubscribe at any time.

www.bookouture.com/natali-simmonds

Although *While My Baby Sleeps* is a work of fiction, Lu's struggles are sadly all too real for many. Sleep deprivation in new mothers is not taken seriously enough and can lead to extreme mental health issues. If you or someone you know is suffering with any aspect of motherhood, please don't feel ashamed or worried. Reach out to friends, family or a medical professional and seek help right away.

I hope you enjoyed reading *While My Baby Sleeps*. If you would like to recommend it to others, I would really appreciate your review. Your comments make such a difference helping new readers discover one of my books for the first time, plus I love hearing from my readers.

You can also get in touch with me and share your thoughts through social media or my website.

Thanks,

Natali Simmonds

www.njsimmonds.com

- facebook.com/NJSimmondsAuthor
- x.com/NJSimmondsBooks
- bsky.app/profile/natalisimmonds.bsky.social

ACKNOWLEDGEMENTS

While My Baby Sleeps is my tenth published novel yet the hardest book I have ever written. From 2009 to 2012 I struggled with extreme sleep deprivation. My daughters were born less than two years apart and they didn't like to sleep (they've made up for it now as teenagers). Much like Lu, I'd moved to a new area, I was home alone all day pregnant and caring for a baby, and I was losing the plot. Thankfully I didn't reach the extreme psychosis Lu does, but I was certainly seeing and hearing things that weren't there. I struggled so much that entire months during that time have been deleted from my memory, and writing this book brought a lot of it back.

It's been a difficult project, but equally this is one of the most important books I've written because the more I talk about postpartum sleep deprivation, the more I realise how many mothers are suffering in silence, and how no one takes it seriously enough.

Psychology Today states, 'Prolonged sleep deprivation is an especially insidious form of torture because it attacks the deep biological functions at the core of a person's mental and physical health. It is less overtly violent than cutting off someone's finger, but it can be far more damaging and painful if pushed to extremes.' Women shouldn't be expected to grin and bear something that is used as a literal form of torture.

I'm proud of this story but, much like raising children, it took a village.

Firstly, I would like to thank my wonderful agent, Amanda Preston, who has championed me and my writing career every step of the way. A huge thank you, too, to my incredible editor, Lucy Frederick, who makes every book I write even better. *While My Baby Sleeps* wouldn't be in the hands of you, the reader, were it not for all the hard work of the editorial, audio, marketing and publicity teams at Bookouture. Plus a massive *grazie/obrigado* to Richard King and his translations team for getting my books into other countries.

I couldn't have written any of this without help and advice from three brilliant clinical psychologists. Thank you to my wonderful writer friend, psychologist and mother of three, Anna Day, who helped me get into Lu's head a little deeper. And to Dr Jenny Banham and Dr Helen Spencer for reading early drafts and steering me in the right direction.

I'd also like to thank the Mums Who Hide In The Loo gang. This Facebook group was a lifeline to me in the early years and it's a testament to how amazing women are that we have all continued to support one another ten years later, this time with our teens. It's your stories, and your struggles, that make me want to keep writing thrillers that matter.

As always, a big thank you to all my writer friends who I've discussed this book with, including Isabella May, Teuta Metra, Rebecca DeWinter and everyone in the Debut23 group, and a special thanks to my bestie and Caedis Knight co-writer, Jacqueline Silvester, whose daily rantings of mum life with a toddler helped fuel this book. My godson is lucky to have you as a mum. Don't forget to appreciate the view.

Lastly, as always, a massive thank you to my own family – my wonderful husband, my mum, my two dads, my sister and everyone else in the family who has supported me not only as an author but as a mother. I'm very lucky to have you all in my life.

And to my two girls, Isabelle and Olivia... you are my

reward for all those sleepless nights. I'm so proud to be your mother – those first few torturous years were worth it. And one day, if you choose to have kids of your own, I promise I'll be there for you, day and night. Always.

PUBLISHING TEAM

Turning a manuscript into a book requires the efforts of many people. The publishing team at Bookouture would like to acknowledge everyone who contributed to this publication.

Audio
Alba Proko
Sinead O'Connor
Melissa Tran

Commercial
Lauren Morrissette
Hannah Richmond
Imogen Allport

Cover design
The Brewster Project

Data and analysis
Mark Alder
Mohamed Bussuri

Editorial
Lucy Frederick
Melissa Tran

Copyeditor
DeAndra Lupu

Proofreader
Deborah Blake

Marketing
Alex Crow
Melanie Price
Occy Carr
Cíara Rosney
Martyna Młynarska

Operations and distribution
Marina Valles
Stephanie Straub
Joe Morris

Production
Hannah Snetsinger
Mandy Kullar
Jen Shannon
Ria Clare

Publicity
Kim Nash
Noelle Holten
Jess Readett
Sarah Hardy

Rights and contracts
Peta Nightingale
Richard King
Saidah Graham

Printed in Great Britain
by Amazon